# Readers love *Sutph[*
## by SANTINO H

"I couldn't put this book down once I started it."
—The Book Vixen

"This was my first contemporary from Hassell, and I am officially hooked. I gotta have more. I'm completely addicted to his writing at this point."
—Reviews by Jessewave

"This book and these characters offer a gritty and realistic view of life while offering a complex and multi-layered story of true friends that become lovers."
—Joyfully Jay

"Get it, drool over it, love it. One of my top reads of 2015."
—Binge on Books

"Every so often a book comes along that absolutely *shatters* you... For me, *Sutphin Boulevard* is one of those books."
—Just Love Book Reviews

"Full of humor, drama, a one-time ménage a trois and a fresh, albeit gritty, look at New York City, Sutphin Boulevard takes readers beyond Manhattan's glitz and glamor."
—RT Book Reviews

# STYGIAN

## SANTINO HASSELL

DREAMSPINNER
PRESS

Published by

DREAMSPINNER PRESS

5032 Capital Circle SW, Suite 2, PMB# 279, Tallahassee, FL 32305-7886 USA
www.dreamspinnerpress.com

Stygian
© 2015 Santino Hassell.

Cover Art
© 2015 "Design by Damonza".
www.damonza.com
Cover content is for illustrative purposes only and any person depicted on the cover is a model.

ISBN: 978-1-63476-500-8
Digital ISBN: 978-1-63476-501-5
Library of Congress Control Number: 2015943921
First Edition October 2015

Printed in the United States of America
(∞)
This paper meets the requirements of
ANSI/NISO Z39.48-1992 (Permanence of Paper).

*For S.K.*

"Never relinquish your terrors. That's when they catch you."
—Poppy Z. Brite, *Exquisite Corpse*

# CHAPTER ONE

THE MANSION was a monstrosity.

Jeremy Black stared up at it, a sweating bottle of beer pressed against his forehead and his drum kit heaped in leather cases by his feet. When the front man of Stygian had declared the band would be going on a summer retreat to work on their sophomore album, he'd neglected to mention they would be staying in a structure over two centuries old.

The place, built in the antebellum style, had only two levels but was wide enough to swallow Jeremy's apartment building. At once lovely and imposing, its pale yellow wood paneling was obscured by a crush of trees, wildflowers, and dangling Spanish moss. The grass scraped past Jeremy's ankles, tall enough to hide yellow-jacket nests and fire ant mounds, indicating a lapse in the property's upkeep. It was surrounded by open land bleeding into a wooded area, which—according to their bass player's obsession with Charlaine Harris novels and atmospheric locales—led to the Sabine River and a couple of swamps. Quince considered it romantic, but Jeremy was 100 percent convinced the mosquitoes would kill him. Or a vengeful Confederate ghost.

The summer was going to be awful.

"Is there AC?" His gaze traced the balconies and arches lining the sprawling wraparound porch. "Because it's literally, according to my weather app, over one hundred degrees."

"No." Kennedy grunted as he set the last of the band's equipment on the ground next to the van. He'd stripped off his shirt five minutes after exiting the van, and the colorful chaos of the tattoos spreading across his body glistened with sweat.

"No?"

"I said no." Kennedy swept his tongue over his lower lip, briefly sucking in the hoop that curled around the side of his mouth. "And don't go whining to Watts about it either. After six hours in this van, I'm tired of his bitchy comments."

Jeremy switched to pressing the bottle against his neck and quit staring at the hard lines of Kennedy's torso. "Where the hell is he, anyway? I thought the people who own this place were supposed to live nearby."

"It doesn't look like anyone lives nearby. He's probably fucking Quince in the woods so he can feel like he's roughing it."

"Dude, it's like one hundred and four degrees in the *shade*, and there's no AC in that piece of crap. This *is* roughing it."

"Talking about it won't change things, so save your energy for bringing your shit to the house. I'm tired of being everyone's bellhop."

Kennedy shoved a cigarette between his lips, lit it, and grabbed his guitar case and an amp. He marched off toward the mansion, his boots trampling the weeds that had sprouted along the path leading to the porch.

Jeremy frowned after him and then down at the many components of his kit. *Great.* He drained his beer, tucked damp strands of platinum-colored hair behind his ears, and began the task.

As he trudged back and forth, Kennedy watched from the porch. After several minutes, he flicked away the cigarette and stood.

"I didn't mean to snap at you."

"It's fine." Jeremy placed the kick drum's case in front of the ornate wooden door that would have been their way inside if Watts and Quince hadn't disappeared.

"I'm just pissed. It's fucking hot, it's my van, yet Watts pulled his bossy front-man crap for the entire drive, and now he's who the hell knows where with Quince. You'd think Quince would have more common sense, but he's too busy doing cartwheels over the fact that someone is finally paying attention to him for more than a one-time fuck in the toilets at a dive bar." Once the words hit the open air, Kennedy winced and ran a hand over the buzz of his dark hair. "That was a shitty thing to say."

Jeremy shrugged. It was also true.

"I'm just saying none of that is your fault. I don't want to add to the problems by taking it out on you."

Jeremy hiked up his shorts and jumped off the top step to stand beside Kennedy. He was nearly a full foot shorter and about half of Kennedy's size.

"I get it. I'm the new kid on the block and replacing someone irreplaceable."

Jeremy's expectations for a smooth transition had faded fast. Stygian's former drummer had died in a car crash not even six months ago. A drunk driver had careened into the vehicle while Watts had been at the wheel. Now he coped by making it snow up his nose on a regular basis and trying to drag Quince into winter wonderland with him. Luckily, Quince was more interested in banging and writing new bass tabs.

"Right."

Kennedy didn't seem too enthused with the excuse, but his stoic mask rarely slipped.

"Do you really think this summer will get the band back on track?"

"I think it boils down to Watts and which way his mood swings on a given day." Kennedy shaded his eyes and peered up at the mansion. "But I took the summer off from the youth center to come finish this album, so I sure as hell hope he pulls it together."

"I had to quit my job."

"At the record store?"

"Yeah. I mean, it's not… comparable to you having, like, a real career and everything, but it was all I had."

"Does your mom know?"

Jeremy suppressed a bristle. "No. I haven't spoken to her in a while."

Those dark eyes returned to Jeremy. "Why not?"

*Because I can't handle her recent descent into lunacy, since I already have to deal with that shit on my father's side.*

"We don't always get along."

Jeremy regretted mentioning his own situation. The last thing he wanted was to be seen as one of the at-risk youths Kennedy spent his time trying to save.

As if sensing Jeremy's discomfort, Kennedy nodded at the van. "I'll help with the rest."

They finished moving everything to the front of the mansion, and Jeremy wondered what had possessed Watts to rent something so large for the four of them. All they needed was a garage, some outlets, and two rooms to crash in, and their retreat would have been fine. Jeremy had to assume the extravagance had a lot more to do with Watts's bottomless trust fund and his desire to feed Quince's need for *atmosphere*. Not that it mattered since Quince didn't appear to care that Watts was using him for sex.

Jeremy wondered what lyrics the twosome would cook up over the next couple of months. They wouldn't consult him, anyway. He was the newest, the youngest, and the least experienced, as Watts reminded him on a daily basis. Jeremy was starting to wonder why they'd offered him the gig in the first place.

Sweat trickled down Jeremy's back and created a damp path along his spine. He surveyed the property, but with the sun burning at the center of the sky, only the mansion itself and the distant woods offered relief from the heat. The mass of open space and the distant trees were beautiful in an eerie way, but Jeremy couldn't say the same about the mansion. His imagination was just as overactive as Quince's, but instead of being excited, he was wary of how isolated they were in such a rural area.

"Fuck, I'm going to call him," Kennedy muttered after twenty minutes went by and the other half of their band were still no-shows. "I'm done with the games."

"Maybe they got lost in the—"

"Need some help?"

"Holy fuck!" Jeremy spun around and set eyes on a man who had seemingly materialized from thin air. He was a tall drink of Southern awesome—lean, rangy build, wild black hair that fell across his forehead, and eyes so pale it was hard to tell the color. Not the sort of person you would expect to wander up to an abandoned-looking house. Or, well, anywhere. He was fairy-tale beautiful.

"Where the hell did you come from?" Kennedy glared at their surroundings before turning to the man again.

"Over there." The guy gestured in the general direction of the trees. His expression didn't warm until he looked at Jeremy.

"Yeah?" The question was sharp enough to slice through any potential pleasantries, but Kennedy's frown made it clear he didn't give a damn. "Where's there?"

"I live near the river. I was taking a walk. Did I startle you?"

Tension stiffened Kennedy's shoulders.

"No," Jeremy said quickly. "I mean—you startled *me*, but I don't think anything can startle Ken-boy."

"Don't call me that."

Jeremy ignored Kennedy and grinned at the stranger. "If you live nearby, you'll be seeing us around for the next couple of months. We rented this place."

"Vacation?"

"I guess." The phrase *music retreat* was especially lame in the face of someone not in their band. "Kinda."

The guy took in the array of equipment littering the front porch. All of the black and metal was obscene compared to the curved arches and centuries-old architecture.

"Musicians."

"Uh-huh." Jeremy shoved his hands in his pockets. "We're waiting on our friend to find his way back with the keys."

Kennedy gave him a crazy look, probably wondering what it would take to stop the endless stream of way too much information given to a stranger.

The guy climbed the steps with long elegant strides and didn't hesitate to stand in grabbing reach of Kennedy's menacing form. "Which one of you is Brian Watts?"

"Neither," Kennedy said. "You the dude who rented this monster out?"

"My sister, Laurel, did. I'm Hunter Caroway."

Hunter extended a hand that Kennedy didn't shake. Clearing his throat, Jeremy squeezed past him to take the offered appendage. "I'm Jeremy. I'm the uh... the drummer."

Kennedy's lip curled, but Jeremy barely noticed once a tiny smile appeared on Hunter's face. At least someone was going to be nice today.

"So you're the owner?" Kennedy asked, continuing with his inquisition.

"The land belongs to our family, but we stay in a smaller cabin in the woods. There aren't enough Caroways left to justify living in this big house."

Kennedy grunted. "Either our friends got lost looking for your other place, or it's not as close as you're saying, because they've been gone for almost an hour." His skepticism was thick enough to join the humidity in suffocating them. "You happen to have the keys on you?"

Hunter brushed past Kennedy and twisted the brass handle without inserting a key. The door opened, and Hunter's smile widened.

"Um." The single syllable earned Jeremy a glare of death.

"Not too many thieves looking to rob this place." Hunter slid the keys from his pocket and handed them to Jeremy. "It was real nice meeting you, Jeremy."

"Yeah, likewise."

Kennedy swore and stormed inside.

"ISN'T THIS place rad?" Quince asked.

"Yeah, it's totally tubular," Kennedy said.

He was sitting on the far side of the room due to an apparent mission to stay as far away from the rest of the band as possible, even if it meant hanging out in dark corners with dust-covered furniture and cobwebs. Jeremy didn't know if there were *actual* cobwebs in the corners, but the place was so old and musty that he figured it was a given. The interior of the house was just as antiquated as the outside, seeming as though it had not been remodeled or redecorated since the original construction.

When they'd entered the foyer, the sunlight had shone into the house like a beacon, exposing expanses of rich, dark wood surfaces covered in a light layer of dust and so many heavy drapes, valances, and rugs, that Jeremy was stifled just by looking around. He had glanced briefly at an old piano before he'd followed the others into a larger sitting room.

"Don't be such a drag." Quince plopped down on a hard-backed chair, running his hands over the velvety fabric. His face lit up, making his blue eyes and sun-bleached strawberry blond hair the brightest points in the room. "Look at this furniture—it's probably a hundred years old. Like legitimate early twentieth century. Do you know how much this stuff would be worth at an antique shop in River Oaks?"

"Do you know how little I care about the price of some dusty-ass chair?"

Quince looked crestfallen but his enthusiasm returned after his gaze landed on the mantel. He leaped to his feet and grabbed an object from the dust-coated clutter of pictures and figurines. After brushing it off, he held up a large silver watch. Only a kid who'd done a dozen stints in juvie for larceny would spot something of value amid all the antique junk.

"Do you know how much this *watch* would be worth at just about any pawn shop? It's an Omega!"

Kennedy released a slow breath. "Just put it back, Quince. You're not pawning these people's shit."

"All I'm saying is, you could get a couple of thousand for it. Probably more."

"And all I'm saying is shut the fuck up and put it back."

Quince recoiled, tight-lipped, and dropped the watch onto the mantel again. "I was only kidding."

"Yeah," Kennedy said. "Right."

Tension blanketed the room until Watts looked up from his sprawl on the floor. He was shirtless and wearing a pair of painted-on skinny jeans that exposed a significant amount of ass as he sat looping keys into multicolored rings. Hunter had given them four copies.

"Chill the fuck out, Ken-boy. Did you rejects even look around? You had enough time."

"Yeah, because you got lost in the woods while we broke our backs dragging all of your crap inside," Kennedy said.

"Nobody got lost, fuckhead. I don't know where the hell that Hunter dude lives. His sister only gave me this address, and some vague directions to their other place but all we found was a cruddy shack." One of Watts's wiry shoulders rose in a shrug. "I got chewed up by mosquitoes while y'all hung out in the house."

"This place is creepy," Jeremy informed him. "I don't want to hang out in here. I didn't even look upstairs. I'm totally cool sleeping right in this room near the front door."

"This is practice space," Watts said. "You'll sleep in the preassigned room, or you'll screw up the vibe."

"Preassigned room," Kennedy repeated. "Are you kidding me?"

"Nope." Watts tossed him a key and then nailed Jeremy in the forehead with another. It had a Mickey Mouse ring. "They keep a lot of the bedrooms locked up tight, and one wing is totally sealed off. Unless you're planning to bust down the door to the other wing, you're slumming it with this little asshole"—Watts jerked his chin at Jeremy—"for the rest of the summer."

Jeremy looked down at his beat-up sneakers.

"Aw, he's blushing," Watts cooed. "Look on the bright side, Ken-boy. Figure out how fluid your sexuality is. This sweet little twink would love to spend the next two months slobbing your knob. I can't think of anything—"

Jeremy jumped to his feet and grabbed his duffel bag. He swung it over his shoulder, vacating the room before Watts could finish the sentence. Quince called after him, but Jeremy hurried farther into the depths of the house. He hated how his hands were shaking and the way his temperature had spiked with every mocking word.

The stairs creaked under his rapid footsteps, but despite his hurry to get away, he paused at the landing. Raised voices drifted from below, but he couldn't clearly hear the exchanged words. It was probably for the best. When Watts was in one of his moods, he unloaded an endless stream of asshole retorts and cruel "jokes." He didn't give a damn that his humor often left Jeremy wanting to disappear.

The retreat had barely begun, but he was already regretting coming along and even staying in the band. During his audition, Watts had claimed Jeremy had been the only one with the energy and style to match theirs, but the closer they got to working on the new album, the faster the positive vibes disappeared. It seemed like Watts wanted to scare him off, and Jeremy had no idea why.

Nothing had changed on his end except unrequited infatuation for Kennedy that he'd been stupid enough to confess to Quince. Quince was too sweet and trusting to guard his own secrets so he failed to understand that Jeremy usually kept his buried beneath steel-plated armor.

He regretted confiding in Quince, but he regretted a lot of things. Putting himself in the position to endure two months' worth of hazing was number one on that growing list. Part of Jeremy wanted to locate the nearest bus depot and haul ass back to Houston, but his stubborn side refused to buckle in front of Watts. After everything Jeremy had been through in the past few years, running from the band seemed pathetic. So he'd stick it out and use the summer as a deciding factor as to whether he'd stay in the band or not.

Jeremy stood in the center of a corridor, the strap of his duffel bag digging into his shoulder blade. The wooden floors shone in both directions, reflecting the rays of sunlight that streamed through an ornate stained glass window dominating the center of the landing. Blue, green, and red shards were shot through with little threads of gold to create an image of a man, surrounded by bay trees, with dogs at his feet and a bow clutched in one hand.

The combination of stained glass, hardwood, and the hushed silence of the vacant upper floor reminded Jeremy of being in church, and a host of uncomfortable memories floated to the surface.

Banishing a flash of bloodstained beads, folded hands, and tear-streaked faces, Jeremy ran a finger along the imperfections in the glass. It was surprisingly cool to the touch, but the entire corridor was draftier than the rest of the house. He tilted his head against the window with a sigh, but instead of providing relief, the increase in contact sent ice hurtling down his spine.

Jeremy jerked away and waited for something to happen, but the corridor was still, and he heard nothing but the distant warble of his bandmates' voices and a faint creaking from within the bowels of the house.

"HEY."

"'Sup," Jeremy said without looking up from his bag.

It hadn't been difficult to determine which bedroom Watts had "assigned" to them. One room was clearly a master, while Jeremy and Kennedy's space was smaller and had less extravagant decor.

Quince slipped farther into the room, arms crossed loosely over a ragged T-shirt that proclaimed "Family Values Tour 2006" in peeling yellow letters. "One bed?"

"I'm taking the lounge."

"How come?"

"Because Kennedy won't fit on it. Your boyfriend thinks he's really funny."

"He's not my boyfriend…."

"Yeah, whatever you say, Q."

Quince flushed. "I'm not an idiot. I know Watts doesn't really care about me. But it helps him forget about things for a while, and I've been fucked by worse people, so what difference does it make?"

Jeremy didn't answer. It wasn't anything he hadn't assumed, but hearing it from Quince's bow-shaped lips was grim.

Quince fiddled with the heavy silver watch now adorning, and dwarfing, his thin wrist. It clashed with everything about his ragtag alt kid persona.

"And anyway, it's not his fault we only have the two rooms. Apparently the girl who rented it to us, Laurel, said the rest of the house is a no-access zone. Watts thinks that's where all of their family heirlooms are locked up."

"Then why are they leaving expensive watches hanging around?"

Quince put his arm behind his back. Sometimes he seemed like a sad-eyed little kid, even though he had about four or five years on Jeremy.

"Maybe someone left it here?"

"That's not really the sort of thing someone leaves behind," Jeremy pointed out.

"No, but it's engraved. Says happy anniversary to someone named Kaiden, and the year is 2010." Quince stopped hiding his hand behind his back and held it up as though Jeremy would be able to read the etching through his arm. "So either the Caroways have got the good stuff locked up, or maybe they just don't want to go through the trouble of cleaning up the entire house."

It wasn't unreasonable, but Jeremy's skin prickled at the idea of half the house remaining uninhabited and untouched. Maybe he wouldn't be so freaked-out if it wasn't for the chill he'd gotten in the hallway. It was a definite overreaction to what probably amounted to nothing more than the contrast of coolness after burning up all day, but Jeremy knew he'd recall the icy spike of dread every time he neared the other wing.

Why did the Caroways even bother renting the house, unless they were hard-up for cash?

"Listen, Jere, I'm really sorry. Watts is just stressed-out, you know? Like with the new material, and he's tired of being indie and really wants to get signed, and the plan was always for Caroline to be here. I know you don't get it, because of how he is now, but he really loved her."

Jeremy couldn't picture Watts loving anyone beyond his drug dealer and the vocalist from the Black Keys.

"Yeah, that's great, Quince, but how he acted in the past isn't changing how he is around me now. Which is the equivalent to how someone would react to a piece of shit." Jeremy heaved a disgusted sigh. "I just don't get it. He's the one who said I was a good fit. If he thinks I'm annoying and I suck, why the hell did he let me join the band?"

"Because...."

Quince's eyes darted to the door, and Jeremy closed it with an exasperated huff. He wasn't sure why Quince was so afraid of Watts. His vitriol was never aimed at Quince, unless he'd already spent the day marinating in a tincture of booze and coke.

"He knew your brother in high school. Before he... you know. Died."

"Oh." Jeremy turned back to his bag, but instead of unpacking anything, he stared inside. Watts knowing about his brother's suicide was a potential disaster. A slew of possibilities converged—all the new insults and snide comments Watts would make if he decided to stoop that low. "Were they friends?"

"I'm not sure how close they were. Watts could have just latched on because he knew you'd lost someone and we'd just lost Caroline."

"Maybe."

Quince sighed. "We never talk about it, but Caroline grew up in the same neighborhood as Kennedy—they'd known each other since they were tiny. They were like siblings. Whenever she had trouble at home, she would stay with him. And after Kennedy convinced her to join the band, well, she and Watts... they were inseparable." Quince came closer, his hands hovering awkwardly over Jeremy's arm. "Stygian wasn't just a band. We were like a family, and we need that. All of us."

"You're comparing Watts's situation to yours?" Jeremy scoffed. "He's a trust fund baby. You're a foster kid, and Kennedy's folks are dead."

"Just because there are some people who share his DNA doesn't mean he has a family."

Jeremy couldn't argue with that. Especially considering how determinedly he avoided his own familial relations.

"Watts just doesn't know how to be sad like normal people. He gets mean. So can you please try to take it easy on him?"

Jeremy's jaw dropped. "You're telling *me* to take it easy on *him*? Dude."

"I know, I know." Quince held up his hands. "But he's not as strong as he pretends to be. I really want this trip to help you guys bond. Maybe it can be like it was before. Okay?"

It was unlikely, but in the face of Quince's imploring gaze, Jeremy couldn't say no. So he shrugged, offered a strained smile, and yanked out a hoodie that he definitely would not be needing.

"Okay, Q. I'll try if he does."

"He will. I'll talk to him."

"And he'll listen?"

"I dunno. Maybe. But I'll never know until I try, right?"

"Right."

Jeremy watched Quince stride out of the room. He wasn't optimistic about this plan.

At best, it would change nothing. At worst, the idea of Jeremy needing mollycoddling would turn their front man into an even bigger asshole. Slight suggestions sounded like an order to Brian Watts. Whether drunk or sober, he verbally eviscerated anyone stupid enough to tell him what to do. Eventually he would be put in his place, but not by Jeremy.

# Chapter Two

THE PARTIAL road extending from the main street of Logansport to the driveway of the Caroway mansion wasn't paved. Loose gray gravel snaked through clusters of trees before it gave way to rutted dirt. No matter how carefully Jeremy walked, tiny pebbles lodged in his flip-flops and dust coated his bare legs. It had bothered him during his entire forty-five-minute journey into town, but now his mind was on other things.

It was a week into their stay, and they still hadn't managed a full practice session. Several times they'd set up, plugged in amps, and been poised to launch into a song, only for it to fall apart at the last moment over an asinine complaint.

The room was too hot. The acoustics were fucked. Most commonly, Watts would cut the session while sneeringly proclaiming that he wasn't feeling the vibe. He'd storm off like a temperamental diva while Kennedy seethed and demanded they practice without the vocals, but by then no one felt like making it work.

Watts's sneers were almost always aimed at him, so Jeremy had come to believe he was the one "ruining the vibe." How he could do so by sitting behind his drum set was a complete mystery, and not one he had interest in solving.

Promise or no promise, Jeremy was determined to avoid his bandmates. It wasn't easy. Although the house looked cavernous from the outside, they only had access to a limited number of rooms. His only escape was the land surrounding the house—trading stifling shadows for aggressive sunshine.

It became a routine for him to slip outside and stretch out on the back porch's swing during the early-morning hours. At least until Kennedy and Watts woke up, and their loud snarling drove him off the porch and into the yard. Mostly he'd climb the massive pecan tree that shaded the roof, but today Jeremy had ventured farther. The desire to find a washateria and a grocery store had led to him walking to one of the busier parts of town.

For his entire return journey, Jeremy's only company had been the drone of insects and the singing of birds, but now the low rumble of an engine joined the other sounds.

A rusted two-toned Sierra Grande trundled along the dirt road. Something in the bed of the truck rattled each time the tires ground over loose rocks or bumps.

Moving to the side, Jeremy ignored the vehicle, but the driver slowed down and pulled up beside him.

"Hey!"

A pair of teenagers, who couldn't have been more than fourteen or fifteen, peered at him from the cab. They both had hair light enough to rival Jeremy's and a smattering of freckles splashed across their noses.

"Do you know your way around here?" the boy in the driver's seat asked. "We're up from Center and are kinda lost."

"I only know this one road," Jeremy admitted. "I'm not from around here either."

"Shoot." The boy slapped his hand against the steering wheel. "We were trying to find this old haunted house. Heard about it from a friend."

Jeremy blurted, "The Caroway place?"

"Shit, yeah! That's it. Do you know where it is?"

The heat of the day did nothing to chase off Jeremy's chill. "Yeah. I'm staying there for the summer with some friends."

The girl nearly climbed over her friend's lap to stare at Jeremy through the window.

"So… you said it's haunted?" Jeremy asked.

The boy nodded once. "That's what they say, but it's probably just bullshit." His smile was strained. "I guess we'll head on back, then. No point in us poking around a full house."

"Wait—"

"You be careful," the girl hollered.

The truck did an abrupt U-turn and went back the way it had come. For as short as the exchange had been, it left Jeremy wishing he wasn't on the road by himself.

He half jogged back to the mansion and climbed the pecan tree instead of going inside. With six weeks left to go on the retreat, he didn't want to think too hard about the place being haunted.

It was easier to lose himself in the therapeutic repetitive motions of climbing. Trying to keep his balance or grip while moving branch by branch reminded Jeremy of his childhood. Summers exploring the fields outside of Houston, races through tall grass and stalks of ragweed, followed by a frantic climb to the top of a tree where he and his brother, Luke, had watched the setting sun. Everything had been an adventure, a game, and the vivid fantasy worlds they'd created had made it easy to forget how odd they were and how poor they'd been.

Jeremy had been unaware of their poverty until junior high, and that was when everything had changed. A steady decline in the magic of climbing trees and going on adventures until childhood had abruptly ended with the edge of a serrated blade.

Jeremy pulled himself onto a low-hanging branch of the pecan tree. Letting his legs dangle, he looked down at the acre of land surrounding the Caroway house. Apart from a rickety shed with chipped red paint, the yard was empty and melded into a dense wooded area. Miles of dry grass interspersed with overgrown weeds and trees led to the Sabine River, warming beneath the merciless sun.

Despite Quince's wheedling, Jeremy had yet to explore the woods, but now he was tempted. If he'd walked all the way to town, he could find his way to the river. He analyzed the woods from his vantage point and wondered if he could map a route that would not end with him becoming hopelessly lost.

As Jeremy peered into the distance, a flash of movement through a break in the trees caught his eye. He squinted, trying to follow the motion, but breaking glass and a shout drew his attention away.

The back door burst open, and Quince raced out. He jumped down the stairs, stumbling into the grass, and barely caught himself before Watts barreled out of the house. He was shirtless, barefoot, and red-faced. No mistaking the furious set of his mouth or his baleful glare.

"You little shit—that was the last one!"

"I told you it was an accident."

"You're a fucking liar. I saw you dump it!"

Each time Watts took a step forward, Quince jumped back with his hands raised in surrender. He didn't look concerned as he danced out of the way of his lover's lunges, but Watts's stormy countenance put Jeremy on edge. He climbed down the side of the tree and dropped to the ground, moving closer to the spectacle. Just as he reached the porch, Kennedy appeared at the door, flicking a cigarette between his fingers.

"What's going on?" Jeremy asked.

Kennedy lit his cigarette and inhaled deeply. "Quince poured out the last of the vodka."

"Why?"

"Because Watts is worthless with it in the house. He's bad enough with the coke."

No disputing that.

"What's the point of him chasing Quince? He'll just get hot and bitch some more."

"Yeah, no shit." Kennedy exhaled a cloud of smoke into Jeremy's face. "Probably has something to do with him being twenty-five going on twelve."

Watts chased Quince halfway to the line of trees before tackling him to the grass. The sound of their bodies slamming together was especially loud with the area so deserted. Jeremy started forward, concerned, but paused when half-drunken complaining descended to murmurs. The stillness of Watts pinning Quince to the ground turned into subtle rocking and, within seconds, Quince rolled them over to transform their argument into a rough kiss. They didn't break apart, and Jeremy stole a glance at Kennedy. He was still smoking, his hooded eyes trained on their bandmates.

Kennedy seemed as unaffected by the sight of Watts and Quince writhing against each other as he was by everything else. Only when a belt buckle clinked and Watts groaned did Kennedy shift his gaze to Jeremy.

He was giving Jeremy the stare that set a thousand groupie hearts aflutter, and caused die-hard fans to wait show after show for Kennedy to notice them. Jeremy wasn't sure if he was reading into things because of the smoldering heat and building tension, but he didn't want the moment to end. Which meant, of course, that it did.

Kennedy strode around the side of the house, and Jeremy sagged against the banister. Ignoring Quince and Watts, he wondered why he still expected anything to happen between him and Kennedy. At times it seemed possible, when Kennedy's eyes lingered, or when his fingers slid over Jeremy's bare shoulder after a show. But those moments only led to Jeremy's filthy, late-night fantasies and fast, heady jerk-off sessions in cheap motel bathrooms when they were forced to share a bed.

No longer interested in listening to the sound of fervent rutting, Jeremy returned to the house. He tried to drown his frustration in a cold shower, and lay down to put his churning thoughts at rest. Jeremy dozed off on the bed with Kennedy's smell saturating the sheets around him. He awoke feeling queasy and dehydrated when Watts's surround-sound voice boomed through the mansion.

"Get your faggot ass down here, Black. Practice time!"


IT DIDN'T go well.

If Quince had intended to fuck the aggression out of Watts, he'd failed. The session was brutal.

Jeremy was off-kilter and it showed. They started with a ballad, but he was drumming too loud and too fast, and Watts's snarling complaints poisoned Jeremy's ability to concentrate enough to adjust the rhythm. He started overthinking, and when that happened, he inevitably screwed up in embarrassingly simple ways. His hands were so sweaty by the last part of his solo that he nearly dropped his stick, and he flinched when Watts leaned backward to sneer at him over the kick drum.

The next song wasn't any better. The snare inexplicably began to give off an awful ringing noise that made Jeremy want to slam his head into the wall. Everything sounded so shitty that at one point even Kennedy looked over with annoyance. Watts leaped at the chance to bring the entire session to a screeching halt. He shoved his mic stand against the wall.

"What the fuck is your problem, Jeremy?"

"Nothing." Jeremy wiped his forearm across his damp forehead. "I'm not feeling well. It's too stuffy in here, and—"

"I don't give a fuck. You're screwing us up and slowing us down after we finally got our shit together."

The drumsticks clattered when Jeremy slammed them down. "You mean now that you've finally gotten *your* shit together. It wasn't me slowing us down for six days, dude. You were the one starring in your own one-man lush show."

Quince bounced on the balls of his feet, looking from Jeremy to Watts. He chewed on his lower lip, clearly wanting to intervene but hesitating. All Kennedy did was roll his eyes and unplug his guitar from the amp with more force than was necessary.

"Yeah, but you know what?" Watts's mouth turned up at the side. "I can still sing when I'm drunk. You can't even play stone-cold sober. I guess that's what I get stuck with when I let some dumbass kid in the band just because I knew his—"

Jeremy sat up straight on the throne. Every synapse in his body set off sparks and sent electricity firing through him. "Knew my *what*?"

Watts ripped a hand across his sweaty face but didn't tone down the glare. "You know I felt sorry for you because of Luke. You look just fucking like him. I recognized you as soon as you shuffled your emo ass up to the audition."

Would Watts finally unleash the gossip and air it in front of Kennedy—revealing just how fucked-up and weird Jeremy's family was? The pools of blood, Jeremy breaking down in school before being sent away—what exactly did people know about it, anyway? It'd been all over social media at the time.

"Stop."

Jeremy's fingers curled into fists.

"Leave the kid alone." Kennedy's low, curt tone brooked no room for argument. "If you want to pick a fight, you can pick one with me. I'm tired of this shit."

Watts didn't look away, but now that a new voice had intervened, the freight-train roar in Jeremy's ears lowered. The desire to lash out disappeared.

"He shouldn't start a fight he won't want to finish," Watts spat.

Kennedy had already begun to wrap the cord to his amp around his hand. "I could say the same about you and me, *Brian*. You've been a toolbag since we got in the van back in Houston. Talking shit to me, bossing me around, but yet you back the fuck off once I get in your face."

"Oh, okay," Watts said. "Next time I'll let you punch me so you can feel like the manly one in the queerest band since One fucking Direction."

"It has nothing to do with me being manly and everything to do with you being a pain in the ass." Kennedy brought his shoulders up in a sharp shrug. "We have all summer to practice, so we can wait for a day when you're not in a shit mood. Although I thought shoving your dick into your favorite outlet would cheer you up."

Quince blanched.

"It did for twenty seconds." Watts didn't spare Quince a glance. "But then I was reminded of this trip being a huge waste of money since my band can't even play their own instruments properly."

"Watts, can you please stop! Why do you have to be this way?"

Quince's shout caught Watts off guard enough for him to pause. It was a rare occurrence for Quince to stand up to Watts for anything, let alone for a slight aimed at himself.

Jeremy got to his feet. Even if Quince and Kennedy were intervening for the first time... ever, it wasn't enough to keep Jeremy behind his drum kit like a giant target for Watts to aim at as soon as he got a wild hair up his ass.

"Great practice, guys," Jeremy said without emotion. "I sure don't regret quitting my job to show that I'm a team player."

"Oh God, quit being so dramatic. If you can't take *this*, your twink ass won't make it anywhere once we start playing outside of our little fucking niche," Watts said. "Do you know how brutal people are to nobody bands that open for the headliners? How do you think they'll respond to a band of guyliner-wearing fags?"

"I know the deal," Jeremy snapped. "But those people are a bunch of strangers. I guess it's asking too much not to be treated that way by my front man."

Watts rolled his eyes, but instead of shooting back a snide remark, he crossed his arms over his chest. Nobody else spoke.

Having no interest in patting them on the backs and reassuring them that he wasn't so mad after all, Jeremy left the room. It was a pitfall he'd fallen into early on—taking crap and then apologizing for being visibly upset. Like he was the one with the problem. Jeremy had gone so far trying to fit in with Stygian that somewhere along the line he'd given them the impression that he was a subservient doormat, and he didn't know how much more he could take.

He stormed up to the bedroom with Kennedy trailing behind. Jeremy said nothing and stood next to the window, wishing he wasn't being inspected while on the verge of flipping out. Their proximity heightened a sudden urge to flee the house, which was confusing since Jeremy spent 80 percent of his time wishing the guitarist would pay him more attention.

Sometimes Jeremy couldn't decide if Kennedy was part of his problem with the band. Watts was a douche, but Kennedy was a complete enigma. He was an untouchable brooding mass of simmering discontent, but strangely accessible when he was trying to be helpful. Unfortunately, it wasn't pity or guidance that Jeremy wanted. The very notion ratcheted his frustration up to unmanageable levels.

Again, he thought about finding a bus depot and again he tamped down on the idea before it flourished. He wouldn't run away. Not yet.

"We should start switching off."

Jeremy glanced over his shoulder. "What are you talking about?"

Kennedy gestured at the lounge. "You've been sleeping there every night. We should switch off. Or… we can share the bed. We've crashed in closer quarters."

"I'm not sleeping in the bed with you."

Kennedy's expression didn't so much as flicker. "Suit yourself."

"It would suit me better if Watts had let me crash with Quince."

Jeremy looked out the window again. The canopy of trees swaying in the breeze rallied him into motion. He swapped his T-shirt for a black tank and grabbed a notebook, a pen, and a pair of headphones.

"Where are you going?"

"Outside to write. It has to be cooler in the woods."

"I thought you didn't like being out in the middle of nowhere."

"Like I'll be able to avoid it?" Jeremy slipped the headphones around his neck. "Besides, I walked to town today, and it was fine. And Hunter and Laurel aren't too far away. I won't be totally alone."

Kennedy paused with his hands poised on the zipper of his bag, the whorls of ink on his knuckles flashing skulls and symbols at Jeremy.

"That guy was weird. Maybe don't get too friendly, okay, kid?"

"I'd prefer three weirdoes like him to you assholes at this point. And I'm not a kid. I'm twenty-one, and y'all are barely four years older. I may be the youngest, but that doesn't mean the rest of you get to treat me like I'm helpless or stupid."

Kennedy opened his mouth to say something, but then he just looked away, shadows slanting across his face.

An apology welled in Jeremy's throat, a need to soothe the burn he'd just inflicted, but he swallowed it and instead hauled ass out of the room.

He sped up after reaching the hall and cast a cursory glance in the direction of the abandoned wing. As much as he tried to ignore the fight-or-flight instincts that kicked in every time he was near the corridor, it was an impossible task. It was worse in the early-morning hours or late at night when the house was quiet and the others were asleep.

The place was too big, too old, and reminded him too much of another hot summer spent trapped inside an eerie house after Luke's death. His mother had thought a forced spiritual intervention would fix the things in him that had broken after finding Luke dead, but all it'd done was give Jeremy a whole other slew of memories to repress. And Watts ripping the scab off by mentioning Luke only made it worse.

Jeremy headed to the back of the house and into the kitchen. Even with rays of deepening sunlight flooding the room, the sable wood and rusted pots were somber. Everything was too dark, too cluttered, and it pushed him out the metallic portal of the back door.

He glanced at the sky, measuring the time it would take before the sun set fully, and took a few tentative steps off the mottled wood of the porch. He bypassed weather-battered wicker furniture, and plants that had shriveled in their pots until nothing remained but tiny brown skeletons that would disintegrate the moment someone moved them.

The plastic band of Jeremy's headphones rubbed against his sticky skin as he began his trek into the woods. He almost put them on but decided against it, uneasy at the thought of wandering around while the shrieking of Bring Me The Horizon masked every other sound. Apprehension tickled Jeremy's spine at first, but after a while, he welcomed the solitude of being surrounded by cypress trees. The land was untouched and pure in a way he rarely encountered in the riot of strip malls and shotgun houses crowding his neighborhood in Houston.

His ears caught the soft, distant rush of water, and as he wandered aimlessly, his chest loosened. The knot of his anger unfurled so easily that Jeremy was struck by the sudden lightness of his shoulders. He'd entered the woods with the intention of pulling himself from a pit of despair, but now he just itched to jot down fragments of lyrics and coinciding tabs. To memorialize a moment of being removed from the rest of the world, and the strange enshrouding sense of safety he felt in the woods.

Jeremy's sandals weren't made for tramping through trees and brush, but he walked without thinking, and somehow this method worked. He found his way to the river as if an internal GPS had set the path. After one look at the undulating currents, Jeremy toed off his sandals and set his notebook, headset, and phone aside. He'd just peeled off his tank when movement flashed in the corner of his eye.

"Jesus, you sure know how to sneak up on a dude!"

Hunter's black curls were wet and combed back from the striking planes of his face. Up close, his eyes were paler than the sky, the irises ringed with black. He was shirtless and damp, his willowy form muscular without Kennedy's rippling cuts or Watts's wiry sinews, and completely at home in the middle of the woods.

"Sorry." Hunter raised his hands. "I wanted to warn you about swimming."

"Warn me? Why?"

"Alligators."

"*Oh.*" Jeremy took a step back and peered uneasily down at the water. "And to think I was all worried about swamp serial killers. I didn't even consider actual beasts of the wilderness."

Hunter smiled, and Jeremy's stomach flipped. He was often surrounded by gorgeous men in the music scene, but his body responded differently to Hunter. Jeremy found himself taking a step closer, then another, until he was crossing the boundaries of personal space.

"You just have to keep an eye out."

"Right." Jeremy's eyes strayed helplessly to Hunter's tapered waist and the lines of his torso. "Anything else I need to look out for?"

"No. Not in the woods."

"So I do in the house? I heard it was haunted."

The smile froze on Hunter's face. "Who did you hear that from?"

"Some kids in town." Jeremy wrestled with the desire to say more and eventually added, "And a feeling I get."

"A feeling?"

"Yeah." Jeremy gestured in a vague direction since he'd already forgotten the route he'd taken to the river. "I get weird vibes from the sealed-off wing."

He expected Hunter to refute the story, to cocoon him in reassurance the way any other landlord would, but Hunter just looked at him quietly as they stood in the silent golden-green haze of the woods.

# CHAPTER THREE

"SHOULD I take that as a yes?"

Hunter chuckled. "Would you like to take a walk with me?"

Jeremy nodded, trying to act normal and not like the absence of a response had every hair on his body standing on end. "Where to?"

They returned to the shade of the trees so Jeremy could retrieve his belongings. The sharp edges of a rock dug into the bottom of his foot, and Hunter pressed his fingers against Jeremy's shoulder, steadying him as he tried to dislodge it. After his shoes were on, Hunter pulled away and Jeremy was left oddly bereft.

"I can show you where my house is. In case you need me."

"To save me when the ghosts start their reign of terror?"

"You should be ready for it. Your band seems used to battling."

"What's that supposed to mean?"

"I picked up on the tension easily enough. I may be isolated out here, but I'm perceptive when it comes to people, and your guitarist wasn't exactly welcoming."

Jeremy turned the words over in his mind as they began walking. The area didn't have a trail so much as a path that had been worn over time into the tangle of gravel and leaves. Even so, there were very few signs of inhabitants except for their own light footprints and the occasional brown butt of a cigarette crushed into the loamy soil.

"Kennedy isn't a bad guy. He just doesn't trust many people."

"Including you?"

"Me? Why would you say that?"

"I couldn't help but notice the look on his face when you spoke. He seemed to be expecting you to say the wrong thing."

How could strangers even tell his own band didn't particularly like him? Maybe it had always been obvious. Maybe he'd just been deluded for those first couple of months.

"I'm sorry." Hunter paused in his stride. "I don't think before I speak."

"No." Jeremy shrugged, refusing to show his hurt in front of this flawless stranger. "Nah, you're just honest. It's okay. I like it."

"Okay." Hunter's graveness fell away, and another of his tiny smiles broke free. "I don't want to upset you."

"There's no reason to be upset. It is what it is. I'm new to the band, and I'm still trying to fit in."

"I understand."

Hunter pushed drying hair out of his face—an unconscious movement that enraptured Jeremy. He traced the elegant lines of Hunter's wrist, his long, thin fingers. Who the hell was this guy? Why was he living out in the damn woods like a recluse?

"You understand what?" Jeremy asked a beat too late.

"About fitting in. Laurel and I don't fit in… anywhere, really. We're odd."

"I doubt it, man. Beautiful people always fit in. It's like a rule."

"If that were true, you wouldn't have any problems."

The extravagant compliment was spoken so bluntly that Jeremy almost didn't process the words. When he did, he turned away. Maybe if Hunter didn't focus on him for long periods of time, he wouldn't notice how inaccurate it was.

Jeremy knew he wasn't troll material, but he was also very aware of his slight stature. He'd inherited the irritatingly fae-like Black family features—pale blond hair, dainty nose, wide mouth, big gray eyes—but unlike most of them, Jeremy had come out runty. Barely pushing five feet five and skinny as a whip. He looked more cartoonish than sexy. A lot of the other bands joked that he was Stygian's little mascot.

"So," Hunter ventured. "Tell me about yourself. Are you talented?"

Jeremy released an awkward chuckle. "I've never had someone ask me that before. I don't really know. I'm no Tré Cool, but I'm getting better."

"I don't know who that is."

"The drummer in Green Day!"

"Ah."

Jeremy had the feeling Hunter still had no idea who he was talking about. "What type of music do you listen to?"

"I don't particularly like music."

"What! How is that possible? I would die without music."

"Somehow I doubt that."

Cocking his head, Jeremy considered Hunter. "How old are you?"

"How old do I seem?"

"You *seem* totally out of the loop for all that is culturally pertinent to my generation, but you look like you're in your late twenties."

"Which matters more to you?" Hunter began walking again.

"I don't know, dude. It's too hot to be thinking this seriously about small talk. My brain is charbroiled in my skull."

Jeremy's foot slid on another long, flat rock. He felt like a legitimate damsel after Hunter steadied him again. "This is getting embarrassing. Maybe I should just cling to your arm."

"You could if you wanted."

"Dude. I'm joking. Badly, at that."

"I wouldn't mind if you clung to me. I told you I think you're very beautiful."

"You're pretty high up on the spank bank list yourself."

The joke once again failed to translate, but judging from the way Hunter slid their fingers together, he got the idea. Walking around in inappropriate footwear in the woods had definitely been one of Jeremy's better ideas.

They walked for a while—aimlessly, Jeremy thought—and he wondered how long it would take to return. The shafts of sunlight were growing deeper in golden hue, and the sky smudged pink as daylight waned. He looked over his shoulder with a jolt of anxiety, but they'd left the river behind and had gone deeper into the woods.

More than once, Jeremy nearly suggested they return to the mansion, but a single glance at Hunter chased all doubt away.

"Look," Hunter said, nodding at a break in the trees. "This is what I wanted to show you."

They approached a shack so poorly tended, Jeremy couldn't believe it belonged to the same family who owned the mansion. The area was absent of the waist-high weeds that climbed some parts of the woods, but cobweb-covered vegetation pressed in around the sun-bleached porch. Although the ground was paved down with gravel that led to an actual trail, the structure itself looked on the verge of falling apart. The lattices of the roof were shot through with a riot of vines, and the air smelled of damp rot and fungus.

If Hunter had not taken Jeremy there, he'd have assumed it was abandoned.

"This is where you live?"

"Yes. If you need anything, I'll be here. You can follow that trail"—Hunter pointed to another less obvious break in the trees—"back to the house."

"Oh." Relief struck hard and fast. "Good. I should get back."

"So soon?"

"Yeah, I mean...." Jeremy rubbed his damp palms together. "Before it gets dark and I get lost and starve out in the woods."

"I could give you something to eat."

Jeremy switched his gaze from the cabin to the trail. "I don't know."

"Come on."

Hunter climbed the short set of stairs and pushed the door open. Jeremy hung back, fingers hooked into the belt loops of his shorts, and offered a halfhearted smile when Hunter looked back expectantly.

"Scared?"

"No." Jeremy was unwilling to explain his reoccurring feeling of unease. "I just think I should get back before the sun sets."

A woman became visible in the shack's doorway, and Jeremy was struck by her appearance. She was younger than Hunter and soft, petite, and curvy where he was long and lean, but the dark pitch of her hair and the rain color of her eyes marked her as family. She had to be Hunter's sister—Laurel.

She walked around Hunter and propped her arms on the railing. Neither of them seemed concerned about the glistening cobwebs and arachnids creeping along nearby.

"Don't come on so strong, brother," she said, staring at Jeremy. "You'll spook him."

"Ha. Nah, I'm not that easily spooked." Jeremy rocked on the balls of his feet. "I mean, not by people. By dark woods? Yes."

"No worries," she said. "I'm sure my brother will have plenty of time to fawn all over you this summer. I wouldn't mind fawning over some of your bandmates, myself."

Jeremy wondered if she meant Kennedy but knew a hookup between him and Laurel was unlikely. Kennedy didn't do complicated regular fucks, and that pretty much ruled out their landlady.

"It's nice to finally meet you."

"Likewise."

Both siblings watched him intently.

"Well," Jeremy said. "I'll see y'all later, I guess. Maybe we can have a drink up at the house sometime."

"Great. I haven't had a drink in ages." Her words came out in an easy drawl, but Hunter tensed. She ignored him, lips curling higher, and wiggled her fingers. "See you later."

"Yeah, later."

Jeremy started up the path leading to the rest of the property, and was grateful that it was more discernible than the trail they'd followed through the woods. For the first time, he was anxious to get back to the mansion. While he'd enjoyed Hunter's company, the easy companionship and comfortable silence had vanished as soon as they'd arrived at the cabin. Having both siblings so focused on him had been unnerving.

Jeremy unconsciously quickened his steps as two sets of eyes burned into the back of his head. He didn't shoot a glance over his shoulder until he reached a bend in the path.

A ribbon of unease constricted his chest.

Hunter and Laurel were gone, but the weight of their scrutiny lingered to prickle his skin.

Redoubling his pace, Jeremy almost expected Hunter to show up during the walk back, but despite the nagging feeling of being watched, there was no sign of the older Caroway.

SOMEWHERE IN the depths of his dream, someone was playing the piano. The notes were faint, but with each quiet step down the hallway, Jeremy could hear more. The increasing tempo, the growing intensity, the way something so beautiful could almost sound like a threat— Liszt. The piece about the gondolas. The one Luke had always played.

The music washed over him, halting his careful footsteps. It grew louder, more sinister, and his stomach coiled before the piece ended abruptly. The notes faded, and from somewhere close by, someone whispered his name. Jeremy spun around.

"Luke?"

The hallway behind him stretched long and empty with only a faintly moving shadow at the far end disrupting the stillness.

He ghosted toward it, but a sinking feeling told him the shadow was not his brother, and there should have been no strangers here. The dream had always been a lasting connection to Luke, and now.... Now, the stability of that link unraveled. Maybe these dreams were nothing more than products of wishful thinking; or maybe they were signs that he was going down the path of his father's family.

Either way, he needed to know.

The shadow started to detach itself from the darkness, but before it escaped its veil, the whisper returned, and Jeremy opened his eyes.

The sheets he'd pulled over the chaise lounge were damp with sweat, the room unbearably hot despite the lazy swishing of the ceiling fan. The hallway was gone. The music was gone. He was back at the mansion in Louisiana and far away from the past.

Jeremy sat up, and his body protested in response. It was hard to fully awaken when everything had an unreal quality to it. He blinked and told himself the shadows of the room were not the shadows from the dream. That sunlit hallway was not from this house. It was the middle of the night, and Kennedy should be in the bed a few feet away. Jeremy was not trapped in a waking dream, the kind where he thought he was conscious but was still lost amid memories of being locked away after Luke's death.

He was in the real world.

To reassure himself, Jeremy peered at the bed but it was empty, the sheets wrinkled and trailing halfway off the mattress. The only sign that Kennedy had recently been in the room was the smell of cigarette smoke hanging in the air.

Jeremy got to his feet and left the room, hurrying to the bathroom. As he hunched over the sink and stared into the mirror, the invisible crawl of nerves returned. Mirrors set him on edge—he always expected someone to appear behind him or for his face to shift and change, for the glass to reflect all of the raw, ugly things he hid inside. He'd held those fears since childhood—that there was more to the world than what was visible on the surface.

He splashed the icy water on his face and slicked it through his hair, forcing the disorientation away. It was an attempt to bury the nagging worry that, once again, his stitched-together pieces were coming undone.

Inhaling deeply, Jeremy focused on the sounds of the mansion. The random creaking, the night insects, a breeze jingling the wind chimes on the porch, and… a steady knocking sound.

Jeremy left the bathroom and walked down the length of the hall. By the time he realized it was emanating from Quince and Watts's room, he knew what it was. Moans joined the knocking sound, echoing in the otherwise silent house.

Jeremy slunk away, but Quince's frantic voice piqued a perverse sense of curiosity, and he backtracked to their room. The door stood open as it often did when they had sex.

Quince was on his stomach, hips raised, as Watts fucked him with such force that each thrust slammed the headboard against the wall. The tangled pleas falling from Quince's mouth rose in volume after Watts reached around to jerk him off.

The combination of roughness and wild abandon bowled Jeremy over. Watching the two men rutting against each other reminded him of how long it had been since anyone had shown such a burning need for his body. Months. Maybe over a year.

He retreated a step, and his heel landed on a spot in the floor that elicited a loud creak. Watts looked over his shoulder, eyes locking on Jeremy. He smirked, and flexed his hips faster.

Quince's cries chased Jeremy down the stairs.

Returning to his room wasn't an option for the foreseeable future. Knowing Watts, he was keyed-up on coke and would nail Quince all night. It could only lead to Jeremy jerking off while fantasizing about Kennedy making *him* scream. It wouldn't be the first time a Quince-and-Watts sexathon sent him spiraling in that direction.

Thinking about music, especially about learning to play the guitar, was a good alternative to obsessing over sex. Jeremy tried ineffectively to switch gears, but it all crashed back like a tidal wave once he wandered to the kitchen and saw Kennedy through the open back door.

He was sitting on the porch swing, smoking a cigarette and wearing only a pair of black boxer briefs. His muscular thighs were splayed open, and Jeremy tried very hard not to seek the outline of his bulge.

"Hey."

Kennedy exhaled a cloud of smoke. "Hey."

When Jeremy didn't move, Kennedy raised an eyebrow.

"You coming outside?"

Jeremy let the screen door shut behind him, and it banged louder than he'd expected. Making an idiot of himself was going to be the theme of the night, so he made it worse by looking hesitantly between the steps and the spot next to Kennedy.

Kennedy scooted over, but one of his arms remained extended on the back of the swing.

They were almost too close together given their lack of clothing and with Jeremy's thoughts still firmly positioned in the gutter. To distract himself, and to avoid fidgeting, he snagged a cigarette from the box resting on one of the armrests. Leaning in to light it off Kennedy's, their eyes locked, and Jeremy steadied himself by bracing a hand on Kennedy's thigh.

The cherry of Jeremy's cigarette flared, and he reluctantly pulled away.

"Can't sleep either?"

"Nope," Jeremy said. "Not with Quince and Watts going at it like animals down the hall."

"Yeah, they'll be at it all night." Kennedy pressed the sole of his foot against the side of the porch. "That's not what woke me up, though."

"What did?"

"I'm not sure. I kept hearing a weird sound and went to check it out. Then the porn stars started up, and I came out here."

Jeremy looked out at the woods. There were no lights in that direction or even in the backyard itself. If not for the moon, they would be sitting in pitch darkness. "You know, looking for the source of a mysterious sound is generally how people die in scary movies."

"You have a point. Which is why I'm surprised to see you wandering around." Kennedy slumped down. "Are they that loud?"

"Now they are." Jeremy tried not to react when Kennedy's hand fell on his shoulder. It was a light touch, but it was enough to spike Jeremy's heartbeat. Especially once Kennedy turned the graze to a massage. "I... uh, that's not what woke me up either, though. I had a shitty dream."

"Is that why you're on edge?"

Jeremy stole a look at Kennedy, but the man gazed back calmly. Maybe for Stygian, it was normal to massage your bandmates while sitting half-naked on the porch in the middle of the night. The band had always possessed superflexible boundaries about space. Or a complete lack of boundaries.

Even before joining, Jeremy had watched them perform from the corners of dive bars and all-ages clubs. He'd been fascinated by how handsy they were with each other. Whether it was Watts grinding up on Quince or Caroline while he sang, or writhing on the floor at Kennedy's feet like he was begging to be touched, there had been no denying the group had chemistry.

Kennedy smiled. "You gonna answer?"

"What?" Jeremy blinked. "Sorry. You're distracting me."

"Do you want me to stop?"

"No. It feels good."

For the second time in as many days, Kennedy gave him that look. The up-and-down stare that could be an eyefuck or just another example of how unintentionally sexy Kennedy's intensity was. Either way, Jeremy had to return his attention to the moonlit woods surrounding them before he did, or said, something foolish.

The ensuing silence was heavy with the ambiance of night. With the breeze rustling the trees and tall grass, and the answer and call of crickets and frogs, there was nothing to do but smoke and share a mostly warm bottle of beer that Kennedy had brought outside.

The tension melted away, and Jeremy became a boneless thing as sure, steady fingers worked the kinks out of his neck and shoulders. He sank down, tilting his head against Kennedy's shoulder, and let their bare knees brush. The massage turned into an idle, repetitive pull of long fingers through Jeremy's hair.

"I could get used to being somewhere like this," Kennedy said. "I like the quiet."

"I don't."

"It doesn't seem that way to me." Kennedy squeezed Jeremy's neck again before pulling away. "I haven't seen you this relaxed since I met you. Well, when you're by yourself on the porch or up in that damn tree."

"I didn't think anyone saw me climb up there," Jeremy admitted.

"I always see you, kid."

Jeremy curled his fingers around the edge of the swing. "I—I do like the quiet, but this house brings back weird memories for me. When I was younger, I spent months locked up in a place like this. Not a big mansion, but an old church out in the country. It had stained glass."

Kennedy picked up the beer bottle but didn't bring it to his lips. "Why were you there?"

"I was with my uncle. It… wasn't a good time." Jeremy felt Kennedy go rigid and added quickly, "He didn't do anything to me. I mean he did—but not like that. He wasn't a pervert. Just a religious zealot."

"So, why were you there? What was he doing?"

Jeremy turned sideways on the swing, one leg beneath him. "It has to do with my brother. Luke." He focused on the cigarette burning between Kennedy's fingers, the cherry working its way up the white stick. "After he died, I didn't handle it well. I had… problems. My mom wasn't too good at dealing with problems, so she sent me to my uncle. She thought because he was a pastor, he could help me."

"I'm guessing he didn't."

"Not so much. Being locked up with him made me worse. His delusions about religion just made my delusions about everything else more vivid. I thought I was losing it. I was in denial about Luke being dead, and sometimes I thought I could feel or hear him…. So, yeah, not a good time."

"Jesus, Jeremy. I had no idea."

"Most people don't. I don't even know why I'm telling you now."

The pangs of regret were already scraping beneath his skin. There was nothing to gain by discussing his temporary psychosis, but Kennedy was easy to talk to.

"You don't mention your family much," Kennedy said. "Are they that bad?"

Jeremy woodenly raised one shoulder. "My mother's family is full of religious fanatics, and the Black family, my dad's side, is made up of drunken, depressed lunatics who… believe in weird mystical shit."

The last part came out in a rush, but Kennedy only nodded, seemed to consider asking something, and evidently decided it was none of his business.

Jeremy sagged on the swing again. "I guess it's good I told you before Watts has the chance to mock me about it."

Kennedy tilted the neck of the beer bottle back, draining the liquid in one gulp. He licked the remnants from his lips and set the bottle on the floor. "Maybe. Maybe not."

"Oh, come on, Kennedy."

"He's unpredictable. It could go either way."

"He hates me. Admit it."

Shaking his head, Kennedy said, "He hates himself more than anyone, but I'm probably a close second."

"What?" The information did not compute. "Why would he hate you? I can't believe that's true."

"Believe it."

"But *why*? I know he's all bent out of shape because he wants to be in control of everything, but—"

"It's not that." Kennedy's gaze burned across the yard and into the surrounding trees—a laser beam that could set Jeremy afire. "He knows I resent him for Caroline dying, and he wants me to pat him on the shoulder and be supportive because of his fucking survivor's guilt, but I can't."

If there was a right thing to say, Jeremy didn't have a firm hold on it. Kennedy never spoke about Caroline. Not at length, anyway. It was always fleeting comments and aborted statements about something she had done or said in the past, but then the shutters would slam down on Kennedy's face, and he would return to his typical laconic self. During those times, Jeremy wondered if Kennedy had been different before the accident. If this gorgeously quiet and smoldering man was just a shell of someone he'd once been.

"Was Watts… drinking? Is that why they crashed?"

"Unless his mommy paid off the cops, I don't think so." Kennedy's mouth twisted in a hard mockery of a smile. "But hey, anything is possible if you've got the fucking money, right? I could totally see Watts or his mom palming over a big wad of green and some fat Friendswood cop letting a BAC test slide. Pretty easy to stop giving a shit about some dead white-trash girl under those circumstances."

"Dude." Jeremy touched Kennedy's jaw. After a brief resistance, Kennedy looked at him with eyes glittering wetly in the darkness. "Fuck, I'm sorry I suggested that. He wasn't drinking. A cop wouldn't let him get away with that shit."

"It's not your fault," Kennedy said, but his voice was rough. He tried to chuckle, but the sound was thick, unsteady. "I'm being an idiot."

"No." Jeremy tentatively ran his fingers over the rough stubble shading Kennedy's cheek. "I know how it feels to lose someone. It took me years to deal with my brother's death, and you just lost Caroline."

"But you were a kid. I'm a grown-ass man."

"Even so," Jeremy said. "Grief fucking sucks. Death fucking sucks. There's no acceptable way to deal with someone being ripped out of your life. You can't prepare for that or how to handle the aftermath. Always remembering your last conversation with—"

His increasingly choked words were muffled by the sudden press of Kennedy's mouth.

Jeremy froze, barely reacting, as cool, dry lips moved against his own. It was nothing really. Just a brief graze. But in that moment, Jeremy tasted menthol and warm beer and the more muted flavor of Kennedy. Just Kennedy. It zinged through him until he wanted to clamber into the guitarist's lap and make the kiss hard and desperate.

But he didn't. He knew, beneath the explosion of tingles and warmth, that Kennedy would end this before it really began. And he did.

Kennedy pulled away, casual as you please, while Jeremy fought to suppress the hitches in his breathing and the tremors in his hands.

"Was that—" Jeremy cleared his throat. "Is that how you shut me up?"

"Yeah. You were getting pretty morbid."

Feeling like a fool, Jeremy faced forward again. He wrapped his arms around himself, fingers digging into his own skin, and stared out into the silver-lit night. "Yeah," he said. "I guess I was."

He knew without looking that Kennedy was watching him, but Jeremy refused to meet his eyes. If it didn't matter to Kennedy, that minor bit of intimacy wouldn't matter to Jeremy either.

"Did I weird you out?"

"No. It's not like it was a real kiss, anyway."

Static silence replaced the confidences they'd shared a moment earlier. Strange how something Jeremy had craved for months could create space between them. How it made him feel so low.

"So… what I was getting at is that you shouldn't worry about Watts," Kennedy said. "He's fucked-up. Always has been. The typical product of a wealthy home."

"Got it."

"And regardless of what he says," Kennedy pressed on, "he wanted you in the band. He recognized you when you came to audition, and he said he'd been friends with your older brother. He was surprised you were into the drums instead of piano like Luke."

Now *that* was strange. And more unexpected than Kennedy's meaningless shut-up-the-emo-gay-kid kiss.

"Wait—friends? Luke didn't have any friends. I thought Watts just knew about Luke because they went to the same school."

"Ah. Well." Kennedy sucked his lip ring into his mouth. "Maybe I'm making it out to be more than it was. But Watts knew things about him, so I assumed they were closer."

"Maybe he heard rumors?" Jeremy ventured. "Dude, seriously. My brother had no friends. I think it was partially why he killed himself. Being alone sucks."

"He had you."

Jeremy tried not to show just how sharply those three words socked him in the gut, and redirected the conversation away from Luke. "Regardless, Watts may be fucked-up, but that doesn't mean I can't be tired of walking on eggshells. I don't understand why you've put up with it for as long as you have."

"Because he was there for me when my folks died," Kennedy admitted. "Sometimes loyalty overrides discontent."

The vulnerable wavering side Kennedy had showed while discussing Caroline was gone, and he was as stoic as ever.

"That's fine, but I have nothing to override mine. I've admired Stygian for years, but if I haven't found my place by the time we head back to Houston, it's never going to happen. I won't be his whipping boy just so I can be in this band."

"I see."

Jeremy knew he should say something to add a balm to the proclamation, but being summarily quieted during his last show of compassion hadn't left him charitable. Quiet was safer. In one way or another, words always got him in trouble.

From the corner of Jeremy's eye, he saw Kennedy pick up a slim book that had been wedged beside him. It had a moleskin cover and was tied shut with a short leather cord.

"What's that?"

"I found that under the bed while I was looking for my lighter." Kennedy dropped it on Jeremy's stomach. "I think it belonged to someone who rented the house. Thought you might be interested."

Jeremy undid the tie and flipped through the pages even though he couldn't see any of the writing in the dark. "Why?"

"It belonged to some writer. I only read a few of the entries, but he talked a lot about how writing saves him from himself. How it's the glue holding him together when he thinks everything is falling apart." Kennedy flexed his legs and rocked the swing. "It reminded me of you and your brother. Especially what you said at your audition about why you got into music."

"I figured you guys thought that was lame."

"Watts pretended to, but I'm sure he can relate. Why the hell do you think he holds on so tight to this band and freaks out when he thinks things are going wrong?" The sound of a striking match followed the question, and the smell of sulfur filled the air. "Whether the crash was his fault or not, I do know Watts is barely keeping it together. The music and the band, me and Quince—we're his glue. Even if I'm tired of the responsibility."

Jeremy tightened his fingers around the cover of the journal and looked over the railing again. In the distance, something was steadily moving through the trees—a low rustle, twigs snapping, and far too loud to be a real predator. Jeremy kept watching, but the movement and the noise ceased abruptly.

With nothing else to distract him, Jeremy thought about that reckless kiss, and the lack of care the entire band used with him even though he was in need of some glue of his own. Too bad Stygian seemed to be in short supply.

# CHAPTER FOUR

*SIMON, I hope you use this journal to take down all of those late-night ponderings. Love, Olga.*

The inscription was written on the inside of the journal's cover. With those words alone, Jeremy conjured a blurry perception of Simon—sensitive, prone to overthinking, and needing to record his musings in order to sort them out. The very definition of an artist.

It had intrigued Jeremy enough for him to start reading, and after a couple of days, he understood why Kennedy had given it to him.

Simon wrote in flowing cursive that sprawled across the unlined paper, ensuring a single sentence took up almost half a page. He was a young adult author and told the story of his stories—documenting his characters' journeys, their backgrounds, and how they would grow within the chapters of novels Simon never actually seemed to write. Extensive notes, character sketches, and plot outlines would precede sprinkles of scenes and dialogue that enraptured Jeremy. The start of each story hooked his attention with a combination of grim irony and melancholy, but they always stopped after the first handwritten chapter was complete.

By the time Jeremy got to the middle of the packed journal, it occurred to him that Simon's characters all reminded him of his brother, and he wondered how Kennedy could have known. For all that Luke had yearned for a friend to confide in, very few people in high school had patience for someone so fragile, and years of bullying over their secondhand clothes and rumored town-slut mother had made them both disinclined to share too much with others.

So, how did Kennedy see Luke so clearly in the pages if they had never been friends?

Jeremy knew he should be relieved Luke hadn't been forgotten or that his death hadn't turned into a semi-interesting story about someone's high school career, but he wasn't. He wondered if everyone knew how fucked-up Luke had been, and worried they knew the same about him.

The breakdown he'd had after finding Luke dead. The unyielding waves of denial, even though he'd sat alone, for hours, with the body. How he'd insisted to his mother that Luke wasn't really gone, and the desperate way he'd tried to ground himself with razor blades and sliced skin once the facts had become irrefutable.

Then his uncle's backwoods fanatical attempts to rip the spiraling instability out of him with the righteous force of God. It had amounted to nothing more than an attempt to break him until he became a paragon of a Christian youth instead of a queer alternative kid, and a semblance of normality had returned only recently. He'd found it with the help of counseling and by distancing himself from the past.

But now the Caroway mansion, the country, and the reminders from the band were bringing everything back.

Jeremy wrapped the cord around the journal and rubbed his thumb over the soft moleskin cover. Had Simon Abbott panicked after realizing it was gone? Or had he started a new journal with new characters? A fresh beginning with less tragedy and angst. It was not so different from what Stygian had set out to do by coming here—outdistance the past, release the demons, and escape the pain. Start over.

If Watts let them do it. If any of them ever let Jeremy in.

Gripping the journal in one hand, Jeremy yawned and stood with a languid stretch, relaxed despite the sweat and grime gathered in the creases of his clothing and exposed skin. He scooped up his sandals and returned, barefoot, to the trail. The grass and warm earth beneath his feet was soothing.

It was well after noon, which meant time for practice, but Jeremy was loath to leave the peace of the woods. It was weird to long for something so basic when he usually derived comfort from shrieking song lyrics and aggressive riffs.

He meandered his way through the woods, walking around jutting rocks and the tallest clusters of weeds, and had almost made it to the edge of the tree line when he realized something had changed. No more mockingbird, cicadas, or soft scrabble of an animal. Everything had stopped.

A scan of the area did nothing to explain the unnatural stillness. Skin crawling, he resumed walking, faster this time, but the quiet stretched. Walking turned into jogging until Jeremy was outright running toward the mansion. By the time he made it back, sweat dripped from his face and soaked his shirt.

Watts had been slouched on the stairs but sat up once Jeremy crossed the yard.

"What the hell were you doing? Jogging through the forest?"

Jeremy came up short next to the back porch. "Just... just trying not to be late for practice."

"Calm the fuck down, jailbait." Watts pressed the tips of his toes against Jeremy's wet T-shirt. "Your eager beaver routine isn't going to win you any points."

Jeremy shoved Watts's foot away. "I'm not jailbait, and I'm done trying to impress you. You can keep your cool-kids club, and I'll just stick around until you find a drummer you actually want."

Watts said nothing, and it added weight to the eerie silence.

Jeremy scowled. "Why are you looking at me like that?"

"You're full of shit. You're not going nowhere."

"Think so?" The abrupt, erratic singing of a mockingbird cut through the muted quality of the woods. Jeremy exhaled slowly. "I'm not a masochist, and I'm not totally oblivious. You don't want me in the band now, even if you did before. I'm an outsider, and I'm not up to par. Just find a replacement after the summer, and I'll make tracks. It's not that big of a deal to me."

"Oh yeah?" Watts hopped down and bumped into Jeremy. He put his hands on the hips of his skintight jeans and glowered through a halo of messy black hair. "And where the fuck are you going to go? Try out for an entertainment band at a country club in Pearland? Maybe it's a good idea. You might get play from some rich old ball sac with a taste for baby twinks."

"At least I'd get some steady gigs."

Watts's eyes turned to blue slits. "What are you trying to say?"

"It's not that complicated to figure out, to be honest."

Watts reached out in a blur, and Jeremy recoiled, taking a stumbling step back. He leaned against the side of the porch as Watts's face went from angry to incredulous.

"Now you think I'm going to fucking hit you?"

Jeremy shrugged, face warm and body tense. "I dunno."

"I was going to shake some sense into you, not punch you in the face, you dumb—"

"Everyone cool?" Kennedy stepped out of the house, dark eyes sweeping between Watts and Jeremy.

"We're fine," Jeremy muttered.

Watts turned and stomped up the creaky stairs. "Little bastard is acting real brand-new all of a sudden," he growled as he shouldered his way through the rickety door. It rebounded and slammed shut.

Kennedy didn't flinch. His focus settled on Jeremy. "Where've you been?"

"Out."

"All right. Any chance we can talk later?"

"Sure."

"What's with the monosyllables?"

"I don't have much to say."

The stoic mask cracked, and Kennedy's mouth tipped down. "Look, about the other night—"

"Let's just go practice." Jeremy climbed the steps. "I'll try not to fuck you up."

"Jere—"

Kennedy reached for Jeremy's arm, but he yanked away.

"Jesus, what's with you people grabbing at me all of a sudden?"

"*You people*? What did I do to you?"

"It doesn't matter. Just forget it." Jeremy attempted to walk around Kennedy to get in the house. "It's just not my day."

This time Kennedy didn't touch him, but he did plant his hand firmly against the screen door. "What's wrong?"

"Nothing! Just leave it alone."

He tried to pull the door open, but Kennedy's weight was firm against it.

"It doesn't seem like nothing," Kennedy insisted.

Unwilling to talk about his momentary freak-out on the walk home, Jeremy said, "I'm cool. Let's just go practice before Watts gets more pissed off."

Kennedy didn't look convinced, but he released the door, and they entered the house.

The practice space was more organized than Jeremy had seen since their arrival. While he'd avoided the band, they had made a valiant effort to get the day off on the right foot.

Watts had already sunk into one of his moods, but he kept his comments to himself and contained his annoyance to stony glaring.

"Everybody ready?" Quince asked with forced enthusiasm.

"Start with 'Blue Tabs,' then 'Happy Trails.'" Watts jutted his chin at Jeremy without meeting his eye. "Do it."

Jeremy nodded, grabbing his sticks. He tried to launch himself into the zone—where nothing existed but him and the music. Lately it had been unattainable, but maybe now…. Maybe if he boxed up all those concerns, he could reach it.

"Blue Tabs" started with hyperfast hi-hats, and an up-down rhythm that made his arms ache as the vibrations rattled through his bones. It was one of Jeremy's favorite songs, the first he'd heard by Stygian and the first time he'd watched in awe as a local band tore up the stage like they were playing at the Roseland Ballroom instead of some tiny dive bar in Houston. He'd told them that at his audition, and now Jeremy wondered if Watts was trying to do him a solid by starting practice with this set.

It was unlikely, but it set an awesome tone.

The dim room exploded with sound. Aggressive punk chords were tempered by Watts crooning into the mic as if he was singing about a lover instead of prescription drugs. For him, it was probably the same. The song was more instrumental than lyrical—all chaotic noise before dipping into moody lows—but ended with a wail of the guitar so abrupt the amp's cord may as well have been cut.

They went on to "Happy Trails" and "Up the Road," working their way through a set list that had been created long before Jeremy's audition. It didn't matter, because he knew the music just as well as if he'd been the one to pen the tabs. The rest of Stygian thought they had cornered the market on grief, but Jeremy had admired Caroline since he'd seen her perform at a block party years ago. Jeremy played her parts like he was doing her homage.

The rest of the band keyed in to his energy, and when they wound down, his adrenaline had spiked to a degree that fueled a need to stage dive like he would have after a real show.

"Right on," Quince breathed when they finally stopped for a break. "Dudes, that was *so good.*"

Kennedy nodded his approval, and Watts gave a sharp shrug. He was trying hard to be moody and stolid, but his eyes gleamed with the lust of creativity and the need to perform. He hid it like being pleased was a secret, and dove directly into castigation.

"Little drummer boy finally got his shit together, so we can get a fucking move on, yeah?" Watts paced the small space, aggressively skinny and full of unfiltered impatience. "So we can handle music we've been playing for two years. Fan-fucking-tastic, but that wasn't more than a warm-up. Y'all better believe it's going to get harder than that."

"So where's the new songs, boss?" Kennedy's voice was dry enough to dehydrate the ecosystem in a rainforest. "Lyrics get lost somewhere up your nose?"

"Fuck you, Ken-boy. Where's *your* parts?"

"Written three months ago."

Watts stared, and Jeremy just barely stifled a laugh. He'd watched Kennedy pen guitar tabs in every spare moment, scribbling chords until his long fingers were covered in ink.

"Whatever, Mr. President. I'm tired of your shit." Watts eyeballed Quince and Jeremy in turn, not seeming to mind that his insults and complaints made zero sense.

"Why don't we break to brainstorm?" Quince asked.

"Naw, to hell with that. I don't want to lose my momentum." Watts hopped in place. "Screw it. Let's finish the set. We can figure out the new material tomorrow."

They started up again and didn't stop until the room reeked of sweat and Watts's voice went raw. Instead of guzzling water, he'd sucked lazily on a beer, and by the end of the session, he was close to keeling over.

"This place fucking sucks." Watts ran both hands through his soaked hair. "Who rents a house with no AC in the middle of the summer? That's not even good planning. Laurel is lucky she's a piece of ass."

"I've never even met her," Kennedy said. "So she isn't getting by on charm."

"We've run into her in the woods a couple times. If you scaredy-bitches would stop clinging to the porch, you'd know that."

"I quit clinging to the porch days ago," Jeremy pointed out. "Kennedy hasn't."

"Because a jaunt in the woods would really ease my boredom?" Kennedy scoffed and unplugged an amp. "Unlikely. We just need to make this little retreat musical instead of moaning all the time. Today was a nice change of pace."

Watts flipped Kennedy off, but Quince was nodding in agreement. "Kennedy's right. You know what we should do? I just got a really good idea."

"Oh God." Watts threw himself onto a velvet ottoman, his long fingers trailing along the wooden floor. His leering gaze fell on Jeremy. "I have an idea too. Let's de-virginize our baby drummer since Ken-boy won't."

"Fuck you, Watts." The argument felt like déjà vu. "I wouldn't let you stick it in my ass if you paid me. And I'm not a virgin."

"Yeah? Who've you been with?"

"None of your business."

"Ha! Bullshitter."

"Watts, shut up!" Quince exclaimed. "I have an *idea*! It's a really good one."

"So spit it out and stop talking about how great it is," Kennedy said.

"Fine. Let's go find a decent liquor store, stock up, and party. Just have fun, play some old-school punk, get all of this bored stuff out of our system, and starting tomorrow we focus totally on the new material. I'll even, like, make a schedule for brainstorming and writing and everything."

Watts cocked his head. "That suggestion actually doesn't suck."

Quince beamed and whipped out his phone to search for the nearest liquor store. It turned out to be out of Logansport and farther north. He declared it an adventure and a chance to explore, but both Kennedy and Jeremy declined to go. Being trapped in the van with Watts, even after a successful practice session, would only be an opportunity to ruin everyone's good mood. But when the front door slammed shut and the van's engine sputtered to life, restlessness set in, and Jeremy regretted not leaving the house.

With a low huff, he headed for the stairs while stripping off his T-shirt. He expected Kennedy to finish unplugging the equipment and putting the room back to rights, but Kennedy followed him upstairs. Neither of them spoke until Jeremy threw himself facedown on the bed.

"You were good today."

"Thanks," Jeremy said, his response muffled by the bedspread. He closed his eyes, overly conscious of Kennedy's presence, and jumped when fingers grazed the skin between his shoulder blades. Such a light touch, but it was a power chord straight to his dick. Jeremy bit his lip. "What, Kennedy?"

"I told you that we needed to talk."

"About what?"

"About last night."

Kennedy was still touching him, and Jeremy knew every brush of fingers against flesh would elicit rosy flushes.

"Dude—I don't give a fuck, okay? I know you just think I'm some skinny little kid you have to be nice to and look out for. I didn't take the kiss seriously. You just wanted me to quit talking my emo crap."

More uncomfortable silence, but Kennedy still didn't pull away. He dragged the tips of his fingers along Jeremy's spine down to his tailbone.

"I don't *have* to be nice to anyone. If I'm nice to you, it's because I want to be."

"Okay."

An exasperated sigh came from above Jeremy, and all he could think was *Good. Feel my irritation and confusion and be frustrated.* It was spiteful and childish, but goddamn, Jeremy was tired of being the only one incapable of having a stiff upper lip. He wanted a piece of the Kennedy from last night. The Kennedy who felt things and reacted and shared his fucking pain.

He also wanted Kennedy to stop touching him. Whether he was trying to soothe Jeremy the way he would an agitated colt or he was seeking an excuse to run his hands over Jeremy's back was unknown, but it felt way too good. His dick was already throbbing, and the pressure of the mattress was a tease.

"I wanted to talk about Watts, and after earlier, I think it's a conversation that needs to happen. He went from amped to attitude in the gutter in the space of four minutes, and I wondered why."

The line of questioning skirted the band's belief that, somehow, Jeremy was capable of damaging the fragile psyche of their volatile front man. First Quince, now Kennedy.

"Sorry. Next time I'll roll over and eat his bullshit with the correct utensils."

It was a good thing all talk of Brian Watts had the power to deflate a growing erection, because Kennedy forced him to roll onto his back.

"That's not what I meant."

"So, what did you mean? Quince already gave me the *don't give Watts a hard time* lecture."

"There's a reason for that."

"So, what's the reason?"

Kennedy's expression flickered. "It's not my business to share."

"Right. I forgot." Jeremy raised his hands. "Outsiders shouldn't ask too many questions."

"What the hell is wrong with you?" Kennedy exuded the type of impatience he usually saved for packed all-ages clubs that required wounding and maiming to reach an exit. "You're cultivating your own brand of bitterness at a breakneck speed, and it's a little fucking irritating."

Jeremy's face warmed but he didn't deny it. It was why he typically sucked up insults and snide comments—his own comebacks made it clear he was more hurt than angry. Which was so much worse.

"I don't know. I'm just... something."

"Enlightening."

Jeremy groaned, covering his face with his hand. "I'm sorry, okay? Just tell me what you wanted to tell me, and I'll stop being a brat."

The mattress sank under the weight of Kennedy's muscular frame. They were close—a little too close—and Jeremy swallowed heavily. Proximity to Kennedy was always a distraction, but with them alone in the house, with their bodies tucked close enough for Jeremy to smell the cigarette smoke and clean sweat clinging to Kennedy's skin, it was also too intimate. Too easy to remember the night on the porch and all of the things that could have happened if Kennedy had been serious. If he'd opened his mouth a bit more. Let Jeremy taste the hot wetness inside.

Realizing he'd been staring, and imagining, Jeremy shifted his weight and tried to roll away. Kennedy held him in place.

"You're not a brat."

"Yeah, I know. I'm just a kid."

"Jesus Christ." Kennedy's breath gusted out. "It's not an insult. What do you want me to call you? Baby? Darling?"

Jeremy's face went from warm to burning. "You could just call me Jeremy. Believe it or not, I'm not in fucking love with you like everyone claims," he lied. "I don't need terms of endearment when the three syllables in my name work just fine." Kennedy said nothing, and Jeremy pushed on with a burst of bravado. "And the only time I let a guy call me baby is when he's in my ass."

Peripheral vision gave a clear view of Kennedy's mouth falling open as he did a slow circuit of Jeremy's sprawled body. "And when's the last time that happened?"

"The bathroom of that club in Galveston. When we opened up for the Party Kills."

Kennedy's gaze sharpened. "Are you kidding me?"

"No."

"Who?"

"The drummer."

"You—" Kennedy caught Jeremy's chin between his thumb and index finger. "You let that monkey-sticking kandi kid nail you?"

"He's hot," Jeremy said defensively. "Tall. Hard body. Who cares if he used to cover himself in beaded bracelets in, like, the '90s?"

Disapproval radiated from Kennedy. And something that sent his lip sloping in a mean curve. "You sure know how to pick them. What's next? That creepy bastard who owns this hellhole?"

"Hunter isn't creepy. He's nice. He even showed me how to get to his house in case I need him for anything."

"Oh, I bet he fucking did."

"Dude, what is your problem? Why do you even care whose dick I ride? It's not like you want me to touch yours." Jeremy rolled onto his side. Attempts at being brash kept leading to embarrassment, and he really needed to quit while he was ahead. Or eat cyanide and escape the shitshow of discussing his pathetic sex life. "I'm gonna take a nap."

"Fine."

"Are you ever going to tell me what you wanted?"

The bed rocked again as Kennedy stood. "Did you mention our conversation to Watts? The one we had the other night when I gave you that book?"

"No. Of course not. I don't want to start shit."

"Not the part about Caroline." Kennedy hesitated. "Look, he'd act up if he knew I spoke to you about Luke. He's weird about it."

"Again, *why*?"

"He just is. So please don't mention it."

Something about the force of Kennedy's tone—sharp and brooking no wiggle room for misunderstandings—butted up against the knowledge that both Watts and Kennedy knew more about Luke than they'd initially let on.

Questions and suspicion consumed Jeremy, but Kennedy was gone before he could ask anything more.

# CHAPTER FIVE

IN THE space of time between Watts announcing that he'd invited a few people over and them setting up, there were three brownouts. Jeremy didn't know if it was the unplanned addition of sound equipment, extra fans, or the thunderstorm threatening the power, but it didn't bode well. When the ominous stretch of clouds unleashed torrents of rain, Jeremy was almost positive they'd have a blackout.

Every time the lights dimmed and a hum of electricity filled the air, he waited with a sinking stomach for it to falter and fail. They would be using more electricity than usual with a house full of people, and if they overloaded the wiring, practice would be impossible. The whole trip would be a waste. It was bad enough they were spending time throwing an actual party instead of following Quince's initial plan to unwind together before focusing on writing new music. Quince said it would help Watts blow off steam, but it was clear the others were enabling him, as usual.

"I'm having doubts about this party, dude." Jeremy was wedged in an armchair that had moldered with time and seemed ready to cave in any time he twitched. The cushion was damp and brittle beneath his bare legs. "You should have called an electrician instead of some kid you met on your failed search for a liquor store."

"Don't be such a pussy." Watts grunted as he filled an enormous blue cooler with ice. The day before, he and Quince had gotten lost and wound up in Shreveport. They'd returned with booze, snacks, and apparently the contact information for a group of scene kids. Jeremy didn't know how anyone could be charmed enough by Watts to agree to come to his house. "How can a guy that grew up in the Third Ward be so fucking afraid of the dark?"

Kennedy glanced up from where he sat hunched by a tangle of wires that were a fire warden's hell. He was working diligently to anchor speakers on shelves lining the walls. "You did?"

"Well—"

"Fuck yeah, he did. I was shocked when I found out, since he and his brother went to the private school my parents put me in—"

"Our father's family paid for it after they remembered we existed."

"—but he's a hardcore little piece of ass," Watts went on. "Despite his fear of foliage and shadows."

"First, the Third Ward isn't as bad as it's made out to be. Second, I was talking about this place catching fire, not being stuck in the dark." Jeremy flipped Watts off. "And I'm not afraid of the woods. I walk around out there all the time."

"Why are you so sensitive?" Watts stood and wiped his hands on the front of his signature skinny black pants. It looked like someone had sewn them to his thighs—they were so tight the outline of his bulge was obscene. Quince couldn't stop staring.

"Just leave the ki—Jeremy alone," Kennedy said. "You're going to make the fucking guy leave the band because you don't know when to shut the hell up."

"No way," Quince protested, tearing his eyes away from Watts's crotch. "Jeremy won't leave. It's not like he has some other band waiting for him."

Jeremy shot Quince a venomous stare even though the point was valid. He wasn't sure if he'd join another band if he left Stygian. Figuring out the rest of his life was something Jeremy tried to avoid since he barely made it one day at a time. Music was his passion but, more and more, he wondered if auditioning for the spot in Stygian had been nothing more than a desperate attempt to belong somewhere.

Quince smiled, vapid and oblivious, and a blond, blue-eyed slice of American pie. It was only his clothes and the spiderweb tattoo skating down the length of his arm that prevented him from looking like the preppy kids Jeremy had gone to school with.

"Do you think you could tell your boyfriend—"

"*Boyfriend*," Watts interrupted with a guffaw. "Yeah riiiight."

"—a little more of the stuff I confided in you?" Jeremy raised his voice to talk over Watts. "I don't know what he's going to do without every little detail."

Quince's face clouded over, but his fractured gaze hung on Watts. Not Jeremy. "I know you're not my boyfriend."

"So, then, why's everyone keep saying it?" Watts asked lazily. "Don't start getting delusions of grandeur, baby. I like plugging that hole and would hate to stop."

"For Christ's sake," Kennedy muttered from his position on the floor.

"I didn't," Quince snapped. "I never—"

A rapid knock on the door interrupted Quince and startled Jeremy almost as much as the sudden blast of music that emanated from the speakers. Kennedy winced and turned down the volume a couple notches on his iPhone dock.

"Just in time," Watts crowed, bounding to his feet despite Quince's twisted expression. "Let's get this motherfucker rocking!"

Jeremy had expected the party to consist only of their pissed-off, maladjusted band, and a handful of scene kids, but in under a half hour, nearly twenty people spilled into the foyer. The house filled up with punks, emos, and bangers dressed in the now-standard uniform of skinny jeans, skateboard sneakers or Chucks, and band tees or slinky rockabilly dresses. With all of the eyeliner, teased or combed-over hair, and a dozen voices bickering over bands that had not been active in nearly a decade—it was like being home.

"This place is fucking sick." A guy with a green mohawk watched Quince light candles. "I had a friend who lived in Logansport years ago, and the rumors about this old house were seriously fucked-up."

"What rumors?" Jeremy asked. "The haunted thing?"

"Yup. It's haunted. Bad luck. Devil worshipers hang out here. Etcetera. My friend never had the balls to investigate it himself. None of the Logansport townies come near this place. But I heard the last dude who stayed here took off like a bat out of hell, so they probably have the right idea." Green Mohawk stuck his hand in Jeremy's face. "I'm Kyle, by the way."

"Jeremy." He took Kyle's beer-sticky hand. "What do you mean took off like a bat out of hell?"

"It happened a couple of years back. My friend told me this writer guy—"

"Don't waste time pumping him full of scary stories," Watts called from where he was crouched in a corner, fiddling with an amp. "He's scared of the dark as it is."

"Fuck you, Watts."

Kyle cracked up.

Great. Ridicule from random people. Just what he'd signed up for—not. He debated holing up in his previously claimed armchair when a girl with cat-eye makeup sidled over and slid an arm around his waist. She was rockabilly-pretty in a skintight, yellow-checkered dress with a flip collar and a colorful spread of tattoos that rivaled half his band's. A sugar skull was inked behind one of her ears, and an array of roses blossomed up one arm. Hidden beneath the crimson petals, dewdrops, and tiny spiders were the welts of old scar tissue— jagged lines that had been carved into her forearm in neat rows. Jeremy forced his eyes away.

"Don't let them bug you," she said. "I'm Amy. I'll protect you from the dickheads, if you want."

He carefully unwound himself from her grip. "It's all right. I'll just go, uh, mess with my drums or whatever."

Her ruby lips spread in a thin smile, but it did nothing to mask her disappointment. She inclined her head before slinking away.

With a pang of guilt, Jeremy looked after her, but knew it was better to cut his losses fast rather than lead people on. The party was looking to be awful enough without him having to break the "I'm gay" news after a night of awkward flirting.

As the night wore on, the beer flowed, someone passed around a couple of bottles of rotgut whiskey, and Watts held court in the center of the crowd. He bragged about Stygian's success in the Texas scene until the amps were being plugged in and they were launching into an off-the-cuff performance Jeremy threw himself into. His arms burned with each slam of sticks against skins, and he forgot everything else.

Music flooded his ears—odes to punk rock and Fuck Authority, melodic ballads about loneliness and numbing pain, and, of course, Caroline. By the time they reached their peak, the kids from Shreveport were on fire with enthusiasm. They pogoed like it was a real show, sneakered feet crashing into ancient wood, and went nuts when Watts's spine curled toward their tiny audience, voice gone low with agony.

Everyone in the band was talented, but Watts had the chops to make it big. Between his manic stage presence, the hollowed-out, sharp-edged beauty of a mean punk kid, and a voice that ranged from Morrissey to Oli Sykes—audiences didn't stand a chance once Watts started belting out lyrics. The way his voice could switch from husky and discontent to guttural and thick with rage still gave Jeremy the shivers.

At one point, Quince and Watts pressed together, clutching at each other and sharing the mic, and their audience barely reacted. It seemed natural and always had. No one in the Houston scene had been surprised when Watts and Quince started fucking; the full-on body contact they kept while performing had always been an indicator that it was a coming attraction. And for all that Watts had been a massive dickhead before the party had started, he seemed to crave Quince while performing. Jeremy didn't know if it was showmanship or a faulty short-term memory that allowed Quince to go along with it, but he let Watts grind all up on him for the next several minutes. The song ended with Watts panting pornographically into the mic.

By the time they finished, Jeremy had stripped off his shirt and was buzzed on the excitement from playing a solid set just as much as from the liver-punishing mix of alcohol. He staggered from behind his kit to the feel of hands slapping him on the back and several voices blending together in a cloud of admiration. Amy rushed over to him with a wide smile, crying out with excitement, but he reared away. He was too drunk to come up with an excuse and instead sought out the sweat-slick shine of Kennedy's tattoos.

The sight of him brought everything to a screeching halt.

Kennedy had set his guitar aside and was letting a scrawny emo kid cling to his arm. The boy couldn't be much older than Jeremy, but he was just as thin and pretty in a placid, delicate way. He had zero qualms about running his tanned fingers over Kennedy's arms, rubbing and kneading in a way that was completely unnecessary. But if Kennedy minded he did not let on.

The chest-tightening, lump-swallowing explosion of jealousy morphed into a sharp stab of rejection when Kennedy briefly met Jeremy's eyes. Just a second, barely the space of a heartbeat, and then Kennedy was focusing on his scrawny scenester again. It shouldn't have been a surprise, but it still was.

Jeremy wheeled around and nearly tripped over Amy. She grabbed his hand, but he once again pulled away.

"God, would you cut it out?"

She flinched. "I'm sorry...."

"I'm not interested, okay?" Jeremy gestured roughly before blurting out, "I'm gay."

"I figured you were. I mean, it seems like the four of you aren't very... straight. I wasn't trying to...." Amy trailed off with her cheeks aflame. "You just looked really detached, and I thought—"

"You're right, I am detached. I'm in a really shitty mood. Maybe Quince or—"

Jeremy broke off after looking in Quince's direction. He'd drifted away from their makeshift stage and was caged between Watts and, inexplicably, Laurel Caroway. Jeremy hadn't even realized she'd been invited. Even so, she was ethereal in contrast to the denim-clad scene crowd, and Quince was gazing into her eyes with a dreamy smile. Watts, who was grinding against his ass, did not seem to notice.

"Forget that." Jeremy focused on Amy again. "I'm sorry. Maybe just hang out with one of your friends? I'm not good company right now, okay?"

"Just because I'm with them doesn't mean they're my friends," she murmured.

"Yeah, I know what you mean."

Jeremy sidestepped Amy and grabbed a bottle of moonshine from Kyle's stash. He'd only drunk moonshine once in his life, and it had knocked him out faster than a Long Island Iced Tea laced with Valium, but that was what Jeremy needed right now.

He cringed at the taste and settled on the armchair in the corner, nursing the bottle until his eyes went blurry. At some point, the twink relocated to Kennedy's lap and Watts, Quince, and Laurel disappeared. One moment they'd been engaging in some three-way make-out, and the next they were gone.

Sick of his bandmates and himself, Jeremy sought Amy in the crowd. She'd spent most of the evening by herself but was now lingering near a couple of friends who seemed more aggravated than concerned about her pinched face.

After several seconds of them pointedly ignoring her, she hurried from the room, and guilt urged Jeremy out of his chair.

He was sober enough to walk without stumbling but too drunk to stop himself from setting the bottle on the floor with a clunk. Turning to the foyer, Jeremy intended to find Amy but was instead struck by the sight of Hunter framed in the archway.

The Caroways had a tendency to appear out of thin air, but Jeremy couldn't think too much about that while Hunter was fixated on him. He was radiating the kind of desire better suited for a bedroom than a room packed with young people.

Images coalesced all at once—Hunter pinning him to the ground amid trees and grass and the sounds of the river, kissing down his throat, teeth grazing, bodies writhing. For just a breath, the sensations felt real.

A sound filled Jeremy's ears, and he realized the soft hoarse moan had come from himself.

God. What the hell was wrong with him?

"Nice set," Hunter said once Jeremy approached.

"Thanks." Jeremy hooked his thumbs into the back pockets of his shorts. "Want a drink?"

"No. I don't drink."

"That's cool, but everyone is pretty trashed. I'm only one shot away from the staggering-while-drunk phase, myself."

Looking him over again, Hunter said, "You look fine to me."

Jeremy wished, even with a tan, he wasn't so pale. Every blush set his cheeks aflame. He didn't know what to make of Hunter's intensity, was still unsettled by the afternoon at their cabin, but Hunter's interest and obvious attraction was more than welcome after Kennedy's rejection.

"You don't have to be so heavy with the flattery, you know."

"Flattery is false." Hunter raised an eyebrow. "What I'm saying is truth."

Jeremy wondered if the blush had spread to his full body. "Your sister was having fun." He leaned close to be heard over the music— The White Stripes, "Seven Nation Army." "She had my bass player in a Laurel-and-Watts sandwich. I've never even seen Quince kiss a girl before, but she had him totally bewitched."

Hunter scanned the room for his sister. "Yes, she's like that."

"They took off together. I wouldn't go looking if I were you. I doubt you'd stumble onto a PG-13 scene."

"Did they leave the house?"

"I don't know," Jeremy said. "I doubt it. They're probably upstairs having a good time. And... I seriously apologize for bringing this up. I don't know when to shut up when I'm drinking."

"No worries." Hunter dismissed whatever concern he'd had for his sister in favor of gracing Jeremy with another heavy stare. The guy didn't even glance at the sloshed group of youths currently tearing apart his antique living room.

"I'm surprised you're alone."

"It happens more than you think." Jeremy knew his smile was too big, eyes likely too bright. "I don't have the right cool factor."

"And your friends do?"

"Guess so. Who wants the skinny little drummer when they have tatted-up guys with attitude?"

"More people than you think, Jeremy. I've heard half your band discussing ways to loosen you up. Literally."

A sickening wave of hope unfurled and blossomed in Jeremy's chest. "Who?"

"The ones trying to make it with my sister." Hunter indicated the room behind him. "They came to invite us to the party and had a discussion about how fun it would be to share you."

Jeremy's hope transformed into something closer to nausea. If Watts's perverted ponderings were starting to penetrate Quince's thick skull, it was time for Jeremy to pack his kit and go. He wasn't anyone's band bitch.

"Fuck them."

"Indeed." Hunter touched his cheek. "But they're not the only interested parties."

The attention didn't dim his disappointment, but Jeremy leaned into the touch. Against all logic, Hunter wanted him. That could be good enough. And even if it wasn't, Jeremy could pretend. Maybe in the long, drippy days of summer it would start to be true.

"Do you want to go somewhere and talk?" Jeremy asked all in a rush.

"I've been wanting to talk since I first saw you."

"Good." Jeremy stepped closer. "Let's go."

Hunter grabbed his wrist and gave it a tug, his thumb pressing hard against the spot where the blue-green veins met at Jeremy's pulse point.

Jeremy allowed himself to be pulled, but a hand clamped down on his hipbone and guided him backward. He stilled when the skin of his back crushed against someone's equally bare torso. Without having to look, Jeremy knew it was Kennedy's hands gripping tight and possessive.

"Where you going?" his voice boomed in Jeremy's ear.

Excitement zinged through Jeremy.

"With me," Hunter said with icy precision.

"Yeah."

Jeremy attempted to unmold the hand from his side, but Kennedy's fingers only tightened.

"Why don't you come with me instead?"

Jeremy twisted to look up at Kennedy. He was glaring at Hunter, and was clearly spoiling for a fight.

"Kennedy, what the hell, man?"

"Is he yours?" Hunter's low voice rumbled out in a growl. "Doesn't seem like it."

"It doesn't matter. He's not going anywhere with you."

"What the *fuck*, Kennedy?" The standoff reeked of impending violence, but no one was paying attention. "Look, it's fine. I'm a big boy. I'm not a piece of jailbait you need to protect, no matter what Watts says."

Kennedy's glare turned baleful. "Shut up."

"You shut—"

"Do you want me or him?" Hunter's pupils dilated, his irises overcome by blackness.

For just a beat, Jeremy's surroundings faded. All he saw was Hunter, and then he was drifting forward. One step, then another, and it was only Kennedy's touch that snapped him out of the momentary trance.

Jeremy blinked, attempting to clear the fog even as he hyper-focused on the hot breath brushing his ear and the heat coming off

Kennedy's body. One look, one touch, a few short, blunt words, and Jeremy was back in Kennedy's grasp. Figuratively and literally.

It took so very little for Kennedy to suck Jeremy in, and he probably had no fucking clue.

"Shit," Jeremy hissed. "I'm sorry, Hunter. I'll see you later, okay?"

Hunter's face hardened. "Find me when you're ready." He sidestepped them and, with one last poisonous look at Kennedy, strode away.

The tension bled out of Jeremy, but the reprieve didn't last. Kennedy shoved him forward and out of the room.

# CHAPTER SIX

KENNEDY HAULED Jeremy up the stairs as if his words had laid a claim.

"What are you doing?" Jeremy's voice hushed as they drew closer to the upstairs corridor. Kennedy yanked him into the shadows, opting to go toward the abandoned wing instead of their own, and panic clawed up Jeremy's throat. "Stop!"

They halted, and Kennedy shoved Jeremy onto an antique credenza crammed into a curved nook in the wall. His head snapped back, hair catching on the corners of torn wallpaper strips and crumbling sheetrock.

"What the fuck are you thinking?" Kennedy demanded.

"That I'm tired of being miserable and alone." Jeremy hazarded a glance at the far end of the hall. There was nothing but darkness and the barest glint of ambient light from the windows. "Is that a problem for you?"

"Yes, it's a problem. You don't even know that freak."

"Like you know that miniature twink you were about to bend over the couch?"

Kennedy crowded Jeremy and gave him very little room to think or breathe.

"I wasn't going to bend him over anything! You're jumping the gun just because I let him hang on to me a little bit?"

"Oh, come on."

Kennedy had to be aware of the pheromones he threw off to fans, but he never bothered to deter the railroad of bad ideas that entered their heads if he looked at them more than once. Apparently, that was all it took to develop a full-blown infatuation on Stygian's mysterious bass player. Even if Kennedy didn't seek the attention, he got it. Just by being him. Jeremy knew from personal experience.

"I thought—" Jeremy curled his fingers around the edge of the credenza, his fingers digging crescents into the mottled wood. "I thought you weren't into guys. Or that you weren't into guys like that. Like me. Guys who aren't all butch like you." A harsh, ugly laugh. "Guess I was wrong."

"I don't know what you think you saw," Kennedy said, slow and deliberate. "But you're drunk and you're mistaken."

"I'm not fucking drunk!" It was unconvincing given the slur of his words and the reek of moonshine on him, but it didn't matter. None of this mattered. Whether he was drunk or sober, it didn't change the fact that Kennedy wanted that kid, and he didn't want Jeremy. All of these months, the lack of response, lack of interest, had nothing to do with Jeremy being the wrong gender or physical type. It was just him. "Just forget it. You do what you want, and I'll do what I want."

Jeremy started to rise, but Kennedy planted a hand against his chest.

"I wasn't going to fuck him," Kennedy ground out. "And letting him flirt with me is part of the job. Do you think fans would bother to support us if I barked at them every time they stepped too close? Besides, that's not the same as you going off in the dark to get nailed by a random man. Do you even know how old he is?"

"Oh my God—are you kidding me?" He was starting to sound half-hysterical. "Do you know how old the groupies are before you let them suck your dick after shows? Do you know their fucking... their marital status? No. You know nothing about them, so don't try to pull this overprotective moral crap on me."

A muscle in Kennedy's jaw ticked. "That's different, and you know it."

"How the hell do you figure?"

"Because they're harmless fans, and this guy is—he's—" Kennedy gestured, frustration evident in his sharp movements. "There's just something off about him, Jeremy. I noticed it as soon as we met him. There's something off about him, and there's definitely something off about his sister."

"Like *what*? Why should I take your word for anything?" Jeremy tried to shove Kennedy's hand away but was pinned to the wall tighter. "You won't even tell me how you really knew my brother. You won't tell me why it matters if Watts fucking knows we discussed it. You keep secrets from me and tell me I'm some outsider and then want to scare me off from the first person who's been nice to me on this shitty retreat? No. Fuck you. Fuck Watts. Fuck this stupid party."

His voice was rising, and that was never a good thing. It would inevitably lead to shrill yelling, which almost always devolved into the burn of angry tears bursting free. Jeremy closed his eyes and took a breath. The faint patter of rain resumed outside, and the soft sound provided a calming distraction.

"You're not listening to me," Kennedy said at length. "He's—"

"He's what? Weird? Guess what, so am I." Jeremy scoffed and opened his eyes again. The plinks of rain became more frequent until it came down like a burst dam, sheets of water cascading over the windows. "And you're the one who went all Neanderthal on me in front of a room full of people. You don't even want me, dude. Do you have to make sure I sit in this goddamn mausoleum all summer while Watts uses Quince as a Fleshlight and you either tease or ignore me when you're not outright rejecting me?"

"That's not what—I don't mean to make you feel that way." Kennedy's unflappable mien wavered, and a delicate web of slivers appeared in his self-control. "Fuck, Jeremy. You always assume the worst shit about me."

"What am I wrongly assuming?" There was a flash, distorted from the stained glass, as lightning struck somewhere nearby. Jeremy's shout was lost in a crack of thunder. "What do you want from me? I don't get it. They ride my ass so hard for being into you, and you just stand there and say nothing and let me take all of the heat. I gotta assume it's because you want nothing to do with me."

"That's not true. Believe me, it's not."

"Then why? Why that kid and not me?" It sounded pathetic, mortifying, but Jeremy couldn't hold back now that the wall had weakened. "What's so wrong with me?"

"I just…."

"You don't like guys?"

"I've been with guys," Kennedy snapped. "That's not what this is about. It has nothing to do with your gender." Another short, erratic gesture, ink flashing on large hands in the faint light from the windows. "I'm just not going to fuck one of my bandmates."

"Watts and Quince do."

"Yeah. Exactly. And how do you think it will play out when Quince gets sick of Watts's bullshit? Once he realizes Watts doesn't give a fuck about him and that he'll be inevitably discarded? It will be a disaster, and things will fall apart. The band will fall apart."

"Oh, who cares?" Jeremy snapped. "You can barely stand each other."

"It wasn't always that way. And when I talked about this band being Watts's glue?" Kennedy pressed their foreheads together. "I wasn't just thinking about him. I have nothing, Jeremy. No parents and no Caroline. This shitty band is all I've got."

A bolt of lightning streaked across the sky again, and for one very brief fragment of a second, Jeremy saw Kennedy's strained expression and that vulnerable glint in his eyes.

"You could have me. Even if the band fell apart, we could be together."

"You think I haven't thought about that?"

"No, I don't. Because you act like you don't want me. You kiss me and totally fucking wreck me, and then say you just wanted me to shut up."

"What should I have said? That seeing you in pain made me feel like shit? That I wanted to fucking comfort you, but I didn't know what to say? That I felt like a selfish dickhead for whining about Caroline and bringing all of that stuff back for you?"

"Yes," Jeremy yelled. "That is everything I wanted you to say! But you didn't say it because it's not true. You're just spitting words now because they sound good."

"Jeremy, just stop." Kennedy slammed his hand against the wood, and the rickety cabinet shuddered beneath him. "You don't think I see you when you're behind the drums—sweating and flushed with that gleam in your eye? You don't think I like it when you get all up on me after a show—that I don't notice how bad you want to fuck just to get rid of the adrenaline?"

Jeremy slid his shaking hands over Kennedy's shoulders and drew him closer.

"You think I don't get horny when you sleep pressed against me in those cheap motels?" Kennedy's voice was an octave lower. "That I never get the urge to grind my wood against that ass in the morning?"

"Fuck," Jeremy whispered, digging his fingers in harder. He could see it so clearly—all the things that could and should have been if Kennedy would just give in. All the times they could have touched each other in a motel or in the van while Quince drove and Watts snoozed in the passenger's seat. Stolen kisses and discreet hand jobs, riding Kennedy in the back of his El Camino after a show....

"I see you," Kennedy said. "I've always seen you. And I'm human, kid. If you don't think I want what you're dying to give, you're out of your mind. I just can't stand the idea of it all going wrong."

Each word brought Jeremy's attention to the glint of Kennedy's lip ring in the darkness. By the time realization kicked in and he caught on to what Kennedy was saying, the single-minded focus on the tempting curve of that silver loop spread into the white-hot burn of need. Jeremy leaned in, closing the scant inches between them, and dragged the tip of his tongue across the full swell of Kennedy's mouth until he tasted metal.

Hands clamped on Jeremy's upper arms, powerful and nearly painful, but instead of pushing him away, Kennedy stood stock-still. A hushed sound answered Jeremy's tentatively searching tongue, and despite all of his reservations, Kennedy did nothing to prevent Jeremy from licking at the seam of his mouth.

"Don't start this," Kennedy whispered.

Jeremy spread his thighs wide enough for his hamstrings to burn, but it was nothing compared to the pressure of Kennedy's erection pushing against his own.

"You want me to start it."

"It's a bad idea." Kennedy's fingers quested down to curl beneath Jeremy's ass. "Such a bad fucking idea, Jeremy."

"I don't care." Jeremy's breath caught as Kennedy ground their dicks together through an unyielding layer of denim. "I want you so goddamn bad that I feel like coming every time you say my name."

"*Fuck.*"

"I like you." Jeremy dug his fingers into Kennedy harder. "I've always liked you. Even before I auditioned, I thought you were gorgeous and talented, and so obviously the one holding this band of freaks together. And now I know you are. Without you, Stygian would have fallen apart. Without you... I would have left already."

"Why?" Kennedy asked roughly. "You act like I'm just as bad as Watts sometimes."

"Because you make me so mad, but that doesn't change that you're loyal and strong and such a good person that I just want to be close to you, Kennedy. That's it. I just—I just want us to be... to be something more than we are. I want to be more than just another troubled fucking kid in your life."

Jeremy half expected Kennedy to be turned off by such a raw, desperate admission, but Kennedy kissed him back.

All of Jeremy's brash confidence vanished, and he forgot about rutting and fucking and being nailed against the antique piece of furniture, because the reality of Kennedy's mouth against his was stunning.

Jeremy arched up, wanting more contact, and wrapped his legs around Kennedy so they were one tangle of damp limbs and tattooed flesh. His eyes drifted shut, blocking the occasional flash of lightning while he lost himself to the feel of Kennedy's kisses and roving hands. And when he broke away with a gasp for air, Kennedy nipped at his lower lip and dragged his mouth down the sweaty length of his neck.

"Kennedy," Jeremy whispered. He pressed his palms flat against the credenza and leaned back. "Please don't stop."

It wasn't what Jeremy had fantasized about for months, but the frustrating tease of their covered dicks and the sensation of Kennedy's fingers mapping their way up his spine was more than he'd ever expected to get. It shouldn't have been enough to darken his vision or turn his mind hazy with lust, but it happened anyway, and Jeremy was harder than a frotting session could contend with.

They kissed harder this time, and Jeremy's groan was chased by another crack of thunder. It was loud enough to drag him out of his lust-stricken delirium just as a quieter sound eclipsed the storm.

Low—low enough to be a figment of his imagination, but the ice lancing through Jeremy told a different story. From somewhere down the hall leading to the empty wing, the wooden floor had creaked. The kind of creak made by a footfall, no matter how slight.

Jeremy pulled away and stared wildly into the darkness. He didn't see or hear anything else, but an urgent sense of wrongness swept over him.

"What—"

The rest of the sentence was muffled by Kennedy's mouth, then his hand cupping the throbbing bulge in Jeremy's shorts.

"Oh God."

The creak was nearly forgotten until the air around them shifted. Coldness pooled in Jeremy's gut before piercing his chest and spreading through his body.

"Something's weird," he panted. "I heard a sound."

Kennedy slid down Jeremy's zipper. "What are you talking about?"

"It's just...." Again, the words were lost to an avalanche of sensation—bare fingers wrapping around his aching dick. "Oh.... Oh fuck."

Their lips met again, but Jeremy could do nothing beyond thrusting urgently into Kennedy's curled hand. He wanted to splay his legs wider in invitation, but it was difficult with his shorts still hugging his ass and thighs.

"More." Jeremy could feel Kennedy's heart battering against his ribcage. "I want...."

Kennedy's thumb traced the damp crown of Jeremy's cock. "What do you want?"

"You to fuck me. Please, just for tonight."

"Not here."

"You want it too." Jeremy grasped the belt loops of Kennedy's jeans. "It doesn't matter where."

"It matters to me."

Jeremy shoved himself away from the wall and surged up, reclaiming Kennedy's mouth in a harsh kiss. The hand around his dick tightened with a spasm before moving again, gripping harder and tugging faster, just the right combination of roughness and speed to drive Jeremy wild. He wanted to keep scraping at Kennedy's willpower, plead for Kennedy to stop holding back and sink inside of him, but the unceasing touches brought him to the edge.

"You're gonna make me come."

His voice was high and tight, and he received an answering moan before Kennedy sank into a crouch. Jeremy's eyes widened as his dick was encased in the hot, wet heat of a mouth.

It couldn't be real. It was a dream—or a drunken hallucination. There was no other explanation. No way was Kennedy sucking on the tip of his erection and tonguing the slit while working the shaft with his hand.

Even in Jeremy's fantasies, it had never been Kennedy on his knees.

The storm provided a counterpoint to the noises Jeremy was desperately trying to muffle. The crashing rain and consistent booms of thunder shielded every sound—his heels hitting the credenza, the sloppy sound of his cock sliding in and out of Kennedy's mouth, and Jeremy's agonized cry when he finally rode the wave of his orgasm.

He rocked into Kennedy's mouth until the suction became too much, and he crested while Kennedy swallowed every drop of his release.

Jeremy's thoughts were fractured and disordered. His hands shook, and his stomach was coiled from the force of his ejaculation. Nothing felt quite real. It wasn't until Kennedy stopped licking his dick, taint, and balls, and got to his feet, that Jeremy pulled himself together.

When they kissed, Jeremy could taste himself on Kennedy's lips. He'd just unloaded, but it wouldn't be long before he was ready again. He was always capable of going more than one round, and with Kennedy, he could go all night. The idea of them twisting in the sheets while a storm raged outside caused Jeremy to chuckle nervously because he wanted it bad enough for it to be scary.

He skimmed his hand up Kennedy's back, and smoothed his palm over the slick skin and contracting muscles before dropping it to Kennedy's belt. Jeremy fumbled with the studded length of leather in an attempt to get the buckle unclasped but, before he could achieve his goal, someone cried out below them.

Kennedy started to turn his face toward the staircase, but Jeremy braced a hand against his jaw. "Do you want me to blow you, or are you gonna fuck me?"

"I—"

The scream came again, and half a dozen other frightened voices followed. This time, Jeremy looked down the hallway, eyes widening.

The voices were louder, loud enough to be heard over the storm. Dread washed away any lingering traces of lust, and Kennedy moved to the staircase, already fixing his belt. His boots slammed against the creaking wooden floor as he hurried away.

Jeremy followed, trying to zip his shorts. Just as he descended the stairs, he peered down the corridor they had left behind, and a sharp spike of fear cut through him.

The darkness remained, but farther down the hall the shadows shifted ever so slightly.

Jeremy's heart gave a sickening lurch before starting again, beating in frenzied terror. It thumped with such violence that he thought the muscles might rip apart in his chest.

He sprinted down the stairs and reached the lit bottom floor of the house, but a sense of relief never came.

"Is she dead?"

The question stretched the distance between him and the crowd from the party, but it couldn't be right.

"She's not breathing! Fuck—feel her pulse!"

"How? Her arm—there's so much blood!"

The voices were coming from the kitchen, and Jeremy burst into the room with a squeak of his sneakers against old, curling linoleum. The alt kids were huddled around a pale figure sprawled in the eaves of the fold-out counter.

"What happened?" Kennedy barked, shoving Kyle out of the way. The guy skittered to the side and fell against the counter with a grunt. The space he cleared caused the girl on the floor to stand out in stark relief to her surroundings.

Amy.

She was lying faceup, eyes half-shut and skin iridescent. Her yellow checkered rockabilly dress was skewed half up her thighs, and one of her hands was thrown outward. Blood dripped sluggishly from her forearm and onto the floor. She didn't move, and even in the gloom, Jeremy could see that her lips were powder blue.

Kennedy groped at her uninjured wrist, searching for a sign of life Jeremy knew he wouldn't find.

# CHAPTER SEVEN

"OH GOD."

Quince spun away and heaved into the sink. Jeremy's stomach churned at the watery sound of Quince's vomit. He stumbled back, but he couldn't stop staring at Amy's corpse.

*Oh God.*

"Jesus fucking Christ, someone call an ambulance!" Kennedy shouted. "Watts!"

"On it." Watts had a phone trapped in one bony hand. His gaze was wild and trained on the pooling blood soaking into Kennedy's jeans.

Jeremy wanted to ask what had happened, but he couldn't get the words out. He couldn't take his eyes away. She looked like a broken doll with translucent skin, everything more delicate and vulnerable now that she was still with death and absent of the bubbly laugh and quick, grasping movements.

"Why?" he croaked. "What...?"

"I found her this way," another girl said, voice clogged with tears. A high, pained whine escaped her, and Kyle swooped in to pull her to his narrow chest. "I... I don't understand. She was upset, but I don't understand!" The sentence capped off with a wail.

Jeremy pressed the heels of his hands to his eyes. He didn't want to see any more, but the afterimage of her dead body was burned to his retinas. The need to block out the sight was urgent, but he couldn't forget the ripped skin and pool of blood. The smell invaded his nose, activating a sensory memory that hit Jeremy hard enough to transport him to another place and time. To the bathroom in his mother's house where bloody water had slopped over the side of the tub. His brother's platinum-colored hair plastered across his lifeless face.

Turning away, Jeremy sucked in a breath, then another, but it wasn't enough. His chest was too tight, his lungs demanding too much oxygen too fast. He knew he was gasping, drawing attention to himself instead of Amy, and that only added to the horror already wreaking havoc on him. He needed to calm down, get away, hide somewhere....

When someone steered him away, Jeremy dropped his hands and let himself be guided.

"Stay out of there," Watts said, his voice gruff and low. "You don't want to see that."

They'd only crossed a threshold, but the distance could have been an ocean from the enormity of Jeremy's relief.

He wrapped his arms around himself and stared through the archways, into the foyer, and at the front door. Any moment, the police would come. The house would fill with lights, with voices, with people asking questions and wanting answers.

He reached for a cross he no longer wore.

"Just stay here, Jeremy."

"Okay," Jeremy whispered. "Okay."

Even as he said it, the house pressed in on him, and he felt abandoned once Watts returned to the kitchen.

Jeremy could still hear Quince vomiting and the tormented sounds of Amy's friend. Kennedy's voice was slightly more reassuring—deep, low, and sure in a crisis. As steady as ever. Always prepared to be the one people could lean on when everything went wrong.

Jeremy craved Kennedy's warmth. He didn't want to be near Amy's body, but he didn't want to be quarantined to a room that was empty of everything but antique items and guarded secrets.

He took a deep breath and clamped his fingers over his upper arms. Even when low creaks sounded above him, Jeremy remained locked in the same position. It was safer that way. He told himself that, and kept his back to his band and his eyes trained on the dark portal of the door until the flickering of police lights flashed through the windows and shattered the night.

Policemen flooded the house and separated the group from the death scene. Jeremy hunched in on himself until he was herded onto the porch in the midst of a line of rocker kids who, in Houston, would have glared at the cops with defiant faces. But these kids just looked tired and drawn. They spilled Amy's story when the officers shot off question after question while the pouring rain turned into a faint mist.

"Was she upset about anything?"

"She's been having a hard time with her mom," one of the girls muttered, eyes down and face stained with guilt. "She cuts herself a lot. I thought she was just being dramatic...."

Jeremy barely stopped himself from snarling that people didn't mutilate themselves to be dramatic. It wasn't always just a cry for help. The lonely kids, the isolated ones who felt like throwaways, rarely played those games.

"What about tonight?"

"She looked kind of upset. She said she regretted coming...."

"She was into the band," Kyle chimed in. "Wanted to score with one of them and came down on herself when no one bit. Especially when that one chick showed up. The tall one with the black curly hair and blue eyes—looked like Katy Perry or whatever. She snagged the singer and the bass player, both."

"Did Amy have words with the other girl?"

"Nah. The Katy Perry chick took off before Amy disappeared. I didn't even notice when she left the room."

There were eyes on Jeremy, and he sought out Kennedy who was chain-smoking and slouched against the porch's rail. Compared to the army of Hot Topic-outfitted youths, Kennedy looked like a thug. He dwarfed them in height and muscle mass, broad shouldered and covered in tattoos everywhere that mattered.

The attitude of the cops shifted as soon as they looked at the four members of Stygian huddled together on the far side of the porch. Kennedy stood in front of them like a bodyguard, and with Jeremy too shaken to function and Quince getting queasier with each moment, they needed it.

"Better hope they don't search your room, Watts," Kennedy muttered around his cigarette. "Or we're in a shitload of trouble."

Jeremy had completely forgotten about the massive amount of cocaine Watts must have brought along to last him the entire summer. Somehow, he hadn't thought of it before, even while they'd made the four-hour drive. *Jesus.*

"Just be cool," Watts hissed. "Let me do the fucking talking."

The police conferred among themselves, whispering and throwing the band dark stares before they broke apart. Only one approached.

"All right," he said slowly, sizing up each of them before his gaze lingered on Kennedy. "Why don't you boys go ahead and show me your IDs and tell me what you're doing in this house."

It wasn't the most pressing concern, but they all fumbled in their pockets and handed their identification to the deputy. It was luck alone that Jeremy always carried his wallet. He didn't think he'd be able to handle walking up into the dark corridor alone.

"I rented it, sir." Watts always took charge when they got into a scrape, whether it was being pulled over in the van or a bar fight. He could flip on the upper-crust, rich-boy manners at the drop of a guitar pick. "Me and my friends are musicians. We drove up from Houston for the summer to work on some new material for our next album."

The deputy shone his light down at their ID cards, studying each one. "And how'd you find this place? I don't think this house is advertised on the Internet."

"No, but I saw an ad in a Shreveport paper," Watts said. "My parents brought it back with them a few months ago after going up to the casinos. It was listed for long-term rentals. We're staying for another month."

The deputy pursed his lips. He returned their identification, saving Kennedy's for last. "Tell me how you knew Amy, Mr. Novak."

Kennedy slid his ID card into his pocket. "I didn't."

"How'd she get to be dead in your kitchen, then?"

The set of Kennedy's shoulders was full of old-school fuck-authority resentment, but his words were spoken with flat indifference. "Watts and Quince drove to Shreveport a couple days ago and met all those kids"—he nodded at the cowering group at the other end of the porch—"at the liquor store. Amy was their friend, not ours. She barely said a word to any of us."

"No guesses as to what might have driven her to harm herself the way she did?"

"Are you sure she harmed herself?"

Everyone looked at Kennedy, but he just crossed his arms over his chest. Even when the deputy swung the beam of the flashlight up to shine directly into his eyes. "You want to repeat that, son?"

"Are you sure she killed herself," Kennedy repeated slowly.

"You got another theory?"·

"I don't know. I'm not a medical examiner." Kennedy lifted a brow. "Is there a medical examiner here?"

Watts scowled and took a step closer to the deputy, his shoulder knocking against Kennedy's. "We don't know why she would kill herself," he interrupted. "We met her tonight. I never spoke to her, even though those kids said she was trying to get my attention. Me and my friend Quince were hanging out with Laurel Caroway."

"Uh huh." The flashlight's beam shifted to Watts before gliding over to Quince. It stayed on his pale face, pinpricked pupils, and then dragged along his neck and the rest of his body. "So you didn't hear anything? Never noticed anything about the girl?"

"No, Deputy—" Watts peered at the man's badge. "Deputy Harper. I didn't pay much attention to her all night."

"Seems like that was part of the problem." Harper looked at Jeremy. "What about you?"

Jeremy opened his mouth, but no words came out. He swallowed, balling his hands into fists. "I... she... she tried to talk to me. Hit on me. I brushed her off because um, because I wasn't interested. I didn't want to lead her on." Jeremy's stomach soured. "I saw some cut marks on her arms, though. And... she looked unhappy. Claimed she didn't have any friends." He said the last part in a rush, sneaking glances at the ragged group of teens only a few feet away. Kyle looked away guiltily, but none of them denied it. Maybe she'd just been a tagalong.

"I see."

One of the girls, a skinny thing with a long dog chain hanging from her belt loops, shifted closer. "I've known Amy since we were real little," she said faintly. "But I never thought she'd really do it...."

Harper zeroed in on her and unleashed a barrage of questions. They circled around the issue, the group's belief that Amy had always wanted attention but acknowledging that she'd carried a razor blade in her purse. Why they thought someone would carve tracks into their arms for attention, Jeremy didn't know, but he was nauseated by the similarities to Luke. Lonely, ignored, taken for granted, and finally getting attention in the worst possible way. Turning into a horrible memory or a bloody story to be retold as people tried to attach themselves to the drama. Like it made them more interesting to have known someone who'd died.

By the time it was over, Jeremy was used-up and worn-out with nothing left to give as he sat on the damp steps. Nobody supplied additional details to the moments preceding her death, but Jeremy replayed their exchanged words, turning them over, and couldn't help but wonder if his own actions had pushed her to the edge. It was at once possible and narcissistic, but he was one of the few people to have spoken to her all night.

Once the paramedics removed Amy's body and placed her in the ambulance, the rain resumed, and the police allowed Watts and Quince to go back inside. Just when Jeremy thought it was over, Harper approached again.

"Just so you know, son. It seems like the girl has been on this path for a long while."

Jeremy grasped at any reason to push the regret away, but it still wasn't comforting. "Will, um, her parents come here?"

Harper looked around the perimeter of the darkened lawn. "Her parents will be called to the hospital in Henderson. No reason to drag them out here to this house or to talk to any of y'all. It's pretty clear what happened."

"Not to me."

Harper looked grimly at Kennedy, then unhooked his fingers from his utility belt. "She cut an artery." Harper smoothed two fingers over his own wrist to indicate the area. "Two deep cuts right there. Bled like a sonuvabitch. I don't know if she meant to go that deep or if the liquor made her go too far, but that's what happened."

"I saw the razor blade near her body," Kennedy said. "It was sharp enough to cut that deep?"

"Anything can cut deep enough if you got the intent to do some harm."

"Right." Kennedy didn't relent. "And what about the Caroways?"

"What's that, son?"

"The *Caroways*." Jerking his head to the house, Kennedy said, "Did you talk to them?"

"You sure ask a lot of questions, Mr. Novak."

The deputy shifted his stance and put one hand on his gun. Kennedy's eyes dropped to the motion but his lip just curled.

"An inquiring mind is a healthy mind. And there's a lot to inquire about."

"Maybe you oughta be a cop."

"Maybe I should."

What the hell did Kennedy think he was doing? The last thing they needed was to antagonize a cop. Especially when Watts probably had enough drugs in his room to get them all a couple of felonies.

"Should we do anything?" Jeremy asked, finding his voice. "Call the landlords?"

Harper dragged his pissed-off stare from Kennedy to narrow on Jeremy. His face softened a bit, and he flicked a quick glance up at the house, hand tightening on his gun.

"Look, son, it'd be best if you put this situation out of your mind for now. Worry about yourselves and your music, and try not to get into any trouble, you understand? You're real removed from the town out here, and the nearest hospital is about an hour away. You boys drinking and partying in the woods isn't a smart plan when you're not familiar with the area."

Kennedy didn't respond to the digression, but Jeremy nodded, happy the guy wasn't being a total dick.

"Thank you, sir. We'll be careful."

"You do that."

The cops cleared out within moments, and the cars full of Shreveport kids peeled out of the yard. The Jeep fishtailed and kicked up mud, tearing a gash into the grass before it drove away.

"Seems funny that no one asked for Hunter or his sister, especially since they magically disappeared right around the time this all went down," Kennedy said.

"They probably left before it happened," Jeremy replied dully. "And besides, it wasn't about Laurel or Amy being jealous." He watched the taillights fade into the distance and wished some of them had stayed. "She had problems before tonight."

"That doesn't mean anything."

Jeremy unfolded from his huddled position on the steps. His body protested the sudden motion, knees stiff and back aching from over an hour of sitting in the tepid rain.

"I don't know what you want me to say."

"Just tell me it's not fucking weird that a girl died here and no one wanted to question the owner of the house. Also, why the hell was that cop giving you all this information? I'm pretty sure that's not how shit goes down unless it's different in tiny-ass hick towns."

"Kennedy—"

"And what about those kids? Kyle or whatever the hell his name is? He described Laurel, and the cop didn't bat an eyelash. He didn't ask who she was or what her name was, or seem interested in questioning her. I find it hard to believe the cops don't know the family who own all of this—" Kennedy swept out an arm to gesture at the property "—by name? It was like they didn't have interest at all. Every time I asked, he evaded the question."

"You're right. It's weird." Jeremy brushed past Kennedy to reenter the house. "But what do you want me to think? This whole situation is weird. This place is a freak show, and to be honest, I want to get the fuck out of here. *Especially* now that someone died."

Kennedy flicked the butt of his cigarette onto the porch. "You and me both, kid."

The police had turned on all the lights downstairs, illuminating every room. Even so, Jeremy looked around nervously. He entered the kitchen and shook his head to clear the image of her body wrapped in a body bag and jerking around as the ambulance drove over the largely unpaved road.

Only Watts was in the kitchen, a joint dangling from his lips as he scrubbed the fresh, red stain on the linoleum. He'd barely waited for the cops to leave before getting high again.

"What the hell? They just let you come fuck up the scene?" Kennedy demanded. "What the hell is up with this town?"

"What scene?" Watts retorted. "It was a suicide not a fucking serial killer. Or were you planning to get all CSI and find something they couldn't?"

Kennedy's mouth tightened into a slash, disgust evident in his features. "You two are both in the same boat of obliviousness. If you can't tell that there's something off about this whole thing—I'm done fighting it. Whatever."

Watts stared at him incredulously. "Dude, she killed herself. Relax. I'm sure they know how to identify signs of emo self-harm. Some kids hate their lives and cut self-loathing into their fucking skin no matter what town they live in."

"Like I said—whatever."

Kennedy lapsed into silence, and Jeremy cleared his throat. "Where's Quince?"

"Bed. He's shook up and ain't feeling well."

"I don't blame him." Jeremy braced his hand against the counter, watching Watts sop-up the pinkish white froth of soap and blood with a mass of paper towels. "Listen, Watts...." He trailed off, and Kennedy rolled his eyes, jumping in.

"We can't stay here."

"Fuck that."

"I'm going to take someone bleeding out on the kitchen floor as a bad omen. Staying here doesn't seem like a good plan," Kennedy pressed. "Don't argue for the sake of it. You know it's true."

"I know that you're freaking out like a big girl for no apparent reason." Watts dumped the wad of paper towels into the trash can and sat on his haunches. The sweet-smelling curl of smoke drifted up to where Jeremy stood and grew more pungent after Watts exhaled. "And I know I'm not ruining my chance to focus on writing new material because some drunk-ass chick offed herself in my house."

"Jesus Christ," Jeremy muttered. "Who are you, Phil Spector?"

"No. I'm Brian fucking Watts, and we're Stygian, and we're not going to run the hell out of here just because it's a little spooky." Watts got to his feet with a grunt, wiping his hands against the black Ramones T-shirt he'd pulled on as the cops arrived. "Unless Laurel wants me out, I'm not going. And I'd appreciate it if my band would stop trying to puss out on me about it."

Kennedy's fingers twitched into a loose fist, and he looked ready to argue.

It was obvious to Jeremy how the argument would end. Watts would never back down, and all of Kennedy's logic would drift away as if it had never penetrated Watts's skull.

"You okay, Jere?" Watts asked.

"I guess."

"Good man."

He clapped Jeremy on the shoulder and squeezed, but Jeremy almost hated the approval. Like he was strong for not spazzing when he really just felt like a traitor for not siding with Kennedy.

"Get some rest, kiddo. Tomorrow we rock."

# CHAPTER EIGHT

THE NIGHTMARE resumed as though days had not passed since the last time Jeremy walked through the dreamscape of the old church. Once again, he could hear the ominous notes of Liszt, at once beautiful and frightening. And once again, Jeremy crept along the gleaming hardwood floor to reach the pianist.

"Luke?"

It couldn't be him, but who else would it be? Who else would be playing the funeral piece about the gondolas? Who else latched on to anything that could be transmuted into his own darkness and pain?

But Luke was dead. They had all said it, reminded him of it, and prayed for him to understand it.

Jeremy reached a door at the end of the corridor. Wooden, heavy, and ornate like the rest of the church, a relic of a time when religion was supposed to make people feel safe and protected. As if stained-glass windows and glossy wood denoted the strength of God's love for your parish.

"Luke?" His voice was barely a whisper, but it was still too loud in the silent church. So was the door. It creaked when Jeremy pushed it open. "What are you...."

Jeremy snapped his mouth shut. A scream worked its way up from his diaphragm, but it tangled in his throat before hitting the air.

Blood pooled everywhere. Crimson spatters and scattering spiders, ribbons of flayed skin, and a body in the middle of it all. But it wasn't Luke. It was Hunter. Hunter with darker eyes and tanned skin, and he had blood spraying from jagged seams in his wrists.

Jeremy woke up just as the scream burst from his mouth. He swallowed it and flinched away from the rays of sunlight angling through the window to trap him on the chaise lounge.

His skin was baking in the heat, sweat gathered in the creases behind his knees and beneath each fold of his clothing. It was an added discomfort, but one that brought him fully to reality. He was never uncomfortable or in pain in the dream. Just confused. Lost. Searching for something that didn't exist.

Sitting upright, he plucked the front of his shirt away from his chest before peeling it off entirely. His eyes drew to Kennedy.

The guitarist was sprawled facedown on the bed in his underwear. For the first time since they'd begun sharing the room, Jeremy did not find himself tracing the lines of Kennedy's body.

Not after the night before when he had girded his loins and asked in a small voice if they could share the bed, only to have been flatly shut down.

*"That's probably not a good idea, but I'll switch with you."*

Jeremy had declined the offer and pressed his face into the chaise lounge, careful not to let Kennedy hear the miserable, angry hitches of his breath.

At least the dream distracted him from that hideous moment of rejection. Even if it meant the past was catching up with him.

Before coming to Logansport, Jeremy hadn't dreamed of Luke for years. He'd buried those stolen, confusing moments of wandering in a maze of church hallways. Now, the things he had locked away—that skittish paranoia, the irrational fear of dark corners and lonely rooms—had returned. And he was just as terrified of ending up half-insane like the rest of his family. Jeremy was convinced there was probably a case study about the Black family somewhere even though he hadn't known them for the first ten years of his life.

He'd met his father for the first time on his eleventh birthday. Daedalus Black had arrived with a woman demanding to be called their aunt, both of them looking like older replicas of Jeremy and Luke with pale skin, white-blond hair, delicate features, and gray eyes. His father had reeked of alcohol, barely aware of what was going on, but their aunt had asked them a string of weird questions and stared with clinical detachment before abruptly leaving the house with their father in tow.

After that, Jeremy and Luke had only seen them at sporadic Black family gatherings, which almost always ended up being funerals for people who had died too young. Because that's what happened to people with their genes. Mental institutions or a stalwart belief in sixth senses and the supernatural; suicide or addiction. The latter two seemed to be weapons used to cope with the former.

Stomach churning, Jeremy rose unsteadily, but he got to the doorway without stumbling. Cooler air entered their room from the hall, and Jeremy pressed against the wooden frame. He looked at Kennedy again, concentrating on the rise and fall of his back.

He'd wanted so badly to sleep next to Kennedy, to feel the solid weight of another person nearby. But whatever magic had bewitched Kennedy in the hallway while the storm raged outside had disappeared. When it had all been said and done the night before, Kennedy had barely looked at him after returning to the room.

Maybe their hookup had been another occasion of Kennedy giving him what he wanted just to shut him up. Or maybe Kennedy had been disgusted over Jeremy's failure to voice his own concerns to Watts. Whatever it was, Jeremy couldn't figure it out, and he was too worn and defeated to try again. Especially after he'd bared himself so completely.

In the past, the bubble of excitement that had enveloped him the previous night would have popped and sent Jeremy into a spiral of self-pity. Now, the disappointment was still ripe, but it was overshadowed by the memory of Amy's black rubber bracelets skewing up her long, thin arm and blood pooling on dirty linoleum. Jeremy swallowed thickly and headed for the bathroom.

The shower was just as outdated as the rest of the house, but the water pressure was surprisingly strong. He tried to find enjoyment in the cool water beating down on him, but relaxation was light-years away. He rushed through the shower, retrieved fresh clothes from his duffel bag, and went to check on Quince.

There wasn't a point in knocking since the door always stood open, and he found his bandmates lying next to each other on the bed. Watts was on his back with his limbs splayed out, but Quince had curled into a tight ball. His paleness was made prominent by dark-smudged eyes beneath a wrinkled brow.

Jeremy moved closer, and his hesitant steps were muffled by the rug. When he reached the side of the bed, he brushed his fingertips against Quince's forehead. It was hot. And clammy.

"Damn," Jeremy whispered. Watts's eyes flew open, too large in his gaunt face, and pinned Jeremy to the spot. He froze like he'd been caught fondling Quince, and withdrew his hand. "Is he okay?"

Watts nodded, the barest of motions, and rolled on his side to survey Quince. "It's probably nothing serious."

"When did it start?"

"I got no clue," Watts replied, voice hoarse with sleep. "I thought he puked last night because he's a wuss about blood, but maybe he has a bug."

Jeremy squatted beside the bed and put his hand on Quince again, conscious of Watts's gaze. It was cooler in this room, with heavy curtains blocking out the sun and a ceiling fan spinning overhead, but Quince was still feverish. Other than that, the only thing out of place was a series of purpling hickeys and bite marks on his neck and chest.

"Looks like he had fun with you and that Laurel girl," Jeremy noted. "Maybe she gave him a cold."

"Or something else," Watts sneered. "I'm starting to wonder if that chick just rented this motherfucker out so she could have an array of dicks to choose from."

"Oh, so she's like you?"

Watts's twisted mouth quivered into an almost-smile. "Nah, I wouldn't fuck Kennedy if someone paid me. Your man is a serious asswipe when he gets on a tear about something."

"So he's like you too. I see."

Watts flipped his middle finger, but his chest shook with hoarse laughs. "Fuck off, Black."

Jeremy didn't smile in return. He sat back on his haunches. "I didn't think Quince was into girls."

"He was into her. Literally. Every inch."

"Oh, geez."

Watts smirked. "I won't get too detailed, princess. Don't want to make you blush."

"It would take more than some details about Quince's very first threesome, although a sex story starring you would just give me nightmares." Jeremy stood. "Should I go to the store and get any medicine?"

"How about you go to the kitchen and make me some breakfast. What good's the band bitch if he doesn't perform?"

Hunter's words from the night before returned, the claims of Watts and Quince discussing how they could use him for purposes other than drumming.

"I'm not your bitch."

"Apparently not if your sorry ass can't even whip up some eggs and bacon. I'm getting tired of living on beer and ramen noodles."

"First, your sexist crap is getting old. And second, we don't have anything else," Jeremy said. "And even if we did, I'm not your fucking maid. I'm not going to whip up meals in our haunted kitchen while you people lounge around and nurse your hangovers and pretend like that poor girl didn't die last night."

Watts pushed himself halfway up. Even with his hair sticking out in every direction, clothes twisted and wrinkled beyond repair, and his skin reddened from sunburn and mosquito bites, the guy looked like a rock star.

"Jesus Christ, you get more riled up than a twelve-year-old at a slumber party. Slenderman isn't gonna get you, sweet pea. The only things to worry about here are aggressively emo redneck kids and horny landowners. At least Laurel and her big bro don't seem hard-up enough to start sawing at their arms after a little rejection." Watts grinned, wide and terrible, but his eyes were flat. Tired. "Or else Hunter would have flipped his shit after you took off with Ken-boy."

Jeremy flushed. "Shut up. You weren't even in the room."

"I didn't have to be. The story got repeated like twelve times between me pulling out of Laurel and going into the goddamn kitchen."

"You're an awful person."

"No shit. So, did he bust in your tween ass or what?"

"Why are you so obsessed with this?" Jeremy's voice rose, but Quince didn't twitch. "Do you think if I bend over for him, I'll let the rest of you have a turn?"

Watts's head jerked back. "Uh, no?"

"Then shut up about what happens to my ass."

Watts frowned, eyes skimming Jeremy. "No need to have a titty attack over it. I was just joking."

Jeremy tried to calm his temper. Watts was being himself. Sexist and horrible and insensitive and hell-bent on seeing how far he could push until people snapped. Just like always. It was the reason why most people barely tolerated him until they found out he was loaded. But defensiveness and paranoia were becoming second nature on this trip. At this point Jeremy was just waiting for the other shoe to drop.

"I'll go to the pharmacy," he said. "I think he needs to take something."

"He's fine."

Jeremy frowned. "I saw a Brookshire Brothers when we drove in. I'll go get some medicine. Maybe see if there's a pharmacist I can ask. I'll also pick up some breakfast. I don't care what you say—I'm not cooking or eating where that girl died."

Watts leaned on his palms again, collarbone jutting and making the weight he had lost in the past few months pronounced.

"Thanks. That's real decent of you."

Jeremy shrugged stiffly. "Yeah. Whatever."

Watts's eyes rolled up to the ceiling. "Look, Jeremy. I'm sorry I've been an asshole, okay? I don't mean anything by it. It's just hard. Like you being here... writing new shit, means Caroline is really gone."

Jeremy had started for the door, but the words startled him, and he paused. "I guess I get that."

"Yeah." Watts settled against the cluster of pillows. "And thanks for staying strong last night, dude. I know it freaked you out. I know... what happened to your brother."

The words, said aloud, brought a mental curtain between them.

"Sorry," Watts said quickly.

"Stop apologizing. I—" Jeremy brushed hair from his face and realized his hands had begun to tremble. He wanted to ask what else Watts knew about Luke, but the very idea of discussing it now only made the shaking worse. He couldn't go there when the sight of Amy was still so fresh—the spreading pool of blood, deep crimson where it dripped from the savage slice of a wrist and the bulbous thrust of tissue bursting from the torn skin. Her skin so pale and lips so blue when she'd been vibrant and alive only an hour earlier.... "I'm not going to fall apart every time I get triggered."

Not appearing remotely convinced, Watts said, "Fine. Then get going and don't fuck up the van."

"Will do."

Jeremy grabbed the keys and hurried out of the house.

The mansion was more welcoming at the height of morning. It was almost beautiful with the clusters of shrubs, fruit-bearing trees, and wildflowers tangling together along the sides and vying for attention. It looked harmless, with flecks of dust dancing in sunbeams and shadows only gathering beneath the cornices of the roof like any other Southern plantation-era home.

It didn't look like the scene of a recent death.

Jeremy relaxed. Marginally.

Then his eyes flitted upward and away from the aggressive reach of plant life, and he could swear the curtain in one of the windows of the empty wing moved.

The wheels on the van spun loud enough to draw Watts's attention and ire, but Jeremy didn't slow. He tore out of the driveway and took off onto the road, speeding toward the main street of town before he got enough distance from the house to put the hunted feeling at bay. The adrenaline didn't recede until he was sitting in the parking lot of Brookshire Brothers with his hands clenched on the wheel and pulse still racing.

He was losing it. Again.

Jeremy squeezed his eyes shut and pressed his forehead against the steering wheel. He clung to his self-control, but the layers were already unraveling. Each piece that he'd tried to tie off or tuck away after that summer, after Luke, was loosening and allowing all of the crazy bits to spill out.

Why now? Why now after so long?

He told himself it had to be Amy. It had to be her death, her body, so similar to Luke's, that was triggering him, but that was a lie. The dreams, the hallucinations, and the paranoia that someone was watching him…. All of that had started before she'd died.

Jeremy's eyes slid open, and he stared down at the torn knees of his jeans.

He inhaled and exhaled, counting each time, and reached for the calm center he'd taken years to find. He'd barely gotten his grasp on it even after the extensive therapy following God camp, but it was better than the raw wound that was now gaping in his chest.

His safe place had once been the green fields stretching endlessly in the suburbs outside of Houston. Jeremy had pictured himself and Luke running through the tall grass, going on adventures, and picking wild mushrooms while the sun shone on their backs without mercy. Now, things had changed.

When he reached for a safe memory, his mind dredged up his first real show with Stygian. Kennedy's large palm resting between his shoulders or at the small of his back. Quince's wide-eyed smile when they'd first spent an entire day sharing confidences over cheap beer. And even Watts. Fucking Watts shouting his approval in his brash and reckless style at the audition.

*God.*

How could those false, misleading moments be so grounding? Was that really all he had? Was that the best he could fucking conjure up after twenty-one years of living on this shitty planet?

His answer was a resounding yes.


JEREMY WALKED through the grocery store in a daze.

He was aware of the other customers giving him sideways stares and suspicious frowns, but he did not react. He could barely focus on the pharmacist long enough to translate the word acetaminophen before stumbling over to the cough and cold aisle.

It took longer than was necessary to select one of the various colorful boxes because he was too busy seething over the joke of his existence. How could it be that he had made it this far, scraped through the shit of his childhood and adolescence, and had nothing to show for it except people who didn't want him?

It was a truth he didn't want and a reality he couldn't change.

Weariness slowed Jeremy's steps and weighed down his limbs, and he craved home. His real home. Small comforts like the crowded record store he worked at and his snarky coworkers, relics of a dying punk age, who were a good distraction from the pointless drudgery of his job. The tiny room he rented near Memorial Park, and the clutter of music, books, and art that provided him with a protective wall from the outside world. His real life had enough going on to distract him from things like being alone.

"You one of them boys living up at that old house?"

Jeremy peered over the two brown paper bags cradled in his arms. He'd paid for the medicine and some breakfast in a blur but couldn't even recall exchanging words with the husky, red-haired cashier.

"What? Me? Yeah."

An old man looked at him from under the tattered brim of a gray-and-green Aggies cap. He was wrinkled with age but still wearing the dark-stained work shirt of a roughneck. "You seen that girl when she died?"

"I… I was, that is…." Jeremy's lips and tongue were doing a poor job of forming a coherent sentence. "I was there, sir. I didn't see her do it, though. We all found her after."

"Mmhmm." The man had a Benson & Hedges voice—rough and low. It was oddly soothing. "What're you boys doing in that house?"

"We rented it. For a, um, a music retreat. To write music." Jeremy's cheeks burned. "We're a band."

The man made another sound deep in his throat. It may have been skeptical or just thoughtful—Jeremy couldn't tell. "You came all the way up from Houston to live in a rundown house to write some music?"

"For… the atmosphere. We can concentrate there." Jeremy juggled the bags, and stared down into one of the steamed-up plastic containers of eggs, biscuits, and bacon. How did this guy even know they were from Houston? Was the whole town gossiping about them? "It is a little creepy."

"No doubt about *that*."

"What do you mean?"

"I mean what I said."

"Yeah but, like, why'd you say it like that?"

The old man regarded him with the same skepticism. "You okay, boy?"

Jeremy rephrased what he really wanted to ask. "Do you know the Caroways?"

"Yeah. I know about them Car-o-ways."

"Okay." Jeremy thought about Kennedy's words from the night before. "Are they…. Does anyone know much about them?"

Black orthopedic shoes scraped against the concrete as the man stood up straighter. He towered over Jeremy, taller even than Kennedy. "I know enough. That house has been abandoned for a long while and with good reason, son. Folks from town don't go up there. Not no more. If y'all would have asked a bunch of kids from Logansport to go to that party, they'd have known better. So, you be careful."

"Why don't they go there, though?"

"Just don't. And people around here won't give a good goddamn if you get yourselves in trouble. That old house is bad luck, son. Nobody around here talks about it and nobody fools with it."

"Then why are *you* talking about it?" Jeremy pressed.

"Because ain't nothing gonna bother some old man. But you boys are young, and you're better off going back home."

"What does that have to do with—"

The man's large, warm palm pressed briefly against Jeremy's bare shoulder before he shuffled away. Jeremy stood there long enough for a lady with a quartet of blond children to barrel into him.

The van was hotter already, and the interior was sweltering. He let the door hang open and cranked down the windows, trying to rid the van of the ripe smell of four guys' sweat, fast food, and stale cigarette smoke. It turned into several minutes of impromptu cleaning in an effort to kill time. A desperate measure to avoid going back to the house.

The man was the fourth person to warn him about the house in the past few weeks, but this time it didn't seem like the old man was worried about a bunch of city boys drinking in the middle of the woods. He seemed worried about something else. Something everyone in the town knew even if they refused to say it outright.

# CHAPTER NINE

IF THE encounter in the parking lot had turned Jeremy into a vibrating ball of disquiet, returning to the Caroway mansion heightened the feeling. He visualized Amy's body upon entering the kitchen and was already gagging by the time he blinked away the memory.

After leaving the bags on the kitchen counter, Jeremy grabbed his headphones and Simon's journal, and fled the room. He burst out onto the back porch and, instead of curling up on the swing like he'd planned, wound up jogging across the yard. He moved without seeing and took an automatic route through the woods.

An attempt to find the safe space in his mind—the damn audition with Stygian—resulted in him getting lost in a thousand confusing thoughts about where they were, why he'd come, and whether he should leave. Get away from the mansion and the band and find a bus back to Houston.

Everything blurred together until he was stumbling along in a direction he didn't remember choosing. Jeremy had vaguely considered going to the river, but found himself heading to Hunter's tiny shack. It was almost as though he was being pulled by some magnetic force.

By the time Jeremy got to the sagging, vine-covered structure, his head was aching from the combination of heat and exhaustion.

"Looking for my brother?"

Laurel was sitting in a midlevel branch of a tree. Her curly hair flowed beyond her shoulders, her feet were bare and dirty, and her lips twisted in a red moue. She looked like a fae creature living out in the woods, beautiful and slightly feral.

"Uhh." This was the last place Jeremy wanted to be. He had no idea how to face Hunter after the night before, and the continuous warnings from random people were starting to indicate the Caroways hadn't disclosed everything about the mansion before renting it. Unless it was Watts who had failed to disclose information to the band. "I wasn't looking for anybody. I don't know why I'm here, honestly."

"Since you're here…." Laurel let one of her legs swing down. "We could hang out."

"Er?"

One dark brow arched. "Do you prefer Hunter?"

"I don't know? I guess? I know him a little better."

"Do you now?"

"I said a little." Even as awkward as things would be with Hunter, Jeremy preferred him to Laurel's scrutiny. The Caroways needed to know what had happened the night before, but the words froze on his tongue with Laurel leering down at him. "We hung out once and spoke a couple of times."

"What about?"

"Just stuff and things. Listen, I really should talk to him. Is he in town?"

Laurel smirked. "We don't really go to town."

"Why not?"

"It's just not something we do."

Jeremy wondered if she was just giving him a hard time. "So… is he around? I don't know if he mentioned what happened last night."

Laurel's dangling leg drifted lazily. The sunlight seemed to reflect off her pale skin. "He wanted to fuck you, and the guitarist got in the way." Her gamine smile turned wolfish. "His own fault."

"I wasn't talking about that."

"Oh." If Laurel knew anything about Amy, she didn't let on. "But since we're talking about *that*, I think he should have tried to do you both."

Jeremy recoiled. "I don't think that would happen."

"Why not? I made it with the singer and the bass player."

The guitarist, the singer, the bass player—pieces of meat with instruments attached. Jeremy was new enough to the game for the groupie talk to catch him off guard, but the words rolling off her lips in that molasses accent somehow made it worse. She knew what she was reducing them to, and she didn't care if it made him uncomfortable. Maybe she *wanted* him to be uncomfortable.

"The singer must have fun like that all the time." Laurel lolled her head against the tree, her lashes obscuring her phenomenally blue eyes. "He didn't hesitate to touch me. He wasn't afraid."

"Why would he be afraid?"

"But the other one...." Laurel trailed off, teeth dragging over her lower lip. She leaped nimbly off the branch and landed beside him. "Quince. He was a joy. So pretty and innocent-looking, and he tasted so good...."

Jeremy wrinkled his nose and backed away, but she leaned in until her face was less than an inch from his own. "That's nice, I guess," he stammered. "But I don't get down with kinky threesomes and stuff."

"Hmm." Laurel inhaled. A subtle shift in her expression turned it brittle, and the blue of her eyes seemed to almost... pulse. "Now I get it."

Hunter approached without warning, appearing from between the trees in spectral silence. "What do you get, Laurel?"

She looked over her shoulder. "Why you're acting so different with the little drummer boy."

Jeremy tried to turn his eyes away from Hunter, but the man's mere presence drew him in.

"Am I acting different?"

"You are." Laurel's smile was like the tip of a knife. "Don't let him get under your skin. He won't be around much longer."

The two siblings stared at each other until Hunter sidestepped Laurel and snagged Jeremy's wrist. He didn't suggest they walk away from her; he just made it happen. An automatic urge to resist swelled inside Jeremy but it dissipated just as quickly.

"Sorry about her. She can be strange with people. We're kind of isolated out here. Not too good with society."

"I noticed." Jeremy looked back, but Laurel had already made tracks. No matter how feral her beauty was, it wasn't surprising that her lovely face and dainty limbs had entranced Quince and Watts.

He shook himself. "Listen, we should talk. After y'all took off last night, there was—well, something happened." Jeremy faltered. "There was a girl—"

"The police came to speak to me. I know what happened."

"Oh." So much for Kennedy's claim that the police hadn't bothered with the owners of the property. "Well, I'm just really sorry that some party we threw wound up like this. With someone dying in your house. I'm—I just wanted to apologize. On behalf of my whole band. If you want us to get going, we can."

Hunter stopped walking. "It wasn't your fault. The poor girl was fragile. The deputy told me she had a history of suicidal ideation. I consider myself fortunate to not have seen her body, but then again, I didn't stay long."

The comment was like a punch in the gut.

"I'm sorry."

"Stop apologizing. I shouldn't have assumed anything."

"Things are complicated with Kennedy, and I only met you a couple of weeks ago. But that's really the least of our issues. I've been in this town for less than a month, and already things are completely unusual. Last night was fucking awful." Jeremy started to wring his hands together but stopped himself and shoved them in his pockets. "I'm not good with these things. I have my own history. It's better when I can focus on drumming and listening to music."

Hunter held up a hand to halt the flow of words before letting it drift to the side of Jeremy's face. Not touching, but near enough for Jeremy to lean into it if he wanted. "It's okay. I didn't intend to upset you further, but I'm not in the best of moods myself."

"I know. I know. I'm sor—"

"Stop."

Jeremy toed at the dirt with one sneaker, very conscious of the tickly feeling of spindly legs crawling all over him. "There's something else."

"Yes?"

"A couple of people have made weird comments about your house. They warned me to be careful there. Like… there's something up with it."

"Which people?"

"Just people. It doesn't matter who. I want to know if there's a reason for it."

Hunter made a soft sound at the back of his throat and began walking again. "People gossip about my sister and me all the time. It concerns my family's history. Not you."

It was a near echo of things Jeremy had said to people about his own family. He stumbled over various ways to push for more information without being overly intrusive, and wished he could be as blunt as Kennedy or brash like Watts. But he wasn't, so the conversation lapsed.

He chanced a look up at Hunter and was unsurprised to find their eyes meeting. The urgency to press for details lessened. By the time they reached the riverbank, Jeremy was only thinking of how nice it felt to bask in a comfortable silence with someone who appeared to genuinely enjoy his company.

"Do you want to swim?" Hunter asked.

"I thought you said there were alligators."

"There are, but they don't bother me." A hint of a smile touched Hunter's mouth. "I didn't mean to scare you off entirely. I just wanted you to be aware."

Jeremy looked at the water. He could practically feel it flowing over his sticky limbs and washing everything away. "Are you sure?"

"Positive."

The word was motivation enough for Jeremy to kick off his sneakers and skim out of his jeans and tank. He was left only in a pair of royal blue briefs that were skimpy enough to be marginally embarrassing, but Hunter made no comment as he stripped down to his own underwear. It wasn't the first time Jeremy had seen him half-naked, but he still couldn't get over the breathtaking sight of Hunter's body. So beautiful it was hard to believe he was real.

Jeremy forced himself to stop staring and set his phone and the journal on top of his clothes.

"What's that you have there?" Hunter indicated the small, bound notebook.

"Oh, it's...." Jeremy looked at the journal again and an instinct to lie came out of nowhere. It was preferable to explaining how he found comfort in the scrawled words of a stranger because the sad stories reminded Jeremy so much of his own life. "It's my journal. Where I write tabs and stuff."

"Ah."

An awkward beat of silence passed between them before Hunter turned away.

They padded across the warm earth until the soil became damp and muddy. Brown roots jutted up from the ground at the very edge of the water. Jeremy waded in and swam to the middle of the river. Floating with his eyes shut, hair streaming around him and body warming beneath the sun, Jeremy had not felt so relaxed in days. He couldn't remember the last time he'd swam, but it drained every ounce of stress and unease from his limbs until nothing remained but him, the water, and the sky so blue and wide above him.

"I could stay like this forever."

His only answer was the low *plunk* of a splash.

Hunter had disappeared below the surface, and Jeremy dove after him, his feet kicking up.

With his long pale limbs flashing through the blue-green filter of the water, Hunter glided along as sleek and elegant as a sea creature. For a moment, Jeremy just followed. He didn't know where Hunter was going or how long he intended to stay underwater, but the repetitive slices of his arms and legs soothed Jeremy until all he wanted was to stay close to Hunter.

They swam until the burn in Jeremy's lungs warned he was getting close to the critical point of needing oxygen. The fluid movements didn't come easily anymore, and Jeremy sluggishly made his way to the shore. A few days of very little eating and no sleep were doing him in. Either that, or he was completely out of shape.

Sucking in gulps of air, Jeremy started to haul himself up to the embankment, but the sharp edge of a rock sliced across his finger. He pulled his hand back just as Hunter broke the surface and swam over.

"Are you okay?"

"Yeah. I just cut my finger on a rock." Jeremy frowned and squeezed the offending digit. Blood slid down in a stream. "Damn."

Hunter grasped his hand and peered at the cut.

"I should get a—"

The hot dampness of Hunter's mouth enveloped the digit, and Jeremy inhaled sharply.

Hunter's eyes met his, heavy-lidded and intoxicating as the rough flat of his tongue pressed against Jeremy's cut. This was a bad idea for many reasons, but when Hunter began to suck, the tiny alarms sounding in Jeremy's ears ceased. His world narrowed to Hunter, the swirling of his tongue, and a sudden dizzying warmth. As Hunter's cheeks hollowed around his finger, Jeremy's dick stiffened. He could do nothing but stare while fire coursed through his veins and his brain disconnected from its stem to float somewhere outside of his body.

It wasn't until something sharp pricked his finger, deepening the cut, that he jerk his hand away.

The stain of blood on Hunter's lips gave him the same savage quality as Laurel when she'd stared down at Jeremy from the tree—haunting and dangerous.

Hunter's tongue flicked out. "It's me who should apologize now."

"I... I mean...." Jeremy swallowed hard. "Jesus."

"He hasn't got anything to do with it." Hunter pushed wet hair out of his eyes. "You taste good."

Jeremy's dick pulsed again. "God, just stop. Please." He'd meant it as a joke, but it came out with a ragged edge. With that thought came the damning realization that some dude he barely knew was licking his blood. And he was getting off on it. "Seriously, stop."

Hunter laughed quietly, but the sound was hollow. "At least I distracted us a little?"

"Dude, you don't distract people by sucking their blood."

"I'm sorry. I couldn't help myself."

Jeremy managed to form words only after a struggle. "You don't even know me. I could have... y'know. A disease."

Hunter cocked his head.

"Like HIV? Hepatitis C?"

When Hunter continued to look blank, Jeremy had to stop himself from demanding how anyone could be so out of touch.

"I told you I'm not like other people," Hunter said eventually.

That was an understatement.

Cradling his hand against his chest, Jeremy watched Hunter swim farther into the water. He wondered, briefly, how he'd wound up at the cabin and why he was motionless even though this situation should have launched him out of the river and back to the house, but he still didn't move.

The longer he held eye contact with Hunter, the faster those thoughts floated away like the leaves bobbing along with the currents.

"How's your band?"

"They're… okay, I guess. Quince is sick, and the others were barely awake this morning. Everyone is probably stressed."

"Undoubtedly. It's a frightening thing. Seeing death."

"Yeah, it is."

"It's not the first time someone died in that house."

Jeremy's stomach clenched. "Who was it?"

"My father killed himself," Hunter said. "After he killed my mother."

"Oh. Oh shit."

It wasn't some old relative who had died in his sleep. Watts had rented them a motherfucking murder house. And without asking, Jeremy knew Hunter's parents had died in the blocked-off wing.

"I…." A macabre tableau filled Jeremy's head—imagined scenes of death and gore in a room not too far from the one he slept in. "I'm so, so sorry for bringing this up."

"It's fine, Jeremy." Hunter slid his hand across the surface of the river, causing fallen leaves and small pieces of wood to glide away. "Laurel and I were young. She saw it happen, and I felt like I failed her for not being there right at that moment. She had to handle it all on her own."

"No." Jeremy latched on to Hunter's self-condemnation to escape the disturbing direction of his own thoughts. "You can't blame yourself. You must have been a little kid at the time."

"I know, but feelings are rarely rational. Especially guilt." Hunter looked down at the ripples his fingers created in the water. "I'd appreciate it if you don't tell your band. I already spoke to Watts about what happened, so it isn't necessary for him to know anything regarding my family."

"Wait—" Brow furrowing, Jeremy thought back to the previous night. "When did you call?"

"After I was informed by the police. Watts said they'd just left and he was cleaning up with Kennedy."

A pit formed in Jeremy's stomach and widened with each word. Had there been an occasion for Kennedy to mention this amid the stilted silence following his rejection of Jeremy's plea to share the bed? Yes. There had been. Kennedy could have mentioned it any time, but he'd neglected to fess up about having been proven wrong about both the police and the Caroways.

More half-truths from his supposed friends. What did Kennedy hope to gain by making the Caroways sound shady?

"I won't tell them anything," he said. "I've lost someone too. My brother... he killed himself a few years ago. I found his body."

Hunter swirled figure eights in the water with his long fingers. "Like I said, it's not an easy thing. Seeing death changes you. It changed my sister."

Jeremy watched Hunter's hands, following the slow motions. "After it happened, I was different. I thought... I could still feel him. His spirit, his soul, whatever you want to call it. Sometimes at night, I swore I heard his voice. My mom thought I was going crazy, but it felt so real. I told her it *was* real, and she sent me away. Thought maybe God could save me."

Hunter's hand stilled. "What do you think now?"

"I don't know what I think anymore." Talking about it was an open invitation to scorn, but Hunter's gentle voice created only a feeling of safety. "Sometimes I think it's insanity, but other times, when I wake up in the middle of the night and I'm alone in the dark and nothing feels quite real, it's hard to deny there could be another world beyond the one we're all used to seeing. Pretty weird, right?"

"No." Hunter's chest grazed against Jeremy's. His skin was cool, smooth, and unblemished. No scars, no tattoos, just pale white skin and thick black hair and those mesmerizing blue orbs. "Isolation makes the impossible seem possible. And when you stay isolated, you just accept it. No matter how strange or unusual."

"Like what?"

"Like these woods. The old house."

"Yes. Since I got here, it's been freaky." Jeremy's secrets were flowing forth just as freely as the water. Talking to Hunter wasn't like navigating a field of land mines. "It's just like it was back when Luke died—I feel things, I hear things, I imagine things. After last night, it will be worse. I'll probably start imagining I hear Amy."

"Are you sure it's your imagination?" Hunter pulled a stray leaf from Jeremy's hair and sent it floating back to the water. "Some people are more sensitive to things than others."

It sounded like something Daedalus Black would say.

"Do you really think that's true?"

"I do. Don't be so quick to think you're crazy. I've experienced stranger things than that. You're right when you say there's another world beyond the surface of this one."

The knife of anxiety Jeremy had carried all day dulled. Maybe it was safe to confide in someone who was just as fucked-up as he was. And how horrible was that? Hoping maybe Hunter had his own brand of insanity just so he would let Jeremy unburden.

"Maybe people are always so distracted that they never notice," he ventured. "It's easier to ignore things if you have so much else to focus on. And there's always something else. TV, music, social media, friends, drinking, drama. But out here?" Jeremy drifted closer. "There's nothing."

Hunter nodded, and his singular focus made Jeremy feel like the most important person in the universe. "Maybe that's why you're more attuned to the energy around you. You're not surrounded by people, like you are in Houston."

"Yeah." It would explain why he'd not had these thoughts since the summer in God camp. "It's possible. And it's not like being with the band is much better than being alone."

Hunter dropped his hand, and Jeremy already craved the gentleness.

"Why do you want him if he's cruel to you?"

Jeremy started, and the water lapped around him.

"Kennedy isn't as bad as Watts. He's just… untouchable. So much is going on with all of them that there's not a lot of room left for me. I don't know how to break into their little circle, and I'm tired of trying. I've pretty much accepted that I'll stay on the perimeter of the band until I find something else and move along."

"I thought they'd known you for a long time."

"No. Not really."

Hunter's gaze slanted away.

"What?"

"I don't want to start problems."

The dreamy quality of the moment ebbed, and the protective bubble that had encircled them popped. Suddenly the humidity was too much, the sun's rays too strong, and Jeremy could feel every pinprick of pain where he'd been bitten by mosquitos in the past hour.

"What kind of problems?" Jeremy pressed. "Just tell me."

For the first time since they'd met, Hunter refused to meet his eyes. He watched the swaying fronds of a willow tree as they brushed the surface of the water, moving just enough to be a constant trigger to Jeremy's overactive peripheral vision.

"Now that you've told me about your brother, I realize I overheard them talking about him. I thought they knew both of you since high school."

"They went to high school with my brother, not me." A short, stilted silence. "Why? What did they say?"

"I'd rather not...."

"Hunter, please." Why was Luke coming up at all? He was long dead. A crumbling skeleton somewhere six feet under at a graveyard in Houston, and no one had cared. No one had come to the burial except his mother's bible-thumping family and his father's meager collection of towheaded Blacks. "They don't tell me anything, even when I ask."

*Don't be like them,* Jeremy pleaded silently. *Don't make me regret trusting you.*

"Your bandmates don't notice their surroundings. They think no one can hear them talking if they see no one nearby." Hunter's broad shoulders ticked up. "Kennedy suggested the singer tell you about his relationship with Luke. Watts refused and said it would just make you hate him more because of what he'd done."

There had been no relationship. No friends. No one had cared about Luke until he died. Especially not a rich party boy who had likely fucked and dated his way through high school.

"I don't get it," he said blankly.

"I'm sorry." Hunter was poised to flit away through the water. To escape this awkward conversation and the words Jeremy was forcing him to repeat. "I didn't listen further. I didn't want to intrude."

Jeremy looked at the willow tree and concentrated on the gently swaying fronds. It sent tiny leaves drifting into the water in a soundless descent. With the exception of the branches, the woods around them were very still. Unnaturally still. Once again, the singing of the birds and the shrill of the cicadas had ceased.

"I should get back."

"I'll walk with you."

Jeremy inclined his head. He didn't feel like being alone.

# CHAPTER TEN

THE SILENCE persisted during the walk, magnified every time Jeremy's toe stubbed a rock or his clothing brushed against the gnarled branch of a tree. It wasn't until he parted ways with Hunter by the break in the tree line that the absolute silence was broken by the twang of an acoustic guitar.

Kennedy was sitting on the back porch with a bare foot braced against the railing. The wood of his guitar shone in the sun, and his long fingers maneuvered the strings while he watched Jeremy approach. It was still too quiet, but it didn't hit Jeremy as hard as he climbed the stairs and stood next to the swing.

Kennedy stopped plucking at the strings with the red pick caged between his fingers. His eyes swept over Jeremy's damp hair and clothing.

"You've been gone awhile."

Jeremy bit back a retort. "How's Quince?"

Kennedy's gentle rocking ceased, and he dropped his foot to the porch. "I tried to tell them he should go to the doctor if his fever gets worse, but you know Watts."

"Did he kick the fever even a little? I brought Tylenol and things from the grocery store."

The guitar emitted a hollow thrum when Kennedy set it down. "It went down, but there's something funky going on with him. He's acting weird. Real sluggish and spacey, but has a bad attitude when you try to talk to him."

"Quince does?" It was so uncharacteristic that the very possibility was ludicrous. "What would he even have an attitude about?"

"Everything. He said Watts was being clingy, and I was trying to tell him what to do." Kennedy stood, sliding his hands into the pockets of his jeans. "I think his fever cooked his brain, or banging Laurel has him feeling like some macho man."

Or maybe he really was tired of having Watts the control freak and band daddy Kennedy making all the decisions.

Jeremy knew he was projecting. Even if Quince had those beliefs, the likelihood of him sharing them was slim to none. The guy was as confrontational as a fainting goat.

"He's probably just in a bad mood because he's sick. It sucks having a fever when it's this hot."

"Yeah, maybe."

Jeremy edged closer to the door, not wanting to be subject to Kennedy's invasive stare downs. The previous night felt so far away it was almost like it had never happened at all. Like their lips had never touched, and Kennedy had never brought him off with the kind of expertise that had left Jeremy reeling.

Now Jeremy could barely meet his eye. If he did, the resentment and distrust that had gathered on the walk back from the river would burst out in an explosion of accusations. The last thing he wanted was to make this trip any more dramatic than it was, but questions burned on the tip of his tongue.

He jerked the door open.

"Are you mad at me?"

"No."

Jeremy hurried through the kitchen and avoided looking at the spot where Amy's body had lain the night before. The heavy tread of Kennedy's boots was right behind him.

"What were you doing with Hunter again? I saw him walking you to the house. Is he your chaperone now?"

"We were talking. I figured someone had to apologize for last night."

"What is there to apologize for? They knew about the party. They came to the goddamn thing."

"I wasn't just apologizing for that."

Kennedy grabbed his arm before he could sprint up the stairs, bringing him to an abrupt stop. Jeremy pulled away and wheeled around. He took in the set of Kennedy's jaw, a telltale sign that his blood pressure was rising.

"You apologized for taking off with me?"

"I didn't say that."

"Don't play that coy shit with me, kid. If you regret it, just say so. Feel free to go hash it out with him some more over a dip in the river, and I'll stay out of your way."

And just like that, uncertainty flourished.

Had he read Kennedy wrong the night before? Ascribed Kennedy's withdrawn attitude to a loss of interest when it'd just been stress from the situation and Jeremy's own insecurities whispering in his ear?

But that wasn't enough to cast aside the other things Jeremy had learned about his bandmates.

"You misled me on purpose," Jeremy said.

"What are you talking about?"

"You said the cops never contacted the Caroways, and tried to make them sound all shady." Kennedy said nothing, and Jeremy jabbed a finger into his chest to emphasize the accusation. "I don't get you. I *really* don't. You're hot, then you're cold, I'm just a kid, and then you're ready to piss all over me to mark your territory, and even after we hook up, you feel the burning need to invent stupid lies just to keep me from liking Hunter? Right before you banish me to the fucking couch?"

"I offered to switch."

"That is not the point!" Jeremy shouted. "I just wanted to be close to you. You knew I was freaked out. Shit, even *Watts* knew. But you just tried to make me believe our landlords were psychos before ignoring me for the rest of the night. It didn't even occur to you to reassure me. And I know I'm not your responsibility, but after everything you said in the hall—" Jeremy's throat clicked when he swallowed. "I just don't know why you pretended to give a shit. I'd have let you fuck me regardless. You didn't have to act like I mattered. It's super obvious that you don't really care about me."

"That's not true." Kennedy's only sign of upset was the clenching in his jaw and the stiff line of shoulders so broad they looked ready to burst through the seams of his T-shirt. "You always jump to the worst possible conclusions."

"Bullshit," Jeremy retorted, drawing out the word. "All you care about is yourself and your band and your fucking guitar, and to hell with me unless you're feeling threatened and your testosterone starts boiling over. You only notice me when someone else is paying too much attention. Any other time I can basically go straight to hell."

And to that, Kennedy said nothing. He looked at Jeremy in a way that could have meant he was completely wrong or completely stupid. Or maybe Kennedy was just annoyed that he was having to justify himself to some mouthy, needy bird who would probably be out of the band soon, anyway.

It was the ugliest thought he'd ever had about Kennedy, but the rancid burn of cynicism ate away at every centimeter of Jeremy's already heavy heart.

"I know I come off harsh," Kennedy said after a slow exhale. "But I don't mean it. It's just the way I am, and I thought you understood that about me. I thought you trusted me by now."

"Well, I don't. And I don't know what delusions have convinced you that I should. Putting your mouth on my dick is hardly a guarantee that you won't manipulate me or treat me like shit. Especially since you've already done both in the space of eleven hours."

"Wow, kid." Kennedy's scathing tone made Jeremy cringe. "Seems like you and Quince have been drinking the same Kool-Aid."

"If it's the 'you and Watts are shitheads' flavor, then yeah. Maybe we have."

Kennedy laughed, but he was anything but amused. "Jesus fucking Christ, this is exactly why I shouldn't have laid a hand on you. I knew it was a bad idea."

Every angry word had been leading up to this moment, but his throat still tightened.

"Fuck you."

"No. Fuck *you*." Kennedy stalked past Jeremy. "And fuck you twice if you think what happened to your brother gives you an excuse to be this way. You're not the only one who's lost someone. Not everything is about you."

Kennedy was gone before Jeremy could muster a reply. But he whispered it anyway.

"It's never about me."


FROM THE pecan tree, the view of the moonlit woods was gorgeous. Everything was tinged in silver. He didn't see so many stars in

Houston, for all that he'd been raised in a state filled with wide-open sky and vast fields.

The only time he'd ever traveled outside of Houston had been with Stygian. In the last few months, they'd played a few gigs at dive bars in Texas's major cities. His first trip to San Antonio, Austin, Dallas… that had all happened with Stygian. Before them, he'd not seen the point in going anywhere. And he hadn't had the money to try.

Everything went back to the band, and it fed the blistering resentment that had swelled during the week since Amy's death. They hadn't practiced for the past few days while Quince recouped from his random illness, Watts finally set to writing some songs, and Jeremy and Kennedy watched each other while pretending not to. The tension between them was so high that he often found himself wandering in the woods and listening to music to drown out his chaotic thoughts.

He drew his knees up to his chin and put Simon's journal aside. Even with the diamond-studded sky stretching above him, he could barely see the scrawled words, so he looked at the house instead. The darkness gave it qualities that were at once more sinister and beautiful, but he was determined not to let it get to him. It worked until a high-pitched whine cut through the night. His heart leaped into his throat, but then he realized the sound had come from the back porch's screen door.

Jeremy assumed it was Kennedy going outside for his nightly chain-smoke-athon, but it was Quince's coltish shadow stretching across the silvery sheen of the grass. He looked thin and fragile, but he walked across the yard with long, sure strides.

It took less than a minute to descend the towering tree and jog across the yard, but by then Quince had already disappeared into the woods. He was moving fast for someone who had been stricken with a fever only a couple of days ago.

Jeremy turned in a slow circle and scanned the trees, but he didn't see his bandmate. He didn't even hear the rustle of clumsy footsteps that should have accompanied a city boy like Quince as he stumbled around in the dark. When it came to the outdoorsy stuff, Quince was as bad as Jeremy. They'd never had parents to take them camping or to indoctrinate them into the good-ol'-boy, gun-loving, and hunting Texan spirit. They'd both drifted through childhood trying to find things that made them happy, and the piecemeal collection they'd gathered hadn't included wandering around in the woods.

"Quince?" Jeremy called softly. "Where'd you go?"

He picked a random direction and started forward, but a hand fell on his shoulder. A cry tore out of him, wild and shrill enough to hurt his throat, but it was only Quince. He'd reappeared as silently as a cat.

"Why are you following me?"

"I was just wondering if I could, um...."

Jeremy had a hard time concentrating with Quince looking so guarded.

Kennedy hadn't exaggerated when he'd claimed Quince had woken from his sleep a changed man. His eyes glittered like jewels, but they held no warmth, and his mouth was a flat line in his pale, washed-out face. He looked sickly, brittle, and the bruises on his neck were more lurid than they'd been on the morning after the party.

"Did Kennedy send you to find me? Because I don't need a babysitter. I can go where I want."

His voice was odd. Unfriendly and untrusting.

"Whoa!" Jeremy held up his hands. "You've got the wrong idea, Q. I was sitting up in the tree and saw you leave the house. I figured I could take a walk with you."

"What were you doing in a tree at one o'clock in the morning?"

"Avoiding sleeping in the house?"

Some of the hardness melted from Quince's posture and expression, and once again he was the passive guy who mediated Stygian's fights. "To get away from Kennedy?"

"Yeah, kinda. Long story."

Quince snorted. "It's not that long. Watts bitched about it while I was stuck in that bed. I couldn't wait to get away from him."

Maybe the passive aspect hadn't returned after all. That level of sardonic disdain wasn't typically present in Quince's dulcet tones.

"Bitching about what exactly?"

Quince's gaze had already darted to the woods as if seeking something or someone, or maybe just anxious to get farther from the mansion. "He said Kennedy finally nailed you, and now there would be drama for sure."

Jeremy blanched. "He didn't nail me. We fooled around a little. And there's not—I'm not going to cause drama. Watts is an asshole."

"Good. Don't let Kennedy hurt your feelings." Quince started walking then, clearly expecting Jeremy to follow in his wake. "I let Watts do it to me for too long. If I was you, I would have gone with Hunter that night."

"Why?"

"Because he's better for you."

Jeremy stopped so abruptly that he kicked up a mound of leaves that had fallen in a wet lump during the storm. The sweet smell of rot wafted up from the ground, and dampness seeped between the sole of his foot and the rubber of his sandal.

"How do you figure that?"

Bemusement crossed Quince's face. "I... don't know. It just seemed like the right thing to say?"

"I see."

Jeremy didn't see, but Quince was acting so strangely that it seemed better not to ask.

They began walking again, and it didn't take long for Jeremy to pick up on their trajectory. Even with the trees blending together like towering shadows and the distracting sound of the forest creatures' combined screeching, Jeremy knew they were headed for Hunter and Laurel's cabin.

"So Watts doesn't like the Caroways either?" Jeremy ventured.

"Not anymore. He thinks Hunter is a weirdo and Laurel is a freak." Quince's soft mouth twisted in a tight little slash. "Of course, he decided that after he fucked her."

"If he thinks she's so freaky, then why did he mess around with her at all?"

"Because it was okay while he was getting something out of it. Now, he doesn't need her anymore." Quince got that look again— mean and impenetrable. Tougher than he'd ever been before. "It's kind of funny how I never realized just how disposable I was until I watched him lay it on someone else."

"You're not—"

Quince's glittery stare swung to Jeremy with cold hostility. "Don't even, Jere. You of all people should know what I mean."

Yeah. Because he was disposable too.

Jeremy swallowed the pitiful denials that Watts would ever throw Quince to the wayside. He didn't know if he really believed that or if he just wanted to console Quince. Either way, he didn't seem in need of consoling. He looked pretty content with his newfound dislike.

"What did Watts do to piss you off this bad?"

"What did Kennedy do to *you*?"

"Nothing worth talking about. Just me accepting the facts after they became undeniable?"

"I guess you could say the same for me."

Their traipse through the woods wasn't going as well as Jeremy had hoped. Instead of companionship and a shared adventure, he felt the slow bleed of discontent and saw the looming dissolution of their band. Which was sadder than it should have been. He wanted to get away, but he didn't necessarily want Stygian to fall entirely apart.

The rest of their journey went by without comment until they reached the break in the trees where the cabin stood. Except for the climbing vines and invasive ferns that looked gray beneath the moon, the state of the structure's disrepair wasn't as noticeable in the dark.

"Jeremy."

For the second time that night, Jeremy was startled enough to leap out of his skin.

Hunter appeared from the dark haze of trees just as Laurel opened the door to the shack. Both of them were ethereal in the starlight. Skin pale as bleached pearls and their eyes like summer rain. And the way they moved.... Both of them stalking forward with the tempered steps of excruciatingly beautiful predators.

When Hunter stopped before him and smiled, Jeremy forgot everything else. His worries and fears. Stygian and Kennedy.

"I didn't know you were coming."

"I kind of invited myself," Jeremy said once he remembered to breathe. "Quince—"

Quince was presenting Laurel with a gathered assortment of wildflowers. Beggarticks, catchflys, and primrose. The names came easily to Jeremy, as if Luke was still there to remind him.

"Um. Yeah. I just tagged along."

"I'm glad you did."

Jeremy shrugged, still feeling sullen, but didn't pull away when Hunter touched his chin.

"Are you all right?"

"Not really."

Jeremy watched Quince and Laurel. He wondered how Quince could shun the band so quickly after having been with them for so long. Jeremy was a new arrival, and his guts were still going through the meat grinder.

"I just have some things to think about, I guess."

"Do you want to talk about it?"

*Yes.*

"Nah. Me whining about my problems isn't going to get this party going." Jeremy forced a grin. "We can just hang out?"

"I wouldn't have asked if I wasn't interested." Hunter tilted his chin up. "Just because I was upset the other night doesn't mean I'm not here for you now. I know how it feels to be alone with no one to confide in or trust."

Jeremy looked at Laurel and wondered if the siblings were close. He'd picked up on a strange tension between them after meeting Laurel, and even now, there was a disconnect between the two.

Laurel had looped her arms through Quince's, pulling him so close they were practically one, and was angling him away from Hunter. Her round eyes focused on Quince, red lips curved with a ready smile, and her posture screamed *mine*. It was a little excessive considering she could only have been hanging out with Quince for less than a week.

"We're going for a swim," she said. "Join us if you want. Or meet us at the clearing? It will be like a party. Our kind of party."

Quince only smiled.

"Where's the clearing?" Jeremy watched them slip between the decaying pine trees leading to the river. "And should they be swimming at night? Aren't there, like, alligators and snakes?"

"The water snakes aren't poisonous."

Not comforting. "I'll pass."

"Okay. Shall we go to the clearing?"

"Sure."

They walked in silence while Hunter snagged his hand and threaded their fingers together. Jeremy just barely kept himself from pulling away and swallowed guilt that he had no business feeling. If Kennedy didn't owe him anything, then the same was true in reverse.

He held on to that thought, clutched it tight to his chest, but it still bothered him.

The walk didn't take long, but once they arrived it felt like they'd been transported to another world. The clearing was small and surrounded by trees so large they formed a canopy penetrated by stray moonbeams. Within the trees' circle, the bed of grass and wildflowers blanketing the ground was dotted with silver light.

"Dude. This is some C.S. Lewis shit."

Hunter laughed and lowered himself to the ground with nimble, controlled movements. "It's really magical. I love it here."

Jeremy flopped on the grass beside Hunter and spread his arms above him. The sweet smell of damp grass and flowers was everywhere.

"Has Quince seen this? He would love it."

"I don't know." Hunter rolled onto his side to gaze at Jeremy's profile. "I'm not sure what Laurel has been doing with him now that they've started going off together. I don't ask."

Jeremy kept looking up at the canopy of leaves. The branches were wound together so tight it formed a barrier between him and the sky. "Do you guys not get along?"

"That's one way of putting it."

"What's the other way?"

"We've been stuck together forever. You get tired of a person after a while." Hunter tilted his face up to the sky. Long tendrils of silky hair tumbled into the grass. "Especially when you don't have anybody else."

"Is that why she's randomly latching on to Quince like he's the second coming of Christ?"

Hunter released a startled-sounding laugh. "I guess. She absolutely loathes me, so anyone looks like an angel of justice in comparison."

"That's pretty harsh."

"Maybe. But it's true." Hunter's expression didn't change. His face was as unmoved as glass. "We despise each other most of the time. It wouldn't be so bad if she hadn't alienated us from the town."

A "How?" nearly popped out of Jeremy's mouth, but he swallowed it. He could see well enough how that could have gone down. Laurel was blunt and sassy and sexual, and most people couldn't handle women like that. Even Jeremy's batshit relatives still went around preaching about females being "ladylike." Folks in a tiny town like Logansport were probably worse.

"Can't you go somewhere else? You don't *have* to be together. You're both adults."

"There's nowhere for us to go, Jeremy."

"Why not?" Jeremy sat upright with his palms flat against the damp grass. Sharp blades slid between his fingers. "Sell that behemoth of a creepy-ass house and get a place in Shreveport or Center. Or shit—leave Louisiana. Go to Texas. Start over. You know?"

"What would I start over and do? I have no skills." Hunter's voice had a hint of a smile. "Be a waiter? Go to school? Maybe I'll be a stripper."

Jeremy burst out laughing and probably startled hordes of tiny forest creatures. "Man, you could do it. You're hot, and you have a rocking body. If I looked like you, I'd seriously consider it. I love to dance."

"Then do it," Hunter said easily. "There's no shame in it, and you're gorgeous."

"Not really. I'm a runt."

A shadow fell over Hunter's face. He grabbed Jeremy's arm and pulled him down until they were tumbled together on the soft, wet grass.

"How," Hunter said against Jeremy's face, "can you not see your appeal?"

Jeremy couldn't think with Hunter's delicate eyelashes tangling with his own.

"I don't know who made you feel this way, but they're wrong. You're clever. You're smart. You're sweet. And you are so beautiful that it's difficult for me to keep my hands to myself."

"You don't—" Jeremy took a slow breath, trying to calm down, but failed. How could he steady himself when Hunter's eyes were sucking him into a dizzying abyss? "You don't have to say that."

"I'm not just saying it. It's true. And Kennedy is a fool for not wanting you."

Jeremy tried to rise, but Hunter pinned him to the ground. "How do you—"

"Correction," Hunter said. "He wants you, but only at his convenience. Isn't that right?"

"I… I don't know. How do you know he doesn't want me?"

"Oh, Jeremy." Hunter cupped his face. "Kennedy may act like he wants to keep you for himself, but it seems more about control. He likes the attention you give him, and he'll lose that if you turn to someone else. That's why he dislikes me."

Jeremy fell back against the grass and pressed a hand over his eyes.

"Just like Watts only wants you in the band so he can have a punching bag. Unless you let him fuck you, and then he can have both. Neither of them deserves you." Hunter's voice dropped lower. A siren's song in Jeremy's ear. "They don't want you, and you shouldn't care. You don't belong with the people who hurt your brother. Did something to him they never want you to know."

"Hunter…."

"They're twisted inside from the things they've done, and there's no saving them. Or changing them."

"*Fuck*." Jeremy's shuddering sigh sounded suspiciously like a sob. "Fuck, I know. I *know*. But I don't have anyone else. No family. No real friends. What if I leave the band and I'm alone? I don't even have a job anymore."

"You don't need them," Hunter whispered. "You can do anything you want. All of the things you said to me."

Jeremy kept his eyes hidden behind the safety of his hand so Hunter wouldn't see his pointless, miserable tears. "I've been trying to figure out what the fuck to do with myself for years, Hunter. *Years*. I've got… nothing. No ambition. No goals. Nothing drives me. I don't *want* things. I just want people. People to care about me. And that sounds so pathetic that I can barely stand myself, but do you understand?"

"I do." Hunter kissed Jeremy's forehead, as gentle as a snowflake and just as cold. "Because I'm the same way. Maybe that's why I feel so drawn to you."

"Maybe," Jeremy said roughly. "Or maybe you just pity me."

"No." Hunter hovered above Jeremy, and his hair curtained them both. An added layer of protection from the world. "I know we've only just met, but we have a connection. A closeness I've never felt with anyone else. They may not want you, but I do. Every part of you. Every memory and secret. And I'll give you everything of mine."

Then Hunter wrapped Jeremy in his arms and held him securely to his chest. He didn't appear to expect a response, and Jeremy was relieved because he didn't have one. The internal wound had been picked to bleeding again, and he was too tired to fight against Hunter's declarations of affection or his damning words about Stygian.

# CHAPTER ELEVEN

PRACTICE HAD skipped going to hell in a handbasket and plowed straight into the ninth circle with the force and velocity of a bullet train. They were finally working on new material—tabs written in the previous weeks by the rest of the band were now matched with lyrics hastily penned in the past few days by Watts—but no one could get it together enough to make it work.

The first problem was that Watts kept singing ballads when they'd all decided on an edgier sound for their sophomore album. His crooning, emo lyrics were barely heard over the modified D-beat Jeremy was banging out of his kit. Nothing matched up, and everything was wrong. And, of course, Watts blamed him.

A series of "That's not our sound" and "You're trying to turn us into some bubblegum punk bullshit" comments were snarled straight through the first few songs until Jeremy was so tense and nervous that he started screwing up his own parts. He reversed the kick and crash on two songs, back and forth right and wrong, until Watts was ready to implode.

By then, Jeremy *wanted* to implode. Or to escape this fucking nightmare and return to his new haven—the clearing in the woods.

"Wakey, wakey, Jeremy."

The mic nailed Jeremy in the chest before he saw it coming. It startled him more than hurt him, but Quince reacted with the fierce protectiveness of three lionesses. He cut the bass line short in the middle of a bridge, and caught a squeal of distortion as Kennedy stumbled over a palm mute at the sudden absence of half the rhythm section.

Waifish, strawberry blond Quince should have looked ridiculous as he literally dropped his bass and got in Watts's face, but he didn't. He looked ready for a fight. In less than two weeks, the sweet boy Jeremy had once marathoned Molly Ringwald movies with had transformed into a more vindictive version of Watts, and the shades of his former self only came out in the sun-dappled green of the woods.

"What's your fucking problem?"

"Whoa," Watts said with half a laugh that didn't reach his eyes. He took a step back from Quince. "What's with the mama-bear routine all of a sudden? You all up in tiny twink's cunt too?"

Jeremy rubbed his chest and pointedly ignored the alarmed look Kennedy was throwing at him. If Quince was angry, Jeremy had become completely withdrawn. Lately, he spent more time in the clearing with Hunter than with Stygian.

"Him not wanting you to beat up on me means we have to be fucking?" Jeremy asked. "You're an idiot and an asshole."

"We already knew that," Watts said. "And if you think that's beating up on you, you're more of a fragile baby than I thought. But I guess it's good to know that you're not into the pain-slut routine like Q over here. I haven't seen bite marks that deep since I did community service at the youth center with the specials."

"You're such a piece of shit," Quince said. "You don't have respect for anyone or anything."

"Yeah, no shit. I never have."

"Can y'all just shut the fuck up?" Kennedy shoved a cigarette into his mouth. "I'm sick of all of you."

"The feeling is mutual," Jeremy said.

"Definitely," Quince added.

Watts couldn't have sneered harder if he'd gone to school to study the art. "Oh, check out the twins of cynicism and angst. A random chick dies, and everyone falls to pieces and starts acting all brand-new."

"It has nothing to do with Amy." Jeremy walked around the throne with the mic in his hand. "It has to do with everything that's wrong with the band."

Kennedy's eyes narrowed into slits.

"Oh fuck, now you're on this kick too, Jere? All of a sudden neither of you can shut the fuck up about how much the band sucks?" Watts poked Quince in the chest. "This cockwad has been bitching about every complaint he'd ever held in for the entire length of time he's known me. Everything from the time I fucked his mouth too hard in the parking lot of Jumping World to my motherfucking failure as a roommate. Sorry I didn't think to bring my Roomba."

Smoke seeped out of Kennedy's mouth as he looked between his bandmates. "This is getting us nowhere. Watts—shut up. And Quince, can you back off him?"

"What if I don't want to?"

Watts wiggled his fingers in an *I'm so scared* motion, but his eyes were serious.

"Let's go, Quince." Jeremy put a hand on Quince's shoulder. "Let's take a walk."

"Where?" The question shot out of Kennedy's mouth like a gunshot. "To see your fucking boyfriend?"

Again, Jeremy ignored Kennedy and spoke to Quince. "We can go cool off. It's not like this is a priority anyway."

"How do you figure?" Kennedy again. The first mention of the Caroways shifted him from half-assed mediation mode to possessive smartass. "Because you both plan to quit the band and shack up in the woods for the rest of your lives?"

Jeremy dropped his hand and looked at Kennedy. "That would be hundreds of times better than wasting my time with you."

The stricken wash of Kennedy's features affected Jeremy for a single heartbeat before he remembered something Hunter had said the day before—after an hour spent listening to Jeremy agonize over whether he should keep trying or quit the band now.

*They know how to play on your kindness, and you let them do it.*

Jeremy clenched his jaw. "Quince, let's go. Please."

"Fine."

Quince gave Watts another cold onceover before striding out of the room.

Kennedy set down his guitar with a hollow thud. "Are you really going to keep running to Hunter and acting like you fucking hate me?"

Jeremy half turned to the archway that led to the foyer. "I don't know."

Kennedy's eyes blazed. "I don't know how we got here, kid."

"That's part of the problem."

"No. The problem is you trusting some freak we just met instead of someone who—"

"Someone who *what?*" Jeremy swung fully around and pointed. "What have you done for me? What do you think you should be to me?"

Kennedy started to speak, but slammed his lips shut after glancing at Watts.

"Don't worry, Ken-boy," Watts sneered. "I'm fucking off right now."

Jeremy was on the verge of following Quince out the door, but Kennedy's presence prevented him from drifting further into the hateful chasm that had formed.

Watts shouldered past Jeremy and stomped up the stairs. Kennedy didn't speak until a door slammed shut.

"If I'm nothing to you, then why are you still standing here?" he asked quietly. "Why aren't you running after Quince to go meet your boyfriend?"

*Why aren't you?*

Jeremy glanced over his shoulder and immediately felt foolish. The question had clearly been in his head.

"I don't... know." He should be leaving. The door was right behind him. Escape was so close. But with Kennedy hurt and confused, Jeremy forgot why he was supposed to be escaping. "I don't know what's happening."

Kennedy frowned. "What do you mean?"

Jeremy's mouth was so dry. He swallowed thickly, but it didn't help.

"You make me so angry. All of you do. It's why I want to stay away until we can get back to Houston where I can isolate myself in my fucking apartment."

Kennedy crossed the room in two long strides and was pushing Jeremy against the wall before he could evade. "You think I'm going to let this drop once we're in Houston?"

"You always did before."

"And I told you why." Kennedy braced his arms on either side of Jeremy's face. "Every fucking word I said the night of the party still stands, Jeremy."

*He pushed you away.*

"Bullshit." Jeremy kept himself still, but he was painfully aware of the hardness of Kennedy's torso. The heat of his breath. "The night of the party, you were an asshole an hour after you had my dick in your mouth."

"Maybe because none of my bandmates will listen to me!" Kennedy's voice rose to a shout. He flicked a glance at the door before lowering it again. "Do you know how frustrating it is to have none of you fucking trust me when it's actually about something important?"

"I've always trusted you," Jeremy blurted.

It was the wrong thing to say. He'd sworn to himself, and Hunter, that he wouldn't make himself vulnerable. That he *wouldn't* trust them. But the strength of his feelings for Kennedy rose to the surface and overtook all of those late-night promises. It shot through the dark abyss like an arrow made of sunlight.

"You're not just this hot, tattooed musician who I want to fuck me. You're—you're a good person. You care about people. You... used to look out for me when I first started doing gigs with you guys. If you didn't want me falling for you, you shouldn't have been so nice to me. It *meant* something. Don't you understand? One of the things I hoped for this summer was to get close to *you*." As soon as he stopped speaking, Jeremy wanted to crawl in a hole somewhere. "Please, Kennedy. Just let me go."

"No fucking way."

Then they were kissing. It happened too fast for Jeremy to pull away, but he didn't want to. Not when his world had dwarfed to this moment—Kennedy shoving him against the wall, tonguing him hungrily, and moaning once Jeremy kissed back.

*He hurt Luke.*

Jeremy recoiled as if Kennedy's lips had burned him. "Stop!"

Kennedy breathed hard against him, his eyes wild. "What's wrong?"

"I can't do this." Jeremy ducked under Kennedy's arm and tore away. "I can't fucking stand here and do this with you."

"Why? You want me. You just said—"

"I know what I just said!" Jeremy's voice was shrill. He sounded hysterical. "But I just *can't*. I can't trust you anymore. I know you're keeping things from me."

"About *what*?"

"About my brother!"

And just like that, the guard slammed down on Kennedy's face. "See? I fucking knew it."

"You don't know anything," Kennedy said sharply. "Whatever ominous shit you're assuming is wrong. I'm just afraid to increase the level of fuckery when we've already jumped feet first into a shitshow."

"That doesn't tell me anything!" Jeremy sucked in a breath and tried to find his calm center, but it was unattainable. If anything, Kennedy's evasiveness was drawing out the rage that had so briefly retreated. "I want the truth."

Kennedy took a step closer, his hands pressed pleadingly together. "Jeremy, pl—"

"Tell me."

"Just give me time. Let me talk to Watts—"

*Liars. All of them.*

"Why? So you can concoct a fake story to pacify me?" The lingering remains of Jeremy's desire burned away and left only distrust. He closed in on himself until his feelings were buried and there was nothing left but weariness and the voice in his head. "No, Kennedy. Just stay away from me until you can."

AFTER LEAVING the house, Jeremy took a meandering route to the river. A swim sounded wonderful. The repetitive motion of his arms cutting through cool currents would ease his chaotic mind.

But he still ended up at the Caroways' cabin.

Each time Jeremy stepped into the woods, he lapsed into a foggy dreamlike state. He didn't know if his mini fugues were caused by stress or the increasingly hot days, but he always wound up going somewhere he hadn't planned to go. Like the cabin. Or the clearing. At the moment, it was hard to care.

Hunter was sitting on the stairs as if he'd been waiting all along. His face broke into a slow smile.

"Jeremy," he said. "How was practice?"

"Miserable." Jeremy sat, and rested his head on Hunter's shoulder. "Things are getting worse."

"How so?"

"I keep thinking all of these terrible things, and it makes me act like an asshole. Even when it isn't necessary. I'm starting to think I'm paranoid. Like making it bigger than it is. For all I know, they barely knew Luke, and this is all a misunderstanding."

"Jeremy...."

Jeremy winced. "I know. Why would they hide it if it was no big deal?"

"Exactly. Don't play their game. Don't let them manipulate you."

This had been the reoccurring conversation since the first night Jeremy had followed Quince into the woods. Entire afternoons in the liquid heat were full of the nonstop conversation about his bandmates. It was impossible not to suspect Kennedy and Watts of wrongdoing after those hours of rumination, and he often heard the reverb of their discussions even hours after returning to the mansion.

"I won't. And I'm so sorry I keep bothering you with all this, but I keep wondering what they may have done to my brother or what they want from me, and it feels like I'm going insane."

"You're not." Hunter shifted his position to kneel in front of Jeremy. Their gazes locked, and Hunter's eyes dilated. The ghostly blue shrank to a thin band around his pupils. "You're seeing them for who they are. People who will use you and hurt you and lie to you as long as you can do something for them, and then they'll discard you."

It was impossible to do anything but nod and absorb the words.

"Now, stop doubting yourself. And stop trying to find excuses for them."

"I will. I'll stop."

"Good." Hunter brushed his lips against Jeremy's cheek. "Do you want to go to the clearing?"

As soon as Hunter's intense stare broke away, Jeremy's doubts returned. "I need—I was going to...." What had he been going to do? The entire walk to the cabin now felt like it had been taken by someone else. "I think I need to get some sleep," he managed. "Is that okay?"

"Of course it's okay." A cool note slipped into Hunter's tone. "I'll see you later?"

"Yeah. Maybe tonight."

"Tonight it is."

It had been stupid to walk all the way here just to return to the mansion, but Jeremy couldn't handle talking about Kennedy anymore. He didn't want to wonder. He just wanted to sink into the oblivion of sleep.

Except when Jeremy returned to the mansion he couldn't bring himself to go back inside. He climbed the pecan tree and found Simon's journal nestled in the branch where he'd left it that morning. He reread an aborted chapter about one of Simon's lonely, sensitive queer kids, but his mind inevitably returned to Kennedy. The things he'd said in the corridor while the storm had raged outside, and now that kiss.

Hunter would be disappointed by his weakness, but Jeremy couldn't forget the private moments when Kennedy opened up, and the connection between them felt so real. And Jeremy couldn't stop his heart from beating a little faster every time Kennedy strode into the room wearing his customary skintight black T-shirt and ripped jeans. He couldn't suppress those things no matter how often Hunter's words lingered in his mind.

Jeremy stayed out of the house until exhaustion seeped into his bones. By then, Watts had likely drunk himself to oblivion, and Kennedy had lapsed into stoic chain-smoking on the back porch while plucking out an acoustic version of a Manic Street Preachers song. It was easy to avoid him by entering the front door, so Jeremy did so before going to their room and claiming the bed.

Falling asleep was a hard-won battle, but the dream hit him hard.

Now, Hunter was almost always in the church. Sometimes it was a frightening version of Hunter who was hurt or hurting, but more recently Dream Hunter was always healthy and alive. Sometimes he was simply repeating the words he'd said that day in the woods, but other nights, like this one, he was touching Jeremy with incredible focus.

Sex dreams with Hunter were singularly intense. Even after waking, Jeremy's body was achy or tired, mostly from pleasure and pain. Some nights Jeremy woke and swore someone had really been touching him, pumping his dick and dragging teeth over the delicate purple-green tracery of his veins, and that was almost always the case when he'd slept in the room alone. A frequent occurrence since the tensions between him and Kennedy had flown high.

Tonight was no exception.

In the dream, Jeremy was naked and sweating on the sun-bleached floor of the old church while Hunter's pale, lithe body hovered above him. Wet, nipping kisses trailed down Jeremy's body and led to a blowjob that felt so real it ripped Jeremy straight out of his dream.

The sensation of a mouth moving over his cock continued. Hot and unbearably wet.

"Oh fuck."

Jeremy's toes curled in the sheets. He arched into the waiting mouth even as he stumbled through bleary awareness to figure out how... who...?

His first thought was Hunter because of the lingering vestiges of the dream, but Jeremy rejected that notion even in his delirious state. Hunter wasn't in the house. He couldn't be. And even after that one stolen encounter in the dark corridor, Jeremy recognized the shape of the mouth currently wrapped around his cock. He knew the sting of that stubble. The tight grip of those big hands as they hooked under his knees and held his legs apart.

A confusing mix of emotions ripped through Jeremy. A voice hissed *Push him away. Don't let him touch you. Who the fuck does he think he is?* even as Jeremy bucked his hips to get his throbbing dick farther down Kennedy's throat. Angry thoughts, resentful and bitter, bubbled to the surface, but Jeremy had a hard time listening to the tiny voice that ordered him to shove Kennedy away.

The other part of him, the traitorous part that wanted Kennedy like it wanted clean air and water, reached down to grip the back of his head. Kennedy still managed to pull away, and Jeremy nearly shouted in frustration. The urge dissolved when Kennedy sucked his balls.

"Oh my—*mmm.*"

Saliva was everywhere. It was all so fucking sloppy and amazing. And then Kennedy's fingers were slicking through the mess and toying with the dripping slit of Jeremy's cock before sliding down to push into his ass.

Jeremy lifted his hips and rode Kennedy's fingers until he saw stars. The stubborn, furious voice was still whispering, but Jeremy couldn't hear it. He could only feel Kennedy's mouth latching onto the junction between his groin and thigh and feel the sweet, sweet slide of fingertips against his prostate.

"Kennedy." Jeremy's voice was nothing but a shattered, undone sigh. "I want your dick."

"Yeah," Kennedy whispered. "Fuck yeah."

Reservations and worries that existed in the light of day had no place in the near-pitch blackness of the bedroom. Jeremy was drugged with lust and a raw hunger to be fucked hard and deep and recklessly. He flipped over onto his hands and knees, wrapped his hands around the headboard, and presented his ass for Kennedy to breach.

The mere seconds it took for Kennedy to tear through his open duffel bag to find a condom were torture. But then he got it on with a soft groan and was slipping inside of Jeremy inch by inch. The feel of that dick going in deep and stretching Jeremy wide was everything he'd imagined it would be.

Gripping Jeremy's hips, Kennedy slid in and out with pounding, unrelenting thrusts. Jeremy braced himself against the headboard and slammed back. All he felt was the delicious brutality of being filled absolutely while sweat slicked their bodies, and all he heard was Kennedy's voice so deep and urgent in his ear. Groaning, gasping, and repeating Jeremy's name in such a wrecked, hushed way that it was almost a prayer.

Beneath the layers of bullshit and anger and hurt, their bodies being together was a relief. An overwhelming fucking relief, because *finally* this was happening. Finally Kennedy was sheathed tight in his ass. Finally Kennedy was moving in him with short hard strokes and angling for the spot he seemed to know would white Jeremy's brain out the fastest.

And it worked. God, did it work.

Kennedy dragged him back with a fierce urgency that sent Jeremy over the edge. Amid the slap of their hips, the damp slide of warm skin, and the harsh, panting breaths Jeremy could hear even over the rush in his head, he came. He came hard—harder than he ever had with the one-offs in crowded bathroom stalls and dirty motel rooms—and his voice crumbled into a hoarse, unintelligible moan as he went tense and still with tears welling in his eyes.

Kennedy released with Jeremy's name once again on his lips. After, he tugged Jeremy into a tangle on the sweaty bedding.

The roar of his own heartbeat, white noise, and the echo of Kennedy's voice, filled Jeremy's ears. A raw feeling moved through him, something exposed and vulnerable, and for a minute he clung to the sheets as the tears dried on his face.

Kennedy closed a hand around his hip and kissed the sweaty stretch of skin between the wings of his shoulders. That one gentle touch undid Jeremy faster than anything else.

He bolted upright.

"It's okay," Kennedy said quickly. "We're okay."

"No, we're definitely not." Jeremy threw his legs over the side of the bed and stood. He was loose-hipped and dizzy from the pounding he'd just taken. But with reality settling around their naked bodies, he needed to get away. "I'm so fucking stupid."

Even stricken with confusion, Kennedy looked beautifully debauched in the swaths of moonlight pouring in from the windows. "Please don't leave. I'm sorry."

"What are you sorry for? We fucked, right? You got off." Jeremy wriggled into a pair of shorts and realized they were Kennedy's. They sagged on his narrow hips, but he kept them on. Too late now.

"I'm sorry that I laid a finger on you if it was going to send you running out the goddamn door. But you were... all worked up while sleeping, and when I kissed you, you kissed me back. I thought you wanted me."

Those words held enough self-doubt for Jeremy to pause in his search for additional clothing. He chanced a glance at Kennedy, and his chest tightened.

Again with that wrecked fucking *hurt* look....

Naked and lacking a hint of modesty, Kennedy stood up and moved closer. He was so broad and strong that it was difficult to picture their bodies crushed together on the bed. They were completely different, but they'd still fit perfectly.

Jeremy swallowed and continued hunting for a shirt.

"We just can't do this, okay? Last time—"

"I fucked it up last time, but the circumstances were shit. Can't you just give me another shot?"

"To do what?" Jeremy yanked on a dirty white tank and slid his feet into sandals. "We fucked. It was fun—"

"It was fun," Kennedy repeated flatly. "You're really doing your best to crush me to dust, aren't you?"

"No." A fine tremor stole through Jeremy's hands before spreading to the rest of his body. "I'm not trying to do anything but get out of this room."

"What the hell for? Just come to bed with me."

Jeremy's stomach hollowed. "Because that shouldn't have happened. I don't even want to *be* here anymore, let alone be begging for you to dick me out like that."

"But it did happen, and you fucking loved it, and so did I." Kennedy reached for him. "What happened that was bad enough for you to flip out like this? What the hell did I do to you?"

"You lied to me. You and Watts."

"Is this about Hunter?"

"He's only part of it."

"Then what's the rest?" Kennedy's voice rose again. "Stop playing games with me!"

"It's not a game." Jeremy yanked away and retreated a step. "Nothing has changed since this afternoon, Kennedy. Just because you got me off doesn't mean I forgot."

"So that's it," Kennedy said. "You're going to *him* after you were with me."

Jeremy bristled. "You can go to hell twice over if that's what you think of me."

"I'm already fucking there, kid."

Jeremy paused, wanting to defend himself and reassure Kennedy, to figure all of this out, but he couldn't resist the lure of the shadows beyond their door.


THE SPRINT to the clearing took half as long as usual with Jeremy trying to outrun what had just happened in the mansion, and an enormous sense of relief bloomed in his chest as soon as he was within the protective circle of their moonlit wonderland. It vanished just as fast.

Something was off.

Jeremy didn't see anyone, but he felt the heaviness of other presences nearby. He wandered to the perimeter of the clearing and paced around until a soft, muted sound caught his ear.

Down a sloping hill and on the damp embankment were Quince and Laurel. Two filthy, stark-naked figures covered in scratches and small traces of blood as they fucked next to the river. They were so close that Quince's body was half-sunken into rising water as Laurel rode him.

And boy did she move.

Her breasts bounced as she slammed herself on Quince, up and down faster and harder, until the speed picked up, and she....

Jeremy blinked, staring hard, and could not come to grips with the fact that Laurel's movements had blurred.

"What the—"

"Where have you been?"

It was a testament to how entranced Jeremy was that he didn't jump at the quietly spoken question behind him.

Had he really seen what he thought he'd seen? Was his exhaustion kicking in and making him imagine things again? That was the more likely answer, but even watching now with both eyes focused on the couple thrashing around in the mud, a growing sense of unease snaked through Jeremy.

Despite Quince defending Laurel left and right and Jeremy spending vast amounts of time with her brother, something about her got under his skin. The way she looked at him with cold analytical eyes until he grew uncomfortable and moved away. Her pointed, distrustful questions, as if she thought he had a motive for wanting to spend time with Hunter. And now—the way she slid up and down on Quince even as he twitched in the shallow water and looked close to passing out. Had they been fucking all day?

And she'd been so fast. Inhumanly fast.

Jeremy shivered. He tried to look away but ultimately failed. "I just woke up."

"Whose clothes are you wearing?"

What did that matter?

Jeremy couldn't stop gaping at the spectacle by the river. Quince's eyes were partially open, but he could barely keep his hand braced on Laurel's hip.

"Your sister—"

"I don't want to talk about her. I told you that we don't get along."

"I know, but Quince doesn't look good. He's been sick off and on for the past few weeks and—"

"Jeremy." Hunter's voice cracked through the night and, around them, the frogs, crickets, and cicadas went silent. "Look at me."

Jeremy looked. Really looked. And he regretted it.

Hunter was different tonight. His face was harder, and he looked older. Like his features had been carved from rough stone centuries ago and had never been tended. And there was something wrong with his eyes. For just one moment, Jeremy thought he could see a pale, ghostly haze emanating from those colorless orbs. But then that changed too, and Hunter just looked angry.

Jeremy's stomach sank. How was everything going to shit in precisely the scariest ways? Laurel's stark-white body blurring through the night, Quince dashed into the dirt like an abandoned corpse trying faintly to animate itself, and Hunter looking like a stranger.

What was real anymore?

"I should go," Jeremy blurted out. "I should take Quince and go."

"She won't let you have him."

"He's not a belonging. He'll go if he wants to."

"And he won't want to," Hunter said with flat authority. "She made sure of that."

Below them, Quince appeared to have snapped out of his daze. His fingers were combing gently through Laurel's shiny black hair as she curled into his side with her lips brushing his neck. She didn't look witchy and frightening anymore, but the cast of her porcelain features was unnatural against the muddy brown riverbank.

"You fucked Kennedy."

Jeremy didn't owe Hunter explanations, but he still flinched. "It just happened."

"How?"

With Hunter towering over him, Jeremy felt defenseless as his thin body swam in too-big basketball shorts and a grimy tank. He wasn't prepared to handle an interrogation about the bout of frantic, dirty fucking he'd just engaged in.

"How do you know we had sex?"

"I can smell him on you."

Jeremy's brows drew down. "Uh...."

"I can smell his sweat and your come."

"Dude, what the fuck? I'm not talking about this with you."

"So you've decided to let him use you, then." Hunter guided Jeremy backward until he was flush against the rough bark of a tree. "You decided that you didn't care about everything else?"

Jeremy didn't struggle as Hunter held him against the tree. He couldn't focus enough *to* struggle. He was too caught up somewhere between humiliation and frustration. "I didn't decide anything, okay? I know I talked your fucking ear off about how I wanted to get away from him, and I know you gave me a lot of good advice, but it seriously just happened. I was having a sexy dream, and I guess... he kissed me while I was all in the throes of it? And it went from there."

Hunter stilled. His lips moved wordlessly while his hand clamped around Jeremy's wrist. Then he said very softly, "So he forced himself on you."

"He—what?"

"If you were asleep and he started fucking you, you didn't give your consent."

The air sucked out of Jeremy's lungs. He sagged against the tree and stared into Hunter's bottomless rain-colored eyes. Eyes that could soothe his pain and slice out his secrets in equal measure. "But...."

"Did you tell him yes? Clearly and plainly? Before he started to touch you?"

"Well... no...."

Everything was changing. The fresh memory was shifting. The night was a living thing that swarmed in on Jeremy, invaded every pore and socket, turned things inside out, and made them raw and ugly.

"He forced you, and I doubt it was the first time he's done such a thing."

Jeremy shook his head without speaking.

"This could be what happened to your brother." Hunter's edges gentled, and he was beautiful and sad once more. So understanding. Tranquilizing and sweet. "Maybe they both did him, and he killed himself as a result."

It was hard to work out the exact meaning of all of those statements at first. Difficult to assign actual words to the low, hypnotizing cadence of Hunter's voice. It made Jeremy feel things. Bad things. All of the worst things. Even if he didn't understand exactly what he was hearing. He just knew that Watts and Kennedy were horrible. They wanted to hurt him. They'd hurt Luke.

"Maybe that's why they brought you here. It's possible that next time they'll do it to you too. And then they'll make you hate yourself until you hurt yourself. People commonly feel shame after a sexual assault."

*Sexual assault.*

The two words were a bucket of ice water. Jeremy emerged from his spellbound daze with Kennedy's pleas echoing in his mind as a reminder of just how fucked this conversation was.

"Dude, Kennedy didn't rape me. That's just—no. That didn't happen."

"You said you were sleeping."

"Yeah. Sleeping. Not roofied. I woke up and begged him to bang me." With each word spoken, Jeremy grew more and more enraged, and this time it wasn't focused on his band. It was focused on the mindfuck Hunter was laying on him. "Just because he's a secretive asshole doesn't mean he's a rapist."

"You're blinded by your infatuation."

"No, I'm not. But you're trying to—"

Hunter looked cold again. "What am I doing besides helping you?"

He was trying to ruin it. Ruin Kennedy's hoarse whispers, his tightly gripping hands, and the searing heat that had swept through Jeremy once they'd melded together. It had been fucking perfect. And Hunter was making it horrible and violent. A violation instead of a few stolen moments of bliss before Jeremy had stomped all over it.

*Fuck.*

"I gotta go."

"No. You don't."

"Dude, yes, I do. I'm sorry, but I really need to go."

Jeremy attempted to push Hunter away and achieved zero result. He may as well have been shoving a mountain for all that Hunter budged. He simply stared down at Jeremy, his black hair a shroud around their faces, and dug his fingers into the centers of Jeremy's wrists. The crescents of his fingernails chipped at the veins.

"Let me go," Jeremy said again.

"I don't think I'd like that."

Surprise washed over Jeremy, but then he wondered why. A couple weeks of spending several hours a day with Hunter had fooled him into thinking they were closer than they were. It had felt like they'd known each other for longer than they did.

Hunter pinned Jeremy's arms above his head, pressed him against the tree, and invaded Jeremy's mouth with a quick, darting tongue. He moaned, but Jeremy was repulsed. His disgust was truncated by a short burst of fear when the sharp edge of a tooth pricked his lips and the taste of iron filled his mouth. With it came a sudden rush of realization.

While Hunter nursed on the newly opened wound on Jeremy's puffy lower lip, Jeremy saw himself as he'd been for the past two weeks. A trusting, open fool who'd let a strange man stroke him and woo him and fill him with all of the things he'd always been too afraid to hear. His own paranoia had created a sieve in his logic—allowing it to drain away until nothing but Hunter's negativity remained.

But *how* had it happened so easily?

Jeremy shoved Hunter away and this time it worked. Without waiting for a response, he fled the clearing and didn't stop until he was free of the woods.

# CHAPTER TWELVE

THE WATERY splatter of violent vomiting jolted Jeremy out of sleep and sent him stumbling out of the bedroom before his eyes had fully opened.

Without thinking, he knew Quince was sick again. And without considering other options, Jeremy knew it had something to do with the night before. The image returned even with him still functioning at minimal capacity—Quince barely conscious as Laurel blurred atop him on the soggy embankment....

Jeremy shuddered.

He found the bathroom door wide open and Quince clinging to the porcelain bowl. Watts hovered in the doorway of their bedroom, confused and rumpled, in boxers and an oversized D.A.R.E T-shirt. He looked as bad as Quince. Rundown and sleep deprived from days of nonstop fighting with his lover.

Jeremy tore his eyes away from the oddly vulnerable vision of their front man and knelt next to Quince. He was upchucking vile pale yellow liquid and breathing with such difficulty that he sounded near to hyperventilation.

Sitting on the cool tiles, he rubbed Quince's back until the heaving stopped. When it did, Quince shuddered and slumped against the toilet seat. He elicited a single, tortured moan.

Kennedy entered the bathroom and knelt beside Quince, his brow creased. "Let's get him to bed."

After effortlessly picking up Quince and carrying him to the bedroom, Kennedy gingerly placed him on the tangled sheet. He backed off with his lip caught between his teeth and concern exuding from him in a wave.

"Has he been like this all night?" Jeremy asked as he tucked Quince into the sheet. He looked at Watts from his new position at the edge of the bed. "And you didn't think to say anything?"

"I was sleeping all fucking night, so how should I know?" Watts shot back. "I'm not his guardian."

"You sleep in the same bed!"

"Not anymore."

Jeremy started to snap but checked himself after catching sight of Watts's pinched face.

"I'm sorry," Jeremy said, looking down. "I'm just worried about him."

"I've fucking tried to worry about him, but he just tells me to go slit my wrists."

"He would never say that."

"Maybe not a few weeks ago."

Grimacing, Jeremy stood up too fast, and his head swam. He'd barely slept after returning from the clearing, and the exhaustion left him disoriented.

"I'll go get some water and toast. He needs to sponge up all the acid in his stomach."

"If he wakes up."

Kennedy was standing in the doorway with his hands braced on either side of the frame. His attention had been glued to Quince, but now it shifted to Watts. "What's that supposed to mean?"

Watts shuffled to the window with a battered pack of cigarettes crushed in his hand. "He wanders off all night and sleeps all day. Or hadn't you noticed that he's a straight-up zombie these days?"

"I've noticed." Kennedy's eyes flicked to Jeremy and away. "I've noticed a lot."

The single muttered sentence held too many unsaid truths, and it increased Jeremy's need to get away. From Quince's fragile form, Watts's quiet bitterness, and all of Kennedy's knowing, softly spoken words.

When had this become such a clusterfuck? When had he and Quince become the problem?

"I'll be back," Jeremy choked out.

With the previous night's horrors still shimmering beneath his eyelids, it was easy to ignore Kennedy's heavy footsteps trailing behind him. He couldn't stop thinking about Laurel, but also Hunter.

How his perfect face had seemed inhuman in the darkness. The way his teeth had drawn blood from Jeremy's lip.

He nearly missed a step, but Kennedy steadied him.

"Thanks," Jeremy muttered. He hurried down the last few steps and charged toward the kitchen, only to stop abruptly in the doorway.

"Do you want me to do it?"

"What?"

Kennedy crossed the threshold of the kitchen. "Do you want me to make him something? I know being in here freaks you out."

"Oh. No. It's… it's fine."

And, oddly, it was. There was no gripping panic or vestiges of fear upon entering the room. Amy's body having lain in the kitchen was more grounded in reality than what had happened the previous night. He understood death and suicide. He didn't understand savage beauty tempered by false-sugar words and tricky benevolent smiles.

With mechanical movements, Jeremy slid two thick slices of wheat bread into the toaster and removed two bottles of water from the fridge. He'd heard somewhere that room temperature water was better for stomachs, but he didn't know if it was true.

"Jeremy."

Maybe if he let the water sit out for a while. By the time Quince woke up, it should be fine. And it wasn't like the fridge was the coldest, anyway.

"*Jeremy.*"

"What?" He kept staring at the label on the water bottle. "What do you want?"

"I've been trying to talk to you."

It was like thinking through quicksand. "Okay. So talk."

A lag followed, so Jeremy looked up. At some point Kennedy had stepped well within his personal space. He seemed bigger than usual—maybe because he was broad and hard where Hunter was lean and soft. Or maybe it was the warmth Kennedy exuded, like huge swaths of burning sunshine. Hunter didn't have that either.

"I don't know what's wrong with me anymore." Jeremy spoke past the knot swelling in his throat, sounding choked, but he didn't stop the rush of words. "I was pissed at you after the party, but for the past week… I fucking *despised* you. I hated being in the same room as you. I kept thinking these horrible things."

He was crying, and he hated it, yet he didn't dash the dampness away. And he didn't back off when Kennedy held his shoulders. He was a watery vision before Jeremy, but the usual stoic mask didn't hide his expression. He just looked weary. And worried.

"What were you thinking?"

"That you and Watts were fucked-up, awful people." Jeremy twitched, but Kennedy's dark eyes held him in place. "That you'd never liked me or cared about me, and you just wanted to use me. That you were a liar. That you'd both… hurt my brother."

Kennedy's fingers dug harder into Jeremy's shoulders.

"I thought about leaving the band," Jeremy went on in a whisper. "I thought about hurting you. But mostly I thought about staying here instead of going back to Houston. I don't have anyone there."

"And you have someone here?" Kennedy's voice was like the crack of a whip. "You were going to stay in this seedy house with Hunter?"

"I don't… know? None of it makes sense to me now."

"And it made sense to you then?" Kennedy gave him a single full body shake. Jeremy's head snapped back, and hair fell across his face. "Thinking about hurting me made sense in that moment?"

"No!" Kennedy was holding him so close, and so tightly, that Jeremy could feel the quickening beat of his heart. "That's not what I meant."

"Then why the fuck were you thinking about it?" Kennedy released his shoulders to cup his face. "What's *wrong* with you?"

"I told you, I don't know!" For the first time in days, Jeremy's perception cleared, and he was brutally aware of how overblown everything had become. How Kennedy's and Watts's little transgressions had run riot in his mind until they were conspiracies and plots. And now he couldn't figure out why. Except for the constant ruminating with the Caroways and Quince. The clearing had become a chamber of echoes that had infected him with the worst kind of lies. "Maybe I'm crazy."

"No, you're not." Kennedy's hands loosened again, but he was just as fierce. "But you and Quince have sure as shit been doing a good job of isolating yourselves in some hateful little circle jerk, haven't you? With that Hunter douchebag serving the jungle juice."

Despite everything, defensiveness sliced through Jeremy's misgivings, and he was protective of the Caroways again.

"You don't understand because you're not like us."

"*Us*? Who is *us*?"

"Me and Quince. And, yeah, even Hunter and Laurel. You're not alone the way we are. You don't know how it feels to be cast aside."

"Cut the shit, Jere." Kennedy dropped his hands. "You don't fucking know him. And I have never cast you aside."

"I haven't known him for long." The words fell out of Jeremy's mouth as though he'd rehearsed them. "But for a little while, I felt like I knew him a hell of a lot better than I know you. I was more comfortable talking to him than having a basic conversation with you or Watts."

"Yeah?" Kennedy's voice rose, but there was no sarcastic edge to it. Despite his hulking stature, he didn't try to intimidate Jeremy. "What changed?"

"It doesn't matter. He's not—that's not the issue. I'm sick of feeling like I'm not safe with Stygian."

"Feeling safe is nothing more than a state of mind." Kennedy brushed a rough hand over his short hair. "I've never done anything to you to make you feel that way. *You* tell yourself you can't trust me, so *you* don't feel safe. That's it."

"How can you expect me to trust you?" Jeremy broke free of Kennedy's grasp and retreated a step. "Just because I see Hunter for what he is doesn't mean the problems I have with this band don't exist."

"Then let me fix them, for God's sake! You won't even give me a shot."

"Dude, this whole fucking summer is me giving you a shot. I wanted us to get along. I wanted things to get better. And you guys were *worse*. Even before shit started with the Caroways."

Hands clenching at his sides, Kennedy's lips parted but he swallowed whatever he'd been about to say once the toast popped up. Jeremy threw the slices onto a paper plate, and grabbed the water.

"Tell me how to fix this, Jeremy."

"Like you don't know?"

Jeremy strode out of the kitchen, clutching the bottles hard enough for the plastic to cave in beneath his fingers.

He was halfway to the staircase when Kennedy shouted, "I haven't tried to manipulate you!" The statement likely floated up the staircase and through Watts and Quince's door. "I said the cops were shady not Hunter. It was weird that they acted like they didn't know the Caroways. I don't give a shit if they thought it was suicide. Deputy Asshole didn't even make a meager attempt to find out more about everyone in the goddamn house, including the only two people from *their* town who *own* it."

"Maybe they think the Caroways are okay people. You've wanted to believe otherwise from the start. Besides, Hunter said the police went to speak to them."

"Yeah, I'm sure that's what Hunter said. Doesn't mean it actually happened." Kennedy stalked up the stairs so he was standing just below Jeremy. "I'm getting sick of this shit. First Quince and now you. What, do they have you both hypnotized?"

"Yeah, that's it exactly," Jeremy retorted, even as a chill stole up his spine with creeping icy fingers. "Or maybe I just don't get your irrational dislike. They're strange, but so am I, and they have good reason to be."

"Oh, so now you're an expert?"

"No, but at least I made the effort to find out more about them."

"Maybe I made a different kind of effort." Kennedy's dark eyes sought out the shadowed corners, moving across decades-old clutter and investigating every suggestive groan of the house. "That other wing," he said.

"You broke in?"

"I got in," Kennedy corrected. "And I saw why they have it all locked up."

"Dude, that's really not cool. We already literally threw killer parties, and now you're breaking into their shit? Why don't we just wave a banner that says 'come arrest us'?"

"Calm down." Kennedy's voice lowered. "And if you don't believe me, I'll show you."

"Show me *what*?"

"Just how weird this place is. I found these articles about James and Sarah Caroway. I'm guessing their parents. They—"

"Stop." Jeremy held up a hand. "Just quit, okay? I already know, and I don't want to talk about it. They may not be… normal." It was hard to get the words past the invisible force in his head. He practically had to spit them. "But it's still not right."

"You don't even know them," Kennedy repeated explosively. "What the hell is wrong with you? Why can't you just trust me?"

"Because you're on a mission to make me more paranoid than I already am, and yet you and Watts are the ones keeping secrets about my brother." Jeremy wasn't supposed to bring it up, had promised himself not to, but the dam broke. "You made it sound like you guys barely knew Luke, but I know that's a lie, and I want to know why."

"It's not a lie. I didn't know him. I didn't even know Watts knew him at the time." Kennedy raised his hands, but they hovered awkwardly in the air, and he didn't make a move to touch Jeremy. "It's just… it's not my story, kid. And I'm afraid of dredging it all up and pushing Watts further off the ledge when he's barely hanging on."

Jeremy tightened his fingers around the bottle. "You don't have to involve Watts in the fucking conversation. You can just tell *me*. Tell me so I'll stop obsessing over it!"

Another hesitation and another hasty look up the stairs before Kennedy said, "First tell me where all of this paranoia came from. I know I brought it up that night on the porch, but you jumped to some serious conclusions all of a sudden."

Was learning the truth worth ratting out Hunter? The answer was a very easy yes. Hunter wouldn't see them again after the summer, but Jeremy had staggered beneath the questions surrounding Luke's suicide for years.

"Hunter overheard you talking about it."

"That's impossible."

Even now, Kennedy didn't want to talk. He was still trying to divert the conversation.

"Did Watts hurt my brother?"

"Jeremy—"

"Watts was an asshole even in high school, you've said it yourself. Was he one of the shitheads who bullied Luke until he felt the need to bleed out in the bathtub? Because that's how he did it, you know." Without hesitating, Jeremy overshared in the worst possible way. "He filled the tub, cut both arms from wrist to elbow, and then submerged himself in hot water. By the time I found him, he'd bled out so much it looked like the faucet had gushed blood. It was everywhere."

Kennedy's face went white. "Jeremy, please don't do this."

"Do what? Tell you the truth? Lay myself open and tell you how fucked-up he was and how fucked-up I still am, just because it makes you uncomfortable?"

"It has nothing to do with me being uncomfortable. I didn't know Luke well, but Watts did, and I didn't know—I had no idea they had been close until Watts went on a goddamn bender after Luke died, and even then he never told me the whole story!" Kennedy's eyes flicked up the stairs again. His jaw clenched. "Fuck it. Just talk to Watts. Whatever happens will happen."

"You told me not to," Jeremy exclaimed. "You made it sound like a forbidden topic."

"Because even though Watts is an asshole and a piece of shit sometimes, a lot of that started after your brother died. He *did* blame himself for Luke, but it's not much different than him blaming himself for Caroline. The guy thinks he's a fucking jinx. He's so messed up that I can't even begin to explain it, because I don't fully understand it. I'm afraid of it coming up again, but at this fucking point, I'm more scared of losing you."

Every time Jeremy thought he had the thread of the story figured out, someone threw in another twist. Then out of nowhere, Hunter's voice seeped into the crevices of his brain.

*Maybe they raped him.*

*Maybe that's why they brought you here.*

*They'll do it to you too.*

*They'll make you hate yourself until you hurt yourself.*

Jeremy shook his head and the whispers scattered. "I don't know what to think."

"Just go ask Watts yourself," Kennedy urged. "I know I told you not to, but it needs to happen. I can't have you thinking we're these awful monstrous people just because some fucking stranger is filling you with suspicions and turning you against us."

"He can't turn me against you."

Anymore.

Kennedy scoffed. "Don't be naïve. He already has."

Jeremy had no defense to that. After years of priding himself on having the toughness to ride out storms, he'd been effortlessly twisted up.

"You're right. I'm sorry I let it happen, but it won't anymore. I'll deal with you and Watts myself, and if I can't, I'll be on the next bus out of here."

He was trembling with the need to escape the mansion and the forested areas around the Sabine. To get far from Hunter's and Laurel's velvet whispers and fork-tongued lies.

Feeling nauseated, he charged up the rest of the stairs.

"Just promise me one thing," Kennedy called once Jeremy had reached the top landing. "Promise you'll let me show you what I found."

Jeremy didn't look over his shoulder. "Invading their privacy isn't right, no matter how strange they are."

"It's not like I kicked the door down." The stairs creaked beneath Kennedy's feet. "There's a trap door in our closet that leads to a crawl space. I was curious, so I checked it out. And if you'd open your eyes and stop being hardheaded, you'd agree to do the damn same. We have a right to know what's going on around here."

Jeremy looked at the stained glass image of the man beneath the bay laurel tree, and he remembered the bolt of coldness that had shot through him on their first day in the house. After Amy's death and the constant pull of darkness in his dreams, the too-fast movements, boneyard skin, and the mindfuck of ten thousand *I'm on your side* speeches, Jeremy wondered if his initial instincts had been right.

ONLY A thick swath of light filtered through the room from behind a single curtain. The windowsill was wide enough for Watts's lean body to fold up on with his head tilted against the chipped frame. He was lost in his oversized T-shirt, the excess cloth a reminder of how he'd looked before the drugs and the partying and Caroline's death.

"Watts."

"'Sup."

Jeremy placed the water and toast on the bedside table, hesitated, and then sat on the other end of the windowsill. "Did he wake up at all?"

"Yeah." Watts nodded in Quince's direction. "But he was incoherent. His weird-ass virus is screwing up our schedule more than his gnarly mood swings."

Jeremy pinned Watts with an annoyed stare, but relaxed after he caught the rawness on Watts's face. Had Quince seen Watts without his usual smirking guard? Had Quince ever seen him looking so young and frightened?

"C'mon, Jere," Watts said, pushing away from the windowsill. "Let's do a bump. You and me. Like bonding."

"I don't do coke."

"C'mon. Just this once. I hate sniffing the moondust alone."

"Then maybe you should stop."

"Nah. I like myself better when I'm stoned."

It was the realest Watts had ever been in a conversation. Jeremy shot another quick glance at Quince, needing a witness to help him experience the revelation that had come with those words, but maybe Quince was too far gone to have noticed even if he'd opened his eyes.

"I need to ask you something."

"It's really eight inches. No lies. No bullshit."

Jeremy scowled. "I need to ask you something serious. And if you don't answer, I'm out of this fucking band. No lies." He would be calm. He wouldn't be afraid. He wouldn't assume. "No bullshit."

*They'll do it to you too.*

*They'll make you hate yourself until you hurt yourself.*

The metallic flip of Watts's Zippo lighter signaled a change in plans as he lit a cigarette instead of doing a line. "Ask away."

"How did you know my brother, and what did you do to him?"

The cigarette nearly fumbled from Watts's fingers. He sat up straighter, catching it before it could drop to his crotch. "What the fuck? Where did this come from?"

"Just answer the question. Kennedy already gave me the runaround."

Watts seemed to be at a loss for words. He settled for slumping against the windowsill and pressed fingertips to his temple. The brash, hard-assed twist of his mouth was nowhere to be seen as he peered at Jeremy from beneath half-shut eyelids.

"What d'ya already know?" he asked tiredly. "The less I have to fess up to, the better."

"I know you knew him. And that you don't want me to know about it. That's it."

Smoke drifted around them in a blue-gray shroud and triggered Jeremy's rare urge to have a cigarette. He grabbed one from Watts's pack and stuck it between his lips.

"I think you already drew your own conclusions, Jere." Watts's mouth curled in an ugly smile as he flicked the Zippo to light Jeremy up. "I can see it in those spooky gray eyes."

"I did," Jeremy admitted. "I think you bullied him just like you bully me. Maybe something worse. You think it's funny to dig at people, even if they already dig at themselves."

The smile faded. "So that's what you think of me, huh?"

"How could I think anything else?"

"Heh." Watts glanced at the bed. "Fair point."

Jeremy inhaled deeply and watched the cherry blaze before smoke seeped out of his mouth and hung in the space between them. They had never spent time like this, alone, this close, and it was weirdly intimate, despite how little they were talking or touching. Almost like a confessional.

"You got one thing right, sweet thing. I was a fucking dick in high school, and I hated every single person, even if they liked me. I was almost as bad as I am now."

"Why?"

"Why not? High school sucks, and I was smarter than almost everyone in that shithole, even though the teachers flunked me just because they didn't like my mouth." Watts's narrow shoulders rose in a shrug, still looking at Quince instead of meeting Jeremy's direct stare. "All the guys wanted to befriend me because I always had booze and drugs, and the girls wanted to fuck me for the same reason. Bunch of lowlifes, only hanging out with me to see what they could get."

It was easy to picture. The school they'd gone to had been filled with upper class kids, but Watts came from a family that had been around since Texas sovereignty. His siblings were a decade older, and from what Jeremy had gleaned in the past few months, Watts had been ignored just enough to be given free rein to run wild.

"Luke would never try to use anyone for money."

"He didn't. We got stuck together on an art project. It was his first time taking it, and I'd already failed the fucking shit twice because I barely went to class." Watts took another drag from his cigarette, and his gaze shifted to the dusty panes of the window and the distorted view of the trees outside. "As soon as I sat down with my shitty attitude, he told me he'd do it alone and stick my name on it. He'd rather do all the work than have to be around someone he thought was going to bully him."

That sounded like Luke. He'd probably curled in on himself the first time Watts had flashed his customary sneer. The idea soured Jeremy on the conversation, but he focused on slowly inhaling and exhaling smoke, and tried to keep an open mind.

"*Did* you bully him? Everyone else did."

"No." Watts chanced a quick look at Jeremy before resuming his examination of the window. "I respected him for wanting to escape the bullshit, and for some reason I got this wild hair up my ass about carrying my weight. We met up at the library and shit. I didn't know what the fuck was going on, because I was high half the time, but he'd read all of these art-history textbooks while I put my head on the desk and stared at him. It was kinda hard not to. God, he was beautiful. In a way that made him a big ol' target because straight Texas dudes can't handle knowing it's a boy who caught their attention, you know?"

Jeremy *didn't* know. It was hard to think about sensitive Luke with his long white-blond hair and darting, frightened eyes, sitting across from a kid who had likely been covered in all kinds of punk-rock bad attitude and tattoos. And Jeremy didn't believe people had picked on Luke because they'd wanted him. Even if it was true, it wouldn't make it any better.

The cigarette burned away as Jeremy struggled to ask the question bouncing around in his head.

"Did you... fuck him?"

"Yup. It's what I'm good for." Watts smirked. "I called it a thank-you for him getting me an A, but I don't think he saw it that way. Especially since I got stupid and mushy and laid myself open by talking about my alcoholic mom and asshole stepdad. Then all of a sudden, we had shit in common. One time turned into a few times, and instead of rocking his world in my car, we were talking about our feelings." The word came out mockingly, but the breath Watts took was shaky. "He'd tell me how lonely and weird he was, and I'd talk about how much I hated all the fake motherfuckers in my life."

"What do you mean weird?" Jeremy hunched forward and held Watts's gaze. "People in that school loved calling me white trash and a freak, and I know it was the same for him, but...."

"No, it wasn't that. He talked about his depression, and how he'd play piano when he was on the edge. He said it helped calm him down, but one day he knew it wouldn't." For the first time, Watts looked away first. His throat bobbed when he swallowed. "Other stuff. Weirder stuff. Dreams he had and how he sometimes knew what people thought of him, even when they didn't say it out loud. He didn't talk about that too much, though and I never knew what to say. It sounded fucking nuts, but for some reason, I believed him."

Not once in the fifteen years they'd shared a house and a room, a *life*, had Luke mentioned any of that to Jeremy. But then... Jeremy had always scorned their family when they made those claims. Even as a kid, he'd been vocal about his dislike for the Blacks. Maybe his ranting had prevented Luke from sharing that part of himself. He'd probably known Jeremy would have cast it off as another Black family tall tale.

The information was almost impossible to process, so Jeremy stayed quiet and noted every tick in Watts's face—the self-loathing poisoning his quick smile, and string of sardonic expressions.

"So one day," Watts drawled, "he tells me he loves me. You can prob take a stab at what happened next."

"You told him to fuck off?"

"No, you asswipe." Watts stubbed his cigarette on the windowsill. He dragged trembling tattooed hands through his inky hair. "I had a girl, and he wanted to make it some steady thing. Wanted me to save him from himself and the voices echoing in his skull, and all that shit. I couldn't do it. He was the first guy I'd been with, and my stepdad would have blown both our heads off faster than you can say Matthew fucking Shepard."

That fact Jeremy knew for himself. Quince had told him about one of Stygian's early shows. How Watts's parents had shown up, unexpected and uninvited, at the bar. They'd gotten an eyeful of the Quince and Watts grindfest, and Watts had shown up the next day with a black eye and a broken jaw.

"I told him I couldn't do it and said we should probably quit hanging out because I'd never be able to keep my fucking hands off him. I didn't want to lead him on. He didn't take it so well."

"He wouldn't have." Jeremy's voice was almost drowned out by Quince's low snores. "He desperately wanted someone to like him, but no one ever did."

"Yeah." Watts frowned down at his hands. "Yeah, so, that night he killed himself."

Jeremy had seen it coming as soon as the story had begun, but now guilt shredded his conscience into a million pieces. Watts was sitting there examining his chewed-up fingernails and waiting for judgment, but all Jeremy could do was wonder how he'd never known this and why he had leaped to the worst possible scenario.

"I'm sorry I thought...."

"Don't fucking apologize to me after I just told you I killed your brother."

"Dude, no." Dragging himself out of his own misery, Jeremy sat up straight and put a hand on Watts's knee. "It's not your fault. He was—"

"Fuck yeah, it is. Maybe I didn't hold the blade, but I sure as hell nudged him in the right direction." The jester smile returned, large and garish, even though the rest of Watts's face was stone. "Seems like kind of a talent of mine. Get close to people, drive them to their death. Literally, in Caroline's case."

"That wasn't your fault either." Now Jeremy could see why Kennedy had wanted to leave this unhealed scab alone. One conversation, and Watts was already picking it raw. "It was a wrong-way driver. Some drunk."

Watts chuckled. "Yeah, but I was behind the wheel and didn't get one goddamned scratch." He looked like he was waiting to be castigated, or maybe like he wanted to be.

"Watts, you're not—it's not your fault. Neither of them were your fault. You're not some kind of jinx."

"If you knew more about me, you wouldn't be saying that, baby. I've only dated a handful of people in my life and each and every one of them wound up fucked-up or dead." Jeremy was shaking his head, but Watts kept talking while counting people on his fingers. "Luke— suicide. That other girl I was dating while fucking him? Rose? OD'd at a party I took her to. Next up—Travis—" Watts flicked up a third finger.

"Travis from the Kickback Kids?" That guy had suffered neurological damage after using some weird synthetic drug.

"Yup. That's the fucking one." Watts waved his pinky in the air to indicate four. "And then Caroline."

"Is that why…." Jeremy closed his hand around Watts's knee and waited to be pushed away, but Watts didn't move. He just kept watching and waiting for a reaction. "Is that why you push everyone away?"

Watts grabbed his pack of cigarettes but didn't remove one. "Don't try to figure me out. Just accept that I'm a fucking scumbag and put up with it or not."

It wasn't so simple when putting up with it meant Watts unloading on Jeremy and Quince, but it didn't seem like the right time to make that point. Especially not when Jeremy had done what Kennedy had tried so hard to avoid—dredged up a bunch of awful memories from Watts's past.

Knowing the full story and getting a clearer understanding of Watts was good, but Jeremy would have waited until the guy wasn't already so close to buckling under the strain of maintaining his hardass front.

He'd thought they'd bullied Luke until he'd had enough. That they'd poked and prodded until he gave up on getting through adolescence alive. It had seemed like a logical assumption due to out-of-context comments repeated by a veritable stranger, and now Jeremy felt like an asshole. And worse—now he *knew* he'd been played. Hunter had twisted a handful of words into something hateful and ugly.

And Jeremy had believed it. He finished his cigarette with one last exhale of smoke.

"Hey, Jere?"

"What?"

Watts leaned forward. "Can I ask you something?"

Jeremy nodded. "Yeah, anything."

"Do you think…." Watts bit his lip. "Do you think Kennedy's dick is bigger than mine?"

"Jesus fucking Christ, Watts." Jeremy scooted away. The moment was broken by Watts's obnoxious, forced laughter. "You really are a mess."

"Tell me something new."

"You're also totally incapable of having a serious conversation for more than five minutes at a time."

"Well, you know what they say…."

Jeremy moved to the edge of the bed to observe Quince. "What do they say?"

"The more you ruminate, the more cocaine illuminates."

"Right. Nobody says that."

Watts spread his arms, once again flashing his fake smile. It would normally annoy Jeremy, but now it was a little easier to see through the veneer.

The belief that his bandmates coasted through life on their cool factor and don't-give-a-fuck edge was fading fast. Jeremy wasn't the only one being dogged by a past, and he wasn't the only one waiting for scorn once his secrets were aired. He wasn't the only one who was afraid to have people turn their backs.

They were just better at hiding it.

"Don't leave the band, Jeremy." Watts's voice sobered. "I'm hard on you because I'm a douchebag who can't handle my shit, and you look like Luke and play like Caroline. It's a killer combo, but apparently I'd rather make you miserable than wrap my brain around the masochistic streak that told me to give you her spot."

"Why do you want me to stay if it's so hard for you? If you can't stop yourself from being a dick?"

"'Cause…." Watts swung his legs down from the windowsill. "'Cause you're more tolerable than most other assholes on the scene."

"Gee, thanks."

"And I'll try to be better about things. I don't want you to go. Especially since I haven't nailed you yet." Watts threw an arm around Jeremy's shoulders and yanked him close, pressing a sloppy kiss to the side of his mouth. He laughed when Jeremy wriggled away. "Maybe Kennedy will fill me in on what I'm missing."

"Kennedy isn't saying shit," a deep voice said from the door.

Jeremy batted at Watts's groping hand and glanced at Kennedy's tall form looming in the doorway. Even if Watts was throwing himself headfirst into the drunk and slutty role without transition from the vacant stare he'd been sporting only moments ago, Kennedy still looked uneasy.

"Are you both good?"

"Yeah, we were about to make out before you walked in and fucked it up."

Kennedy ignored Watts and kept his gaze fixed on Jeremy. "Have your story straight?"

"Yes," Jeremy muttered.

"Good."

Kennedy left before Jeremy could respond. When Watts just rolled his eyes, Jeremy bolted out of the door. He hurried to their shared room and hovered by the bed when Kennedy sat on the edge of it.

He wanted to fix things, but what could he even say? *I'm sorry I thought you're all assholes? I'm sorry I let Hunter light a fire under my ass that made me hate you all? I'm sorry I lost my shit?*

Even unspoken, the words were pitiful. Living in his own head was already a good way to create worst-case scenarios if something went down, but latching on to a guy who could twist a situation with just the right tendrils of negativity and just-so semantics had created a mess. And that wasn't even the half of it. There had been an indescribable… *more.* Those tendrils and carefully chosen words had transformed him. Just like they'd done to Quince. Were still doing to Quince.

For all that Watts was an asshole and Kennedy could be a closed-mouth, blank-faced motherfucker, Jeremy had ratcheted his resentment up to astronomical levels just because he was the odd man out.

After joining the band, it hadn't taken long for Jeremy to sort out everyone's place—Kennedy was the grim one, tall and serious with don't-fuck-with-me-or-mine vibes; Watts was brash and mean but so talented no one ever cared; and Quince was full of recklessly whimsical smiles, naïve enthusiasm, and the primary force keeping

Watts from flying apart. Jeremy didn't have his place yet, and maybe they pointed it out more than was necessary, but Hunter and Laurel had turned them into life-ruining supervillains.

"Kennedy, I'm sorry."

"You don't have to apologize." Kennedy caught the front of Jeremy's shirt and tugged him closer. "I was so busy trying to prevent Watts from turning into a total basket case that I didn't see how me keeping quiet was making everything worse for you."

"But I get it now." Jeremy didn't resist being pulled into a loose embrace, and the familiar tickle in his stomach returned. "I didn't realize he'd been through all of that. If I'd known...."

"Yeah, if you'd known. I shouldn't have been afraid to tell you. And I shouldn't have let him fuck with you so much for the past month." Kennedy tipped his forehead against Jeremy's chest. "I'm so used to being protective of them that I helped drive you away without realizing it."

Jeremy's hands were unsteady as he slid them up to brace Kennedy's jaw. "It's not too late."

"Are you sure?"

The voice in Jeremy's head hissed, but it was distant and garbled with Kennedy's dark eyes locked on his own. "Yeah. I'm sure. Now that the cards are on the table, I want to try to fix things."

Kennedy's relief seemed to sag his shoulders. "I appreciate you giving us—me—another chance."

Jeremy smiled tiredly and moved to sit beside Kennedy on the bed. "Look, you're not the only one who messed up. I didn't give you or Watts the benefit of the doubt. I'm sorry I let Hunter wind me up."

"I'm sure he was hoping to wind you up in more ways than one."

The guilt scraped at Jeremy again as he thought about the river and him panting like a dog while Hunter sucked on his bloody finger. About their bodies locked together in the clearing. Hunter's mouth crushed against his own.

*Fuck.*

"It's not going to happen anymore. Next time I'm angry or upset, I'll talk to you. No middlemen. No... ruminating. No Hunter. I swear."

"Really? Because you don't seem to trust me enough to confide in me."

"I know." Jeremy hunched forward with his arms on his knees. "I spend my life waiting for you guys to get sick of me. Watts ragging on me is just… the status quo, and I always thought Quince would go along with whatever he says if it really came down to it—at least in the past, but you…. You turning away from me is what I'm afraid of the most, yet I keep waiting for it to happen, so I back off and push you away. I basically do the same thing as Watts even though we have totally different methods. I didn't realize it until now."

"So now that you see it, just *trust me.*" Kennedy grabbed his hand and squeezed. "I know you don't buy it, but I really think there's something off about the people who own this place."

"Dude, I'm not as skeptical as you think."

"Then let me show you what I found. Now. Today."

Jeremy still wanted to say no. A thousand times no. Breaking into Hunter's family secrets was like giving someone unlimited access to his own past, but refusing was as good as admitting he was still under Hunter's power. And the cards needed to be on the table on all fronts.

"Okay."

# CHAPTER THIRTEEN

THE CRAWL space between their room and the locked wing was something out of a nightmare.

It was narrow and smothery-black with skittering noises echoing around them, and Jeremy's heart stuttered each time their clothing rustled or his shoes squeaked against the floor. He had no reason to panic, but a knot was lodged in his throat the farther they went. The sense of imminent danger he'd felt when stepping too close to the east wing tapped into the fight-or-flight instincts of his lizard brain and demanded he get the fuck out of the there *now*.

The crawl space had been hidden behind stacked comforters in their closet and was just wide enough for the breadth of Kennedy's shoulders. He'd gone in on his hands and knees without hesitation, fearless in a way Jeremy would never be.

The twin to the trap door opened with a whine and Kennedy exited before helping Jeremy up. Once steady on the floor, he wiped at the broken cobwebs clinging to his palms.

The opening was next to a bed with a sunken, stained mattress and a sheet gone dark gray from time and a thick layer of dust. The room's single tiny window had vines snaking through and creeping along the walls. A table sat below it, its wood warped and swollen.

"What's the point of having a secret passageway when there's a hallway right outside?"

"Good question." Kennedy nodded at the wall opposite them. "Check it out."

Jeremy followed his gaze and noticed a door-shaped outline. Frowning, he moved closer, and dragged his fingers along the area. "There's no doorknob."

"Exactly."

Kennedy applied pressure to the wall, and it sprang outward. When they stepped through, Jeremy realized the doorway was inset into the wall of yet another corridor and designed to blend with the worn wallpaper.

"A lot of antebellum houses have crawl spaces and hidden rooms."

"Creepy," Jeremy muttered.

"People still use them. Even Watts's parents have a panic room right next to their gun closet. Although this could be slave quarters. Who knows. The South is fucked."

The wing they entered was eerily similar to the one they inhabited, though it was frozen in time. The wallpaper was yellow and curling, and when Jeremy peered into the open doorways lining the hall, he saw rotting furniture and mildew-covered walls. One room had a clutter of cards and papers spilling across the floor and several pieces of luggage crowded in the farthest corner. The zippers were half-undone, and pieces of clothing bulged out of the sides.

In his mind's eye, Jeremy could imagine the chain of events that had led to this level of abandonment. After the murder-suicide of the Caroways, maybe the authorities had arrived and swept the children away from the house. Or maybe the kids had fled in horror and had run the miles to town in the middle of the night. Jeremy wondered if Laurel and Hunter had only returned to pack up their former life before locking away their secrets and periodically renting the mansion.

They halted in front of a large room, probably the master of this wing, and Jeremy's breath caught once they stepped inside.

The blood spatter from the murder had never been cleaned. Dried brown stains streaked the walls and windowsill. A decaying bed sat in the corner, and more stains marred the sheets in droplets that led to what had obviously been a pool of blood on the floor.

Holding out his hand to prevent Jeremy from stepping deeper into the room, Kennedy entered alone and picked his way around the blood-covered floor. He collected a stack of brittle newspapers from the foot of the bed before returning.

It was easier for Jeremy to blank out the dried arcs if he zeroed in on the tattered papers. If he focused on Kennedy's discovery, he wouldn't picture the torn bodies that had lain in the room.

"This is fucking horrible."

"Maybe I shouldn't have brought you in here."

"No," Jeremy said. "It's good to see it with my own eyes or else... or else, I don't know. Maybe I wouldn't have believed you."

The concern didn't leave Kennedy's face.

Jeremy put his back to the murder scene and stared into the hallway, but he couldn't shake the sensation that someone else was nearby. He'd felt the same way on the night of the party and on all of those other nights when he'd jerked awake from fevered dreams that had been half-terrifying and half-arousing.

"So, these articles," Kennedy said. "Someone clipped them and left them here."

"Let's just take them and go."

"Bad plan. It'd be obvious that we were creeping around in here."

"You think—" Jeremy swept the hallway with his darting gaze. "Someone comes in here? It looks like no one's been around in years."

The paper crinkled in Kennedy's hand. "I think someone has in the recent past. At first glance it seems abandoned, but there are places where dust has been disturbed. I don't know how recently, but I'm leery about poking around for too long."

"I don't give a shit if they know we were here. Let's just take them and go. I'll put them back later." Desperation pitched Jeremy's voice higher. "Please."

"Okay. Keep it cool. We're gone."

TO GET through the agonizing crawl to their room, Jeremy thought about music tabs and mentally created a solo that would finally sell Watts on the merits of punk. He was so anxious to block the trap door that he knocked over a couple of boxes and pulled down the clothes hanging in the back of their walk-in closet. When everything was put back to rights, Jeremy collapsed on the floor outside the closet with a loud exhale.

Kennedy dragged a bottle of "clean-distilled" whiskey from his duffel bag and presented it to Jeremy with a half smile as he sat next to him. It was some organic shit Quince had brought along after giggling the entire way from the liquor store, arms linked with Watts's and way too proud of himself for finding what he'd dubbed "hipster booze."

They downed a third of the bottle before tackling the articles.

The first one read like a sensational tabloid story. The headline shrieked *Mystery at the Mansion* and breathlessly detailed the gruesome scene of the Caroway murder. It described the home in detail, how it stood apart from most of the other property in the town, and made careful note of the Caroways' reclusive lives.

The second one claimed there had been signs of a small party at the scene of the murder, but it didn't mention any other witnesses. Another clipping lamented the murder-suicide and how it besmirched the reputation of a typically safe town.

The last square of paper was yellow and wrinkled, the ink smudged but still legible as an obituary.

*James and Sarah Caroway passed away on November 9th, 1983, at the ages of 34 and 32. Their lives will be celebrated at 11:00 a.m. at Benson Funeral Home, 511 E. Grove Street, Logansport, LA, with Reverend John Connolly officiating. There to greet them in Heaven are their parents Richard and Beth Caroway, and Clive and Sandra Fisher. Left to cherish their precious memories are several friends and colleagues, as well as the charities that the dearly departed supported through their wonderful lives. The Caroways were kindhearted philanthropists who touched the lives of all who had the privilege of knowing them.*

Jeremy reread it twice before gently setting the paper on the floor and picking up the bottle of whiskey. It smelled weird and tasted worse, but he drank it because he yearned for the disconnected, floating feeling of intoxication.

"Do you see why it's strange?"

The liquor settled heavily in Jeremy's stomach. "All of this is strange."

"I could be jumping to a shit-ton of conclusions," Kennedy said. "But it strikes me as odd that the obit doesn't mention their kids. None of the articles mention their kids. It makes it sound like the *dearly departed* lived here on their own."

Jeremy read the obituary again, slower this time.

"It does sound that way."

"So you don't think it was that way?"

"Kennedy, I don't know what the fuck I think." Jeremy gathered his knees to his chest. "Why don't you just tell me your theory?"

"Because I don't think you'll believe me," Kennedy said with an edge. "You're awfully fond of that smarmy motherfucker just like Watts and Quince were ready to have a threesome in a hurry with his creepy sister. That's normal for Watts, but the last time Quince looked at a girl, we were sixteen, and he was more interested in her outfit than her tits. And that's not even to mention the way you and Quince have acted in the last couple of weeks. Nothing has made sense since we met these people."

Jeremy released a slow breath.

"All I'm saying is, I've had a bad feeling about those two since I set eyes on Hunter. It wasn't just some fucking jealousy thing." Kennedy's voice was too loud, and Jeremy shifted nervously, wondering if someone would hear. The phantom that collected articles and disturbed shadows in the house. "No one in this town has mentioned them by name, and the cops were all blank-faced and stupid when Laurel was described. Who's to say they're actually who they say they are or he wasn't lying about speaking to the cops?"

Who *was* to say anything Hunter had said was true and not a spin in the direction more fitting for his situation? Everyone else, from the police to the man in the Aggies cap, behaved oddly whenever the Caroways came up.

"I met this old man at the store...."

The rest of the sentence dried up in Jeremy's mouth, and the irrational protective streak reared up again. Even if Hunter was trying to create a rift between Jeremy and Stygian, he'd been kind. He'd listened. That meant something, didn't it? It was Stygian who had alienated him for years. And lied by omission. Now they wanted him to turn his back on Hunter. To betray—

Kennedy snapped his fingers, and Jeremy blinked. The hum of vicious, angry words drifted away.

"What's wrong with you?"

"Nothing." Those whispers couldn't poison him if he let Kennedy's warm brown eyes be his anchor. "The old man said he knew who the Caroways were, but he didn't specifically mention Hunter and Laurel. He just said people from Logansport know better than to come here. And that... no one would go out of their way to help us if we got ourselves in trouble."

"See?"

"See what? I don't see anything other than a bunch of weird fragments of a story that don't add up."

"Fine." Kennedy set the whiskey down. "You think I'm nuts?"

"No, I don't."

"So, you think I'm being unreasonably suspicious about your boyfriend."

Jeremy sat up straight. "Can you stop calling him that? Just because I hung out with him doesn't mean anything happened between us. He was nice before things got weird. That went a long way since I normally feel like everyone just puts up with me."

Kennedy stacked the papers together and smoothed them down at the sides with his thumb. "I never meant to make you feel that way."

"I know that now."

Silence fell between them, but Jeremy wasn't in a rush to fill it with a bunch of pointless explanations. The guys may not be villains, but they'd seriously overestimated the thickness of his skin. Not that it mattered anymore. It was inconsequential with all of the other pressing matters on the table.

Like sleeping only yards away from an aged murder scene that had never been cleaned up, and practicing near yet another dried pool of blood—a stain that hadn't fully come out no matter how hard Watts had scrubbed—and of course the Caroways. How much was real when it came to Hunter and Laurel?

Were they making too much of it? The townies avoided the Caroways, but did that signify anything? If people back home had kept Jeremy at a distance after finding out he was related to the boy who'd committed suicide, how might people in a backwoods town treat a pair of socially inept siblings who were attached to an infamous murder? There could be any number of reasons why the people of Logansport avoided the Caroways. Maybe they just didn't like them.

Yet, in only a few weeks, they'd displayed some serious red flags even though Jeremy had initially dismissed the signs. Both Laurel and Hunter were aggressive, manipulative, and they exhibited a frightening desperation to claim lovers. They were also creepily controlling, but what did that mean? What did any of it mean?

"This trip was a bad idea."

"No, it wasn't. The location was. Watts is a fucking moron."

Jeremy chuckled, but the sound was muffled by Kennedy pressing the cool bottle to his mouth. He parted his lips and the whiskey poured in, potent and sharp. It scorched through him, hot enough to burn a hole in his stomach, but he still reached for the bottle to take another swig. Before he could, Kennedy closed the space between them and pressed a firm kiss to his lips. It tasted like cinnamon and smoke and was slow and gentle, as though it was their first.

When it ended, Kennedy brushed another gentle kiss to Jeremy's forehead.

"I really like you, Jeremy. You know that?"

Jeremy wound his arms around Kennedy and clutched the folds of his ratty T-shirt. "Not really. You never treated me any differently."

"Heh. Have you ever seen the way I act when I'm into someone?"

"Well. No. But you're never into anyone."

"Uh-huh." Kennedy brushed their lips together again. "Remember when you said one of the reasons you came this summer is because of me?"

Jeremy nodded.

"It was the same for me."

"That—what? No way."

Kennedy thudded his head against the wall. "I like being close to you, but we never get the chance in Houston. I was looking forward to spending time together, you know? I thought it was a bad idea, but part of me still wondered if something would spark."

"No, dude, I don't know. We could have been sparking for the past few months. I've been in fucking love with you since I first saw you on stage a couple of years ago, and it only got worse after I was in the band and realized how great you are."

"I'm not that great."

Jeremy snorted. "Right. The orphaned guy who is a youth counselor by day and a superhot rocker by night."

Kennedy's laugh pushed lightness into all of the spaces that had recently been full of shadows.

"I know you think I was being stupid, Jere, but it's hard to consider making a go of it when it could potentially fall apart. If we got together and then broke up, you'd leave the band, and I'm already afraid of Watts driving Quince away. If this shit fails, I'll have nothing."

"Then why can't you just say that? Why do you always make me feel like an idiot for trying?"

"Because I don't know what I'm doing half the time, kid. I've got no clue how to handle any of this, and I don't know how to not lose you."

All Jeremy could think of was cheap motels and cold, harsh sheets and him curled in on himself to prevent touching, even though he'd always woken up with Kennedy's body crushed against his back. Watts had demanded separate rooms for every out-of-town show, and Kennedy had always insisted on bunking with Jeremy. He'd claimed it didn't matter if they had a double—he didn't mind sharing a bed.

It was too easy to picture all the times they could have climbed on each other, been inside each other, while Quince and Watts stumbled to another room or crashed in a tangle of tattooed limbs on the floor. So many opportunities, and now Kennedy was making his move while they were knee-deep in a potential horror story complete with spooky mindfucking siblings who lurked around in blood-covered rooms in the middle of the night.

"It's not fair that you pretended you don't give a shit about me. All because *you're* afraid."

"It's not," Kennedy admitted. "But I'm scared of losing people I can't do without. You seem to think I'm all strong and confident, but I'm a fucking coward."

"What if we just used each other for sex?"

The question earned him a husky laugh. "Maybe you can get away with that," Kennedy said. "But I can't. I like you, and not just because you have a nice ass and a fuckable mouth."

"What's there to like?" Jeremy grimaced at his own question and glanced at Kennedy. "Do you really feel that way about me? All jokes aside."

"Yeah." Kennedy pulled Jeremy onto his lap. "You caught my eye during your audition."

"You barely looked at me twice."

"I'm subtle, but I was looking." Kennedy rubbed circles against Jeremy's back. Slow. Comforting. "Watts had commented that he had a pretty little twink signed up to play next, but I didn't expect you to be so gorgeous. You're unreal, kid. Hair so blond it looks silver, with eyes to match and that hard, wiry body of yours. Fuck. And you were even hotter once you got into the music. It was obvious you live for it. Breathe it. And when you started talking all shy, explaining why you love to play, you had me. I avoided you at first because I thought it was obvious that I wanted you."

Each word sucked Jeremy in until he was moving closer, bringing their faces together, and then assaulting Kennedy's mouth. Despite his fear and concerns, Kennedy didn't hold back. They devoured each other like it was their last opportunity. And when he broke the kiss with a soft gasp, Kennedy drew him in again. His hands roamed Jeremy's body, exploring every hollow and plane as he traced soft kisses from Jeremy's mouth to his jawline.

"I thought you said this was a bad idea," Jeremy whispered. "Especially after the way I acted last night."

"It might be, but I can't help myself."

Kennedy bucked his hips, and sharp slivers of pleasure swarmed through Jeremy's veins like a thousand tiny starbursts.

"I'll stop if you want me to," Kennedy uttered.

"I only want you to stop if you're going to pretend this didn't happen later."

"That's not possible anymore."

Jeremy tried to keep his bearings, but it was difficult with Kennedy grinding their dicks together.

"Don't fuck me over, Ken-boy."

"I swear I won't." Kennedy kissed him again, harsher this time, and said gruffly, "I'd rather quit the band than watch you be with someone else."

With a lump in his throat and burning behind his eyes, Jeremy was full of the kind of emotions that had no place on the floor of this fucked-up house, but he couldn't stop himself. Affection consumed every doubt he'd had since the party.

The rest of the world faded to an ugly memory, and his existence became a sea of sensation and sound. The jingle of a belt buckle and the shifting of clothes being tugged off and shoved away. The liquid sound of exploring tongues, and the slide of bare skin against bare skin—electrifying and triggering sharp pulses of lust.

All of the frightening things were blocked by a cocoon of touch and scorching heat. Jeremy was reduced to a quivering mass as Kennedy sucked on his tongue and slid a hand down the back of his jeans to play with his ass. The sounds they made were hushed and lost in the dark, tiny corner of the room, so Jeremy made his desire known without words and blindly emptied Kennedy's duffel bag to get the condoms and lube.

Kennedy's probing fingers slid away from his ass to rip his jeans off, and Jeremy shifted up to hover over Kennedy's erection once it was covered with a rubber and lube.

"Christ, Jere," Kennedy gritted out as Jeremy impaled himself. "You feel so fucking good."

Everything centered on the focal point of their joined bodies once Kennedy started to move, and every coherent thought was fucked right out Jeremy. He slammed down, and Kennedy thrust up, their skin slapping together damply in the quiet room. Once they got a rhythm going, the air filled with a call-and-answer of rising moans.

Bracing his hands on the floor behind him, Jeremy arched his back and rode Kennedy with increasing speed. The burn in his arms was nothing compared to the explosion of energy that sparked with each deep thrust of Kennedy's pulsing length.

Jeremy was reduced to desperate cries and gasping, half-said words until Kennedy's cock nudged his prostate. The world stopped, and Jeremy's body locked up. His breath caught in his chest and eased out only after he came. Milky ropes of semen covered them both, and when it was over, Jeremy was an empty husk.

His arms buckled, but Kennedy crushed him forward. With their chests glued together, a constant slip slide of dampness, Kennedy flexed his hips faster. The pressure of his thrusts was almost painful after Jeremy's explosive orgasm, but he mouthed sloppily at the side of Kennedy's face and rode out the wave of overstimulation.

When Kennedy finished, it was with a series of low moans ending with Jeremy's name. They stilled but continued to clutch each other and, with Kennedy still inside of him, Jeremy pressed their lips together so they could be connected in every way.

For the first time since their arrival, the house was completely still around them, and Jeremy heard nothing but the slowing cadence of Kennedy's breathing and the gallop of his heart.

# CHAPTER FOURTEEN

WAKING IN the Caroway mansion almost never happened peacefully, and the next morning was no exception.

Loud voices pulled Jeremy out of the first restful sleep he'd had since the summer began. It took several minutes to make sense of the sounds, and a lot of slow blinking as a stream of sunlight trickled across his face and into the corners of his eyes.

The haze departed just enough for Jeremy to squirm out of Kennedy's tightly gripping arms, but a suggestive thump against his bare ass planted another idea.

Pressing back firmly on Kennedy's morning wood initiated subtle grinding that had Jeremy raring to go in seconds. If the previous night was anything to go by, a sideways look from Kennedy could reduce him to a panting, libido-driven teenage boy, but the slide of a cock against the seam of Jeremy's ass made him want to roll over with his thighs spread and knees in the air.

Kennedy slid his hand down Jeremy's side, then his hip and thigh, until he jerked it up just enough to stretch Jeremy open.

"Use a lot of lube," Jeremy muttered. "Sitting in the van for hours is going to suck if you spend the whole morning pounding me."

"You can lie in the back with Quince. Watts will be riding shotgun and screaming in my ear the entire way back to Houston."

If Watts agreed to leave.

Kennedy dropped a kiss on Jeremy's sun-freckled shoulder. "Do you want to fuck me? We could take turns."

Jeremy's dick pulsed, but in an attempt to play it cool he said, "Nah. I'm good."

Kennedy fumbled on the floor for the condoms and bottle they'd abused the previous night, and drizzled some lube onto his fingers. He jammed them into Jeremy without the briefest of warnings and chuckled softly at his high-pitched cry.

"I can't wait to have you in my own bed tonight."

Again Jeremy thought, *If Watts agrees.* It would have been sobering enough for his dick to soften if Kennedy hadn't been reaching for his spot with expert precision.

"I have the rest of the summer off, and I plan to spend the majority of it in your ass."

Tingles exploded in Jeremy that had nothing to do with lust.

"Did it ever occur to you," he panted as the head of Kennedy's cock replaced his fingers. "That I can't have a conversation while we're fooling around?"

"Yeah, but I still like those little sounds you make when I play with your ass."

Kennedy was inside of him before he could reply.

He turned his face to the pillow, but Kennedy caught his jaw and pressed their mouths together. He swallowed Jeremy's gasps and accelerated to a rhythm that prevented Jeremy from caring about anything other than the bursts of pleasure rocketing through his body.

He was vaguely aware of more yelling and loud footsteps marching around outside their door, but the roar in his ears reduced the sounds to meaningless bits of nothing. When Kennedy pulled out to flip him onto his stomach and angled deeper, Jeremy dismissed everything else. Including his short-lived desire to smother his moans.

The previous night, Kennedy had realized quickly that Jeremy was an enthusiastic lover. He got loud and wild, and Kennedy had spent hours figuring out which buttons to press to drive him insane. He'd also figured out that Jeremy had stamina that could take him through the night. Even now, his cries spurred Kennedy to move faster.

Kennedy released with a ragged shout, but he braced himself and reached around to finish Jeremy off with a few rough tugs of his hand.

Lights exploded behind Jeremy's eyelids. His arms nearly buckled under Kennedy's weight, but he managed to shift away from the massive wet spot he'd just created to collapse on his side.

*"What the fuck is wrong with you?"*

The question hurtled clearly down the hallway and shattered Jeremy's postorgasmic zone-out. "I thought Quince would be too sick for this today."

Kennedy groaned. "Me too."

"And it doesn't bode well for the conversation we need to have with them."

"That's an understatement, kid." Kennedy sat up, still breathing hard. "Maybe you can talk to Quince while I tackle Watts."

Jeremy glanced at the closet door and thought about the way Quince had forgotten his existence as soon as his eyes had set on Laurel.

"I don't think he'll listen. I was… sort of counting on him being too out of it to protest."

"Not even if he knows about the other wing? And you realizing Hunter was deliberately mindfucking you?"

Another series of shouted exchanges rang out, and Jeremy flinched. "Not even then. I think Laurel has more of a hold over him than Hunter started to have over me."

Kennedy's dark brows drew down. "What do you mean a *hold*?"

Explaining without sounding insane would have been a feat in and of itself. Jeremy could barely take his late-night ponderings seriously let alone say it aloud.

"They're just really manipulative. But we can try."

"I can't figure out if they're psychotic, obsessive and delusional—" Kennedy swiped his underwear from the floor. "Or if they're fully aware of what they're doing and get off on stirring up trouble."

"It could be either." Jeremy looked down at the damp sheet that had gathered in his lap. "They're isolated out here, Kennedy. And I think they're both really messed up from whatever happened to them. They'll probably do anything to not be alone, even if it means ruining relationships. The way I have it figured, Hunter wanted to play on my insecurities until I felt like he was the only person I could trust."

"I agree on that point." The band of Kennedy's underwear snapped when he finished tugging them on. "But Quince is acting like a different person. Unless Laurel can give instant lobotomies or has the power to brainwash, it makes no sense."

It made sense if you believed in mind control. And Jeremy was starting to think maybe his family's certainty regarding sixth senses wasn't so batshit after all.

"Quince and I were probably easy targets for them. He saw me as weak and desperate to be liked as soon as he laid eyes on me. And I fell for it in a hurry because I was so stressed out by Watts and this place triggering me left and right." Jeremy threw the sheet to the side and reached for his own clothes. "Maybe it was the same for Quince."

"Quince has toughed out this shit with Watts for years." Kennedy pulled on a pair of black jeans and stood with his hands on his hips. "And he has a ton of his own shit, but the guy has always managed to keep his smile. Always tried to make everyone else chin up and be happy."

"He can't be happy all the time," Jeremy retorted. "Everyone has a breaking point. And believe it or not, sucking up Watts's trash talk while worrying about the band combined with what happened at the party—that could have been it."

"You're not wrong. But why would it cause him to turn to a woman he barely knows?"

Jeremy didn't have an answer he was willing to verbalize, so he shrugged and finished dressing.

Kennedy followed the voices downstairs, but Jeremy hung back to peer into the other bedroom. The signs of a fight were everywhere. Clothes were strewn around, a suitcase sat open but empty in the middle of the floor, and it looked like someone had trashed the end table that had been accumulating an impressive collection of bottles and two full ashtrays over the past couple of weeks. Now, the floor was littered with ashes and the cigarette butts. The room also reeked of alcohol.

Spying Quince's stolen watch peeking out from beneath the bed, Jeremy bent to retrieve it. He cast his eyes over the area and saw small dots of blood on the pillow and a slightly bigger stain on the edge of the sheet.

More weirded out by the second, he joined his bandmates downstairs, and paused in the archway of the living room with wide, incredulous eyes.

Watts was standing with his back pressed against the wall. One of his cheeks bore a bright red welt from either a smack or a punch, and Kennedy had a hand pressed flat against Quince's chest. He was several inches taller than Quince, but it didn't look it at the moment.

Quince was drawn up to his full height with his shoulders thrown back and lips twisted in a sneer.

"You hit him?" Jeremy blurted. "*Why?*"

Quince did not seem to register Jeremy's presence.

"Because I told him to stay away from that buck-wild country bitch." Watts's body was coiled in a way that usually meant an impending fistfight, but his voice held no vehemence. "He's flipped his shit over some random slut he barely knows."

"I said not to talk about her that way."

Nothing in Quince's face or body language resembled the happy-go-lucky guy he'd been on their drive up to Louisiana. He even looked different physically—pale despite the sun he'd been getting, and there were dark circles around his eyes.

"Like you have a right to judge anyone?" Quince's voice was full of scorn. "You? Poor little rich boy who inhales coke and drowns himself in vodka because of his *tragic past*? I can't wait until they see some more of your lyrics. A dozen new ways to describe your dimming inner light and a hundred synonyms for tears."

"Quince—" Jeremy started.

"It might have more meaning if they knew how badly you ruin the lives of everyone around you."

Watt's stiffened. "Shut your fucking mouth, Quince."

"Why?" Quince shouldered past Kennedy hard enough for him to stumble. "Don't want them to know the real reason you were speeding down the highway with Caroline that night?"

"Quince, stop," Kennedy said, but Quince kept going. He didn't shift his mocking gaze from Watts's face.

"That you didn't see that car coming because you were *so upset* that your mother finally found out you'd been fucking your stepfather? That all of his homophobic bullshit was actually jealousy?"

Horror flashed across Watts's face.

The situation needed to be diffused before it went nuclear, but to Jeremy's surprise, Watts didn't hurl himself at Quince in a blur of fists. He didn't move at all until his lower lip trembled and his eyes turned glassy. There was a devastating silence before Watts turned to press his face against the wall. The sight of him curling in on himself tightened Jeremy's chest.

Kennedy grabbed for Quince again, but Quince tried to evade and wound up falling ass-first on the floor. His head cracked against one of the wooden side tables, and the tautness left his frame. The hostility slowly bled from his expression.

"Go the fuck away, right now," Kennedy growled.

Quince scrambled to his feet, and the glaze of confusion replaced his mocking triumph.

"*Go!*"

"O-okay." Quince looked at Watts once more before bolting from the room.

Kennedy was still staring after him, so Jeremy moved closer to Watts. He put a hand on Watts's too-thin arm, but the simple touch jumpstarted a downward spiral, and a hoarse sound ripped out of Watts's mouth.

"Fuck him." Watts brushed his forearm across his face. "I don't need that motherfucker. Let him sleep in their shack for the rest of the summer."

"Calm do—"

Kennedy cut him off with a sharp shake of his head, and Jeremy raised his hands, unsure of what to do.

Watts paced the room like a caged animal, his lower lip caught between his teeth and his breath expelling in harsh bursts. It was like watching a stone monument abruptly crumble to dust. Watts had never admitted anything close to what Quince had revealed about his past, and the betrayal would have been shocking if not for the glazed confusion on Quince's face. After hitting his head, it had been like he'd emerged from a fog.

Kennedy took a shot at comforting Watts, but it ended the same way. Watts shoved him back, snarled, and unleashed his rage on the room around him. He kicked the side table and smashed his fist through a pane in the china cabinet. Glass splintered and flew everywhere, but it didn't slow him down. He whirled, still panting, and started for the instruments. Kennedy grabbed him just as his hands curled around the neck of Quince's bass.

"Jeremy, go find Quince," Kennedy said as Watts struggled against him.

Nodding, Jeremy backed away. Leaving was easy. Watching Watts turn stricken and hearing his voice go jagged with pain was the difficult part.

Each step took Jeremy farther from the living room, but he kept watching until the fight drained from Watts's body. The last thing Jeremy heard before entering the kitchen was Watts saying he needed a drink.

The low murmur of voices was reassuring. No more violence, no more overflow of hateful emotions or urges to destroy the things that had meant so much to Watts at the beginning of the summer.

Outside, the sky was dark enough to indicate a serious thunderstorm, but Jeremy still set out to hunt for Quince. He could handle a storm. Quince wandering the woods in the rain while disoriented or having some kind of dissociative episode induced by Caroway mindfuckery was a lot more concerning.

He circled the property around the house, found nothing, and proceeded to search the woods. A curtain fell across the sky after thirty minutes of walking, and the verdant smell of summer rain intensified. It wasn't exactly unpleasant once the drizzle began, but his urgency increased. He kept picturing Quince huddling somewhere damp and alone, thinking about his words and choking on his remorse.

The Caroways' cabin was probably the best place to search, but he was loath to go there. He'd be tempted to interrogate Laurel about Quince, but the real problem was Hunter. They hadn't seen each other since the night he'd fled the clearing, and Jeremy didn't know if he could face him again. He was afraid those velvety whispers would gain access to his brain once more.

Jeremy sought out the subtle trail leading to the clearing and, as he picked his way through the overgrown weeds and ferns, the energy around him shifted.

He'd gotten used to the abnormal moments of stillness, but it being accompanied by scores of birds taking flight was new. Dark shapes launched across the overcast sky to the sound of wildly flapping wings.

Fear clawed at Jeremy's throat, but he kept walking.

There was no sign of Quince, or the Caroways, until a low whimper drifted on the strengthening wind. Jeremy swung around, seeking the source, and his forced calm dissolved once he slipped between the tight huddle of trees encircling the clearing.

A few yards away, a set of writhing figures lay on the ground.

Paralysis tried to root him to the spot, but Jeremy ducked behind a tree and peered around it.

Laurel was on her back, cascades of curly black hair trailing along the damp earth, with a tattered summer dress hiked up around her waist. She looked like some kind of wood nymph except for the way her legs were bent and spread open by Quince. He was trapped between her thighs, his shorts shoved down below the curve of his ass, and he was slapping his hips forward as he fucked her. Judging by the dirt and sweat smudged all over their bodies, they'd been at it since he'd fled the house. It was nothing new, given what Jeremy had seen the other day.

The real surprise was Hunter's lean, pale figure hovering at Quince's back.

He was fixed on Quince, but he wasn't touching. Not until Laurel turned to Hunter and showed her teeth in a horrible smile. She said something too low for Jeremy to discern, but her body language made the meaning clear. Everything from her tone, her expression, and the way she arched her back as Hunter's eyes raked over her, indicated she was speaking to a lover. Not a sibling.

Jeremy froze.

Hunter closed the distance between Quince's back and his own bare chest and crushed their bodies together. He released a long, high moan, and the dread in Jeremy's stomach coiled in a tighter knot.

He shouldn't be seeing this. Intrinsically, he knew it. He felt it in the burst of adrenaline burning through his veins and the trembling of his limbs, but he couldn't move. He couldn't tear his eyes away as Hunter yanked Quince's head back and latched on to the pale column of his throat.

Quince whimpered loud enough for Jeremy to hear the slight quaver in his voice before it went low and deep again. He wound an arm back to thread his fingers into Hunter's wild hair, holding him close.

All the while, Laurel watched and smiled. Even when Hunter dropped one hand to undo his own pants.

Jeremy ignored the influx of chemical messages screaming for him to run. Run or interrupt, because this wasn't right. It wasn't normal. This wasn't Quince.

Quince had always cringed at the sight of blood, but the red tinge on Hunter's lips when he pulled away, and the smears of it on Quince's wrist, made it quite clear that the Caroways were into the darker side of kinky, and they'd convinced Quince to go along for the ride.

Because that's what it had to be. Blood play. Kinky sex. Just a twisted game.

It had to be a game.

Jeremy repeated the words in a mantra even while things passed before his eyes like a montage. Laurel and Hunter's cruel spectral beauty. Their coldness. How fast Laurel moved. Hunter's whispering voice. How it sometimes filled Jeremy's mind.

Hunter pulled away, and Quince keened at the loss, but it didn't sound like him. It didn't sound like anyone or anything Jeremy had ever heard.

Detaching himself from the tree, Jeremy took a step back, then another, and his heel caught on a low branch.

Both Quince's and Hunter's eyes opened, and in the shared moment, they looked the same. Skin chalky white, blue eyes wild, and lips curled in a grimace of pain or pleasure. The only difference was that Quince didn't seem to see Jeremy while Hunter was very much aware. Their gazes locked.

Lightning struck, and a crack of thunder yanked Jeremy from his stupor. He fled.

The trees and shrubbery and the steel stretch of the sky were reduced to blurs as he sprinted through the woods. He lost his way three times, got turned around once more, and nearly an hour passed before he burst onto the property. Compared to what he'd left behind, it was a sanctuary.

Kennedy appeared on the back porch. The sight of him, tall and broad and solid, was enough to tear fissures in the wall of panic closing in on Jeremy. Slowing his pace, he gulped in air, trying to attain a measure of calm, and stopped at the foot of the porch. He started to speak, but Kennedy's attention swung to a point over his shoulder.

Jeremy looked back just as Quince staggered out of the woods. He took three lurching steps, paused, and collapsed onto the wet ground with the rain beating down on his prone body.

# CHAPTER FIFTEEN

"WHAT HAPPENED?"

As Jeremy stood there, still caught in shocked silence, Kennedy laid Quince on the bed and began stripping off his soaked clothes. It had only been about an hour since Jeremy had seen Quince, but he looked so much worse. His skin was bleached of color, and his breath came in shallow bursts.

"What the hell happened?" Watts's voice rose several volumes higher. "Why does he look like that?"

"I have no fucking idea," Kennedy said. "He appeared a minute after Jeremy and collapsed on the ground."

Watts pushed Kennedy out of the way and pressed his hands to Quince's face before they drifted down to his neck and torso. He was covered in bite marks, and traces of blood stuck to him in tiny points of color.

"What the *fuck*?"

Kennedy shot Jeremy a frazzled look. "Where did you look for him?"

"I—" Jeremy's gaze flicked between Watts and Quince. "I found him in this clearing they like to go to. I didn't interrupt...."

"Interrupt?" Quince unconsciously flinched, and his whimper prompted Watts to sit on the edge of the bed. He slid their fingers together. "Interrupt what?"

How could he explain what he'd seen? How could he explain what he was thinking?

"They were—he was fooling around. With both of them." Jeremy eyed the marks on Quince's neck rather than Watts's increasingly strained expression. "They're... I don't know. I just didn't want to interrupt, okay? I got scared."

"Did he look like this when you saw him?" Kennedy asked. "Were they fucking around with him while he was keeling over?"

"No...."

"So then what the fuck went on?" Watts's voice boomed in the room again, and Quince released another tormented sound. Watts clenched his jaw. "You're holding something back, Jeremy. I can tell you're lying."

"I'm not lying." Jeremy wanted to shrink away from the weight of their dual stares, but he stood his ground as water from his drenched clothing dripped onto the floor. "The three of them were fucking around, and it was weird. Really weird. They were biting him, and there was blood, and it was like he was in a trance. At one point he looked up but didn't even seem to recognize me."

Watts gaped, and Kennedy paused in his ministrations. "Quince throws up at the sight of blood."

"I know," Jeremy said miserably. "Look, I don't know what to tell you. There's so many things that have gone on in the past week, and it all sounds insane, but the long and short of it is that we really, *really* should get the hell out of here. Quince needs to get as far away from those people as possible."

Kennedy continued to study him, but Watts turned to Quince. After touching the side of his neck, a hundred tiny fragments of emotions flitted across Watts's face before gathering into a brewing storm.

"I paid this motherfucker out through August."

"The money is gone either way." Kennedy sounded more weary than frustrated that Watts was still in need of convincing. "What have we gotten accomplished while we've been here, man? No new songs, no new material, but everyone is at each other's throats, and now Quince is sick and having radical mood swings. The longer we stay here, the worse shit will get."

"And you want us to travel back to Houston while he's in this condition?" Watts asked. "We should take him to a doctor."

"It's Saturday evening," Kennedy said. "There's not going to be any doctors' offices in this town, and the nearest hospital is far enough away that we may as well just leave for good."

"Shit."

Jeremy could see the bits of Watts's stubbornness piecing together.

"I dunno," Watts said. "I feel like we're running away like some scaredy-bitches. We could hold out and take him to a doc in town on Monday."

"No, you moron, there's way more to it than that!" Jeremy threw his hands up. "There's something wrong here."

"Yeah, you keep saying that, but I'm not seeing whatever you're seeing in that crazy skull of yours," Watts said.

Jeremy threw him an icy look. "I'm not crazy."

"Crazy or not, you're not saying a damn thing that's going to convince me to go running out of here tonight."

"Holy shit, Watts. You're rich. What do you care about—"

Kennedy stood and stepped between them. "Both of you shut up. There's no argument. Watts—you booked us a murder house owned by unhinged people, and now we're stuck with them in the middle of the woods. We're going. End of story. I can hogtie you and gag you if that's what's needed."

"*Murder house?*"

Kennedy spent the next several minutes recounting their discoveries as well as their realizations about Hunter's creepy machinations, but Jeremy kept his mouth shut about everything else. If they were leaving without him admitting to his suspicions, there was no reason to bring them up.

Quince stirred as Kennedy detailed the content of the abandoned wing, and Jeremy moved to the bed. Quince's reddish gold lashes fluttered, and his eyes opened a sliver.

"What's going on?"

"You collapsed." Jeremy caressed Quince's face. He was burning up. "How are you feeling?"

"I don't know." Quince wet his cracked, swollen lips. He shifted on the bed as if planning to rise but settled back without trying. "Everything aches."

"Like flu body aches or injury aches?"

Quince scratched at his neck and flinched when his nails scraped at the tiny, still-raw wounds. "I don't know. I just feel weird."

Jeremy started to ask about Quince's neck, but Kennedy's voice grew louder and cut him off.

"Don't be a dick, Watts." Kennedy prowled the room and threw things into the suitcase that had remained open on the floor. Watts was watching with his arms crossed over his chest, but he didn't move to intervene. "You said yourself the Caroways are freaks."

"They're not freaks." Quince's face was pinched, but he looked more confused than ready to defend Laurel's honor. It was a marked difference from how he'd been only a couple of hours ago. "They're nice to me."

"Yeah, I bet." Watts sneered at Quince. "Just sit there and be vulnerable and sick and don't fucking talk."

Quince tugged the sheet up to his chin. "I'm sorry."

"Can you take it easy on him?" Jeremy snapped. "He wasn't himself when he said those things earlier."

"Oh yeah?" Quince being conscious and responsive was apparently a cue for Watts to revert to dick-mode. "Enlighten me as to *how he wasn't himself* when repeating shit I'd confided in him."

Kennedy's hands paused on a handful of wadded up undershirts, and Jeremy again shied away from the scrutiny of his bandmates.

"I just mean I'm not blaming him for things he said after running a high fever for hours."

Watts scoffed, but Kennedy kept watching Jeremy.

"We're leaving?" Quince asked. "But we didn't do anything yet."

Kennedy dragged his gaze away from Jeremy and dropped the shirts into the suitcase. "Doesn't matter. Things have been bad since we got here, and there's nowhere to take you if you get sicker. We can get out of town and hit up an urgent care or Minute Clinic to get some antibiotics." Smiling reassuringly, Kennedy omitted any further mention of the Caroways. "I know you haven't been yourself lately, Q. And like Jere said, I know it isn't your fault."

"The hell it's not," Watts muttered.

It was difficult for Jeremy not to pick up Quince's hard-backed suitcase and crush Watts's face with it. Whether his bad attitude was a self-defense mechanism or not, Jeremy was over it.

Kennedy jerked his chin at Watts. "You want a summer retreat? Fine. I'll charge a fucking suite in New Orleans, and we can dig some Big Easy atmosphere, but I'm not staying in this goddamn house."

The mention of New Orleans caught Quince's attention, and a glimmer of the old Q peeked through the shroud of misery. "That would be so cool, Ken-boy."

"Don't call me that."

"You know you like it," Quince replied with a wan smile.

The relief at seeing those dimples nearly bowled Jeremy over, but he couldn't stop worrying over Quince's appearance. He was conscious, but his complexion was pasty, and the bite marks on his neck looked infected. They weren't deep, but they were inflamed, and pus leaked at the sides of each prick of broken skin.

As Kennedy sold Watts on retreating to New Orleans, Jeremy thought about the incident in the clearing. There had been something inhuman about it. The way they'd all sounded. How teeth had so easily torn into flesh....

"Quince, do you remember what happened?"

Quince's large eyes drifted away from Watts and Kennedy. They appeared to have reached a consensus even though Jeremy had tuned out the conversation. They left the room talking about prices and hotels, and Jeremy took the chance to press Quince.

"I don't remember. Laurel came and got me last night—"

"She came here?" Jeremy asked, lowering his voice. "In the house?"

"Yeah...."

"But you were so sick yesterday. Why would you go?"

"I don't—I don't remember deciding to go. One minute she was here, and then the next thing I knew... I was *there*. That happens a lot. I just... end up going to her even if I didn't plan on it."

It was so very familiar. Lost time. Walking without knowing where he was going—almost as though an invisible force had been tugging him through the woods. Jeremy had experienced it all.

Quince rubbed his thumb against the edge of the sheet, flashing another wound on his wrist. The flesh around the perimeter of the injury had bubbled up and was also oozing pus. His other wrist wasn't in much better shape; it seemed like the band of his watch had seared his skin. It was so bizarre that Jeremy missed part of Quince's hesitant explanation. How could a watch inflict a second-degree burn?

"—went out to their cabin and stayed up all night. I don't remember much after that. It's all blurry. Like blacking out after drinking, you know?"

"Did you drink?"

Quince continued to examine the folds of the sheet. "No. We just talked a lot. She was being really sweet. I know you guys don't like her, but when you're alone with her… she's different."

It was like listening to a recording of himself talking about Hunter. Jeremy didn't know how the Caroway mojo reeled in sensitive emo boys, but they had a helluva knack for it.

"So, you don't remember coming back here and fighting with Watts?"

"Just parts. It's all hazy."

"Do you remember anything before you ran out?"

Quince shrugged and pulled the sheet up again. Even without the aggression, he was a shadow of his usual self.

The first time they'd spoken, *really* spoken, had been on a Christmas Eve in a dive bar in Montrose. Quince had been all smiles with his spiked-up blond hair, smelling of marijuana and old leather, and had demanded eggnog spiked with a fifth of rum. Jeremy had muttered about having no one to be with on the holidays, and Quince had cheerfully admitted to having grown up a ward of the state. He'd never held back. Never been afraid to speak his mind. Even when things were shitty with Watts, Quince hadn't withdrawn as though he was willing himself to wither and fade away. But he was now.

"Quince, do you remember having sex with them in the woods?"

The corners of Quince's mouth sank. "Parts."

"Do you remember them doing this?" Jeremy ghosted his finger along the infected cuts. "Did they ask you, or did they just do it? I'm asking because blood play isn't really your thing. The sight of it usually makes you sick."

"It does. I didn't, I mean, I didn't really think about it. They kind of… just started doing it, and then for some reason I went with it." Shame crept into Quince's voice. Shame and something else. He stopped and started multiple times as if battling the dueling parts of himself—Quince and the stranger he'd become in the past few weeks. "I don't know why. The whole day was like a dream."

"It doesn't make sense." It wasn't the best choice of words, but Jeremy had nothing else. "You didn't look delirious or disoriented until Kennedy shoved you. It's like he snapped you out of a…

superlucid trance, but then you went right back to it as soon as they were gnawing on you."

"That doesn't make much more sense, but I can't explain it any better." Quince chanced a look at Jeremy before burrowing deeper into the sheet. "I need to sleep, okay?"

It wasn't okay, but he needed the rest. Getting away was better than trying to unravel the mystery. The people of Logansport and their goddamn secrets could keep to themselves, and Stygian would haul ass back to Houston. Normal drama and pasts that didn't involve murder houses, blood-spattered wings, and all kinds of triggery shit that launched Jeremy into a constant, nagging state of paranoia that either the impossible was possible or he really was losing his grip on reality.

"DID YOU notice his wrist?"

Kennedy dropped his duffel bag onto the bed. "What about it?"

Jeremy ran his fingers along the creases in a T-shirt he'd folded into a neat square. The words on the front were old and peeling. "It was blistered from the band of his watch."

"Maybe it's a rash."

"Maybe."

Maybe not. The burn had been in the exact shape of the watch. As though the silver itself had scalded Quince's skin.

With his hands poised on the open flap of the bag, Kennedy looked him directly in the eye. "You're thinking something. I can see the gears grinding away."

"I—" Jeremy shoved the shirt into his backpack. "I don't know. Never mind. Let's just get out of here."

"You don't have to be afraid to tell me what you think. I'm not going to call you crazy."

"It's better if we get into it on the road. I want to leave."

Jeremy felt Kennedy's disappointment seeping into the chinks of his don't-make-a-fool-of-yourself armor, but stubbornness won over. They went back to packing. It should have been a relief, but heaviness settled in Jeremy's gut. Instead of anticipating swapping this alternate reality for a cramped flat near Frenchmen Street, Jeremy wondered what else was going to go wrong. Something always went wrong.

He finished putting away his clothes and found Simon's journal sitting on the floor next to the chaise lounge.

Kennedy's voice broke the silence. "I don't think taking that thing is a good idea. Anything from this creepy-ass place is bad luck. It's no wonder people leave in a rush and forget their shit."

The words sparked Jeremy's memory, and he recalled something the boy at the party had said. Something he'd forgotten after Amy's death and all that had happened after.

"What do you think happened to Simon?"

"Who?"

Jeremy held up the journal. "Simon. And the person who left that watch. And whoever else has stayed here in the past few years. I thought one of the kids at the party said the last guest hauled ass out of town."

"I do remember. It was that Kyle guy. The one with the stupid mohawk."

"Yeah, him." Jeremy flipped through the yellowed pages of the journal and watched the loopy cursive fly by. "He said the last guy who stayed here ran out of town after something spooked him."

Frowning down at the journal, Kennedy moved away from his bag. "I didn't take it seriously at the time."

"I didn't either. We were all too busy fighting with each other."

"Right. Well, there's only one way to find out what the hell happened." Kennedy pulled out his phone and thumbed over the screen. Within a few seconds he said, "Got a hit."

Jeremy crossed the room to hover by Kennedy's side.

"Simon went missing after staying here. He vanished, and his family never heard from him again. It says here the Logansport police stonewalled them, and they never got answers about what may have happened." Kennedy gripped the phone and flicked through the article. "There were some alleged witnesses in town who saw Simon leaving of his own accord, but the family was never told their names, so they couldn't investigate for themselves. The police wouldn't even let them question the owners of the house. Doesn't even mention the Caroways or that it's a murder house, or that it's known to be haunted just to add in that extra drama like papers normally would."

"Jesus fucking Christ." A hurricane-force freak-out had Jeremy's hands shaking. "Fuck, you were so right. About the cops. About this place. About the Caroways. They fucking killed that guy. They did something to him. I bet they lure in lonely, fucked-up people and *prey* on them, and these people in the town let them do it. Who knows how many others they've done it to?"

"Jere—"

"We have to go." Jeremy grabbed Kennedy's bag. "We need to fucking go *right now!*"

Kennedy clamped his hands down on Jeremy's shoulders and wheeled him around. They stared at each other, Kennedy with strained calm and Jeremy panting wildly.

"We're fine. We're almost out of here." Kennedy squeezed him. "Okay?"

All Jeremy could see was bloodstained lips and torn skin.

"I'm so fucking scared, Kennedy."

"We're getting out of here in five minutes, and then it will be me and you sharing a room after stumbling in from Bourbon Street. This nightmare will be behind us and things will go back to normal. We'll tell Watts that we're together, and he'll choke on one of those awful touristy drinks and spend the rest of the night teasing us."

A wry grin touched the corners of Kennedy's mouth, but Jeremy couldn't bring himself to appreciate it. He kept seeing Amy's bloody arm, Quince's bite marks, and skin blistered from a silver watch. Hunter's cheeks hollowing as he fucked his own mouth with Jeremy' finger....

"No more Caroways," Kennedy said. "No more worrying about mysterious disappearances. All of this shit is out of our control. We just need to get gone, and we're doing just that, sweetheart."

"But we can't just not tell anyone the things we know."

"We don't have any proof of anything. Just suspicions. For all we know, Simon ran the fuck out of here after the incest twins tried to induct him into their freaky cult."

No. That wasn't it at all. In Jeremy's heart, he knew it was more.

"If I say why I'm so freaked out," Jeremy began, "I'm convinced you will lose whatever small percentage of respect you have for me."

And just like that, the warmth evaporated from Kennedy's expression. He yanked his hands away. "Do you have to be so fucking passive-aggressive all the time?"

"I'm not. I'm just saying how I feel."

"It'd be nice," Kennedy said stonily, "if you'd just have a millimeter of faith in me."

"I know." Jeremy tossed the journal onto the floor and kicked it under the bed. "God, I'm sorry. I'm so terrified of you finding out what a freak I am. Because I *am* one. There's no doubt about it. I'm just like the rest of the Black family."

"Yeah?" Kennedy lifted his chin. "Try me."

Jeremy moved closer and clasped their hands together in an attempt to leach Kennedy's warmth. His solidness and humanity. With Kennedy tethering him to reality, maybe he could find his own strength.

"The first thing you need to know is that people say my father's family is insane. They're known for it in this tiny-ass town south of Houston. They believe in supernatural beings, dreamwalkers, and all kinds of Cold War experimentation psychic shit. They believe it so hard they spend their lives getting drunk and doing drugs to cope. And usually they end up like Luke."

"That's awful, but what does this have to do with—"

"Let me finish!" Jeremy took another calming breath. "I've never believed in those things. I spent years thinking my genes were a ticking time bomb waiting to do to me what's been done to them. But now I'm wondering if I was wrong. If they're not actually crazy."

To his credit, Kennedy's expression didn't change. "Why?"

"Because there's something wrong with the Caroways. The things I've seen them do aren't natural, and I think they target specific types of prey. Dysfunctional people, outlier kids, anyone who is lonely enough to latch on when they start doing their thing."

Kennedy's hands moved up to grip Jeremy's shoulders again. "What thing? What do you think they're doing?"

"Manipulating and seducing but in a way people can't fight." *Fuck. Fuck.* Did he want to go here now? After Kennedy had started talking about them being together? "They're into blood play. They started it up with Quince during the party, and that's when he started to change. And he got worse the longer he fucked around with Laurel. And then Hunter tried it on me too."

Recoiling, Kennedy's brows crashed down. "You told me you weren't fucking around with him."

"I wasn't! I got a cut on my hand, and he… he sort of sucked on it." How could he describe the sensation of his life force flowing out of him and into Hunter's mouth? How it had been intoxicating instead of alarming. How easy it must have been for Quince to get hooked on that feeling. "It just sort of—it just happened. He didn't get very far."

"Why the fuck didn't you stop him?"

Frustrated, Jeremy began pacing the room again. "I couldn't! It was like he put me in a trance. And when I did manage to pull away, he was shocked. Like maybe he expected me to want more. Or get turned on. Or maybe become like Quince. And it worked for a while. I almost *was* like Quince!"

Kennedy sat there fuming, not hearing the words for what they were and instead focusing on a threat that didn't exist.

"It's more than that," Jeremy insisted. "Think about what I'm saying, dude. He sucked. My blood. She bit. His neck. Then they both fucked him while he was on a beta-sex-kitten mind-control trip. And that girl Amy—her wrist was cut, but Quince also has a big gash on his wrist. The one that's not already burned from a *silver watch*. Not to mention Simon going missing and the town covering it up, and how they flat-out refuse to talk about the Caroways while giving us random vague warnings? I *know* it sounds crazy, but come on!"

Kennedy didn't react, and that either spelled problem or him trying to adopt his usual unflinching stone face so Jeremy wouldn't see him panic. The only sign of the latter was the way his eyes quickly flitted to the closet door.

"Are you saying what I think you're saying?"

"I—yes. I guess. I don't know!" Jeremy's brain screamed for him to abort this little mission. No matter how good the clues were, the explanation sounded psychotic when strung together with inadequate sentences. "We really need to just fucking go."

A tense silence followed Jeremy's declaration, and then Kennedy nodded shortly.

"I'll go help Watts."

JEREMY WAS packed in record time, but even with Kennedy's help, Watts took forever to gather his own belongings. It came to the point where Jeremy moved the instruments, his and Kennedy's bags, and Quince to the van and waited outside. He hadn't thought Watts would waste time if the engine was running, but they still didn't appear after several minutes of Jeremy sweating in the passenger's seat.

The lower the sun sank beyond the horizon, the more Jeremy's paranoia swelled. As time slid by in a molasses crawl, he was in constant motion. He fidgeted with his clothes, the van's radio, and rolled down the window.

A gust of air and the rich, green smell of trees flooded the van. The rain clouds had moved on, leaving the kind of cool breeze that was perfect for an outdoor show. Or just practicing in Watts's backyard. It reminded Jeremy of what this summer could have been like—grilling dinner every night, cold beers in a cooler, and the lazy plucking of guitar strings after a grueling rehearsal with the sun baking the roof of the shed. Carefree summer days in Texas and nothing like the fucking nightmare this trip had become.

Sighing, Jeremy glanced back at Quince.

Curled in a nest of sheets that Jeremy had wedged between the wall and the cases of his kit, Quince was sleeping peacefully. His breathing was deep and even. No wheezing or weird gurgles.

Relieved, Jeremy started to turn away, but he caught a flash of color in the van's gloom. Quince appeared to be asleep, but his glittering eyes were partially open and flashing the same pale hue as the Caroways'.

Jeremy threw himself back with a gasp. Fear held him in an unyielding fist, and by the time he collected himself, Quince's eyes were closed once again.

Had he imagined it? It wouldn't be the first time but, considering all that had happened, he took it as yet another sign that it was seriously time to go.

Jeremy shoved the passenger's door open, pocketed the keys, and jogged away from the van. It was then that he noticed the silence. The muted stillness he now associated with danger.

# CHAPTER SIXTEEN

TERROR MOVED through Jeremy like a predator—quick and merciless.

His hands shook, his knees trembled, and the paltry contents of his stomach nearly spewed from his mouth, but he didn't allow himself to get sick. He would keep it together. There was no other option.

He streaked through the mansion but didn't find Kennedy or Watts, and outside it was only growing darker. The house itself was full of shadows and threatening corners no matter how many lights he turned on.

"Kennedy?" Jeremy's voice cracked and pitched higher. "Watts!"

No response.

Each room was empty, and the absence of their belongings made it impossible to forget what these walls had borne witness to. The murders, the deaths, and the advancing realization that maybe the threat was some inhuman and primordial evil. An evil that may have taken Kennedy.

The terror crystallized into something harder, and Jeremy stopped trembling.

He entered the room that had very briefly been theirs and tore apart the contents of the closet. The crawl space seemed like a definite avenue to a horrific death, but he scrambled through it to enter the abandoned wing and emerged on the other side. He ran from door to door, peering into decayed rooms with blankets of dust and the obscene streaks of blood that covered floor, walls, and speckled windows.

Jeremy could almost smell the putrid odor of death, but he didn't find Kennedy or Watts. What he did find was worse. Evidence of his suspicions in the form of the abandoned suitcases in one of the rooms. Jeremy had glanced quickly inside on his first trip into the wing, but now his eyes caught on a shiny metallic logo hanging from one of the bags.

He opened it, and clothing spilled out. A pair of pants and a wallet. Simon's wallet.

Jeremy dropped it as if his hands had blistered to match Quince's wrist.

He sprinted from the wing but bypassed the hidden room for the bolted door. It couldn't lock from the outside, but he was beyond giving a damn about discretion. He burst into the corridor and stood in the center of the hallway, panting, while listening for any sound of movement in the mansion. There was nothing but his own shallow breathing and the deafening thrum of his heartbeat.

Would Hunter hear it the way he'd heard conversations spoken quietly in Watts's room? It was a stupid thought. A dramatic one. But he still believed it.

Shaking off the clamor of his tangled musings, Jeremy focused on the matter at hand.

If he trekked into the woods, he would miss them if they went back to the van. If he stayed in the van, they might be lost to some unknown fate. It was a double-edged sword, and Jeremy hated his own inability to make a decision. He stared at the stained glass window as though the image of a hunter, the sleek dogs at his feet, and the bay laurels surrounding them could help him configure a plan. Instead, yet another realization slinked through him to wrap around his chest with suffocating force.

A hunter surrounded by bay laurels.

Hunter and Laurel—even their names were a lie.

Jeremy spun away from the window and hurtled down the stairs.

HE HAD no time to consider a real plan or even the question of what he could do if Watts and Kennedy were truly in danger. Nothing mattered except finding them and trying to protect them.

So he ran. Out of the house and into the woods while his body buzzed with adrenaline. With each pump of his legs, a new vision of horror slid across his mind until all he could see was Kennedy and Watts, covered in vicious bites and bleeding out slowly in a cabin that had likely not been lived in for years. And then he manifested other images—bone-colored skin, unnaturally pale eyes, haunting loveliness, and the obsession with blood.

Regardless of how crazy it was, Jeremy knew the impossible was possible even if the reality didn't fit the legends. If this could be called reality anymore.

Strength and speed he'd never known surged through his body and propelled Jeremy forward to crash through the trees to the cabin that looked even less inhabitable now that he knew the truth. He hunkered down behind an ancient tree and peered at the cabin.

No movement. No sound.

Had he gone the wrong way? Overlooked some clue? Should he have gone to the clearing instead of assuming they were here? An answer to his questions came in the form of a deep, raspy groan.

He slunk closer and pressed against the side of the shack. The windows were crusted with dust and years' worth of grime, but when Jeremy craned his neck to see in the far corner, his eyes widened.

Watts was limp and as pale as death. Kennedy lay sprawled, seemingly unconscious, on the floor. Nearby the Caroways stood facing each other, expressions tight, hissing in voices too low for Jeremy to fully understand at first. He pressed closer and heard Hunter saying, "I don't want him. Either of them."

"Too bad," Laurel hissed. "You stopped being in charge of what I do a long time ago."

"I don't give a damn what you do to them, but Jeremy is mine."

Jeremy covered his mouth with his palm and sank down to his knees. The lump in his throat grew painfully large until his eyes burned with the need to release a torrent of emotion that wouldn't help his friends.

He tried to find his anger, but all that came was fear. He was impotent, unable to act, and it was only the sound of the door opening and slamming shut followed by fast, angry footsteps, that prompted him to rise again.

Laurel was alone with his bandmates, but she ignored Kennedy in favor of kneeling beside Watts. She fussed over him, smoothing his hair and shoving him upright against the wall to reveal a red stain on his neck—barely visible—that was streaming blood. She surged forward, mouth attaching to his throat.

The Caroways—or whoever they were—weren't human.

Nausea rose in a sickening wave.

He was trapped by the knowledge that he probably wouldn't be able to stop whatever horrors were happening beyond that door. He'd get killed. Maybe he'd get Kennedy and Watts killed.

Another soft groan filled the air.

It was his own insecurity that had stopped him from warning his bandmates sooner, his fear of rejection that had prevented him from telling Kennedy the full story until it was too late. Now, it was possible that none of them would survive.

Gathering the tatters of his courage, Jeremy scrambled for the door. He pushed it open slowly enough to sneak inside.

Laurel was faced away from him as she nursed at Watts's throat. She didn't react when he stepped inside and didn't seem to notice anything but the man in her arms.

The sounds of slurping, of a strange high-pitched keening muffled by torn flesh and lips, curdled Jeremy's stomach. The urge to be sick all over the mottled wooden floor was strong, but Jeremy sucked in a breath and grabbed the first thing he saw—a rickety wooden chair. He heaved it, and it splintered against Laurel's back.

She spun on him with the speed of a viper, and that was when her face changed. Her mouth distorted, canines extending, and the pale blue of her eyes glowed.

Jeremy fell backward. "Please, just let us go. We won't tell anyone. I fucking swear!"

Laurel grabbed the front of his shirt and lifted him up. "You shouldn't have come here, you little idiot." She tossed him across the room as if he weighed nothing.

His back hit the wall and pain radiated up his spine. "H-Hunter said he wants me. He—he wouldn't want you to hurt me."

"I couldn't give a fuck about what he said." Laurel's voice twisted until it was the same high, inhuman pitch as Quince's had been in the clearing. She grabbed him by the throat and lifted him up to dangle off the floor again. Her teeth shortened as she spoke, sliding up into her mouth until they just brushed her bottom lip. "I knew you would be trouble. I could smell it."

"Wh... wha—"

Laurel inhaled him like she'd done that day outside the cabin, as he'd stood in the dappled sunlight with no way of knowing what kind of monster had leaned so close.

"Are you—are you human?"

"What do you think?" Laurel's lips twisted. "It's not always Dracula and Lestat and sleeping in coffins. But you knew that, didn't you?"

"No, I didn't... I don't—"

"You and the big guy were the wary ones. Already catching on." Laurel pressed her face to his, and her teeth clipped his lips. "But my idiot husband kept bringing you around anyway."

"Husband...."

He gaped at the untamed savageness in her distorted face and the gleeful cruelty in her eyes. They glowed like burning stars, sucking him in but unable to hold him completely. Even so, Jeremy nearly missed the slight movements of Kennedy stirring on the floor. He was too focused on the warped puzzle pieces that were finally coming together.

"You're James and Sarah Caroway."

"We used to be." She nuzzled her nose against his face. "What a clever boy."

James and Sarah Caroway were said to have died in the eighties. They'd been doing this for *decades*.

"Oh God."

Behind them, the door opened and slammed against the opposite wall. Hunter's slim, white form framed the doorway.

"I told you not to touch him."

Laurel's hands opened, and Jeremy slid to the floor. With her distracted and Hunter advancing on his wife, Jeremy sneaked a glance in Kennedy's direction again. He was more alert but focused on Watts. Their front man was slumped over, and his head hung at an unnatural angle.

"And I said I don't listen to you."

Laurel glided across the floor like a wraith. She and Hunter stood face-to-face, features warped, and it was now easy to see how unnatural their similarities were. Whatever mutation had changed them into monsters had also twisted their features into smooth, ivory masks.

Jeremy jerked his gaze away just in time to see Kennedy mouthing something incomprehensible while nodding to the corner of the room. By the window and behind a table sat a rusted toolbox and an ax.

"You should have left it alone." Hunter was quiet and controlled, as though three captive musicians weren't on the floor a few feet away. But then he'd had practice doing this. Enough practice to fill four decades. "This has spun out of control."

"It's been out of control," she sneered. "The spiral started when you killed that stupid little girl."

Hunter stood his ground without flinching. "We can let them go. You already have Quince. Four is too much."

"I don't know if he changed," she snapped. "And it's too late to let them go, you sentimental bitch. We change them, or we kill them."

"It won't work." Hunter ground out each word. "The singer has family. So does Jeremy."

"Then we change all of them." Laurel said it as if it was the obvious choice. "And after, they can check in with their people."

"It won't work," Hunter repeated, louder this time. "Jeremy is resistant to the change."

"Then he's dead," Laurel said evenly. "Get over it."

A low animal growl vibrated from Hunter's chest and escaped the curled corners of his snarled lips. "It's not going to happen."

From his position in the corner, Jeremy saw Laurel's fangs snap out to their fullest extent. She dropped her shoulders and hissed as claws curved from her fingers. The monstrous hand cocked back, ready to claw across Hunter's face or throat, and Jeremy leaped to his feet.

There was no plan. Just an instinctive need to do *something*.

Charging forward, Jeremy slammed his shoulder into Laurel's back and sent her crashing to the floor. Her shriek resounded in the cabin.

It seemed certain they were all about to die. Jeremy expected it, accepted it, and looked at Kennedy. His dark eyes, stubble that had brushed against Jeremy's face only hours ago, the tempting glint of his lip ring, and the tattoos sliding over the planes of his body. All of the parts that had initially attracted Jeremy before he'd even known how worthy of affection Kennedy truly was. How patient and kind and willing to do anything he could to help his friends.

"I love you," Jeremy blurted.

From the corner of his eye, Jeremy saw Laurel crouch, strength coiled in her body. She was intent on Jeremy, and ready to leap.

Kennedy's eyes went wide with naked fear. He struggled to his knees, but before he could make it, Hunter closed his hands around Laurel's throat. His thumbs dug in and she went down in a heap. She looked small and helpless with her body so slack, but the rise and fall of her chest meant the reprieve wouldn't last.

"Jeremy—"

"Just let us fucking go!"

"I don't want to hurt you." Hunter stepped closer. "I only—"

Jeremy balled his hands into fists and got in Hunter's face—ready for a fight that couldn't end well no matter how hard he tried. "Tell me what the *fuck* she did to my friends."

"She wanted a companion." Hunter's eyes dropped to his wife's limp body. "We both did. We changed decades ago and...."

"And what? If you have each other, why do you need *us*?"

"I wasn't lying when I said we hated each other," Hunter said. "The change brings out your basest instincts, but Laurel was always cruel. This place made her that way because she wasn't what people expected her to be. We married, but she was never happy. She had other lovers, and one of them, a traveling musician, was... something like what we are now."

Kennedy got up and stood with his back to the wall. He was steady on his feet, but blood glistened on the side of his face and dripped down to his neck.

"The blood in the room—is it yours or people you've killed?"

Hunter speared Kennedy with a look of such distaste that Jeremy stood protectively between them.

"The musician savaged her, nearly drained her. I didn't realize she'd been changed into *this* until after I'd called the police. By then, she'd attacked me. Forced it on me." Hunter sought Jeremy's eyes again, perhaps hoping the story would draw compassion instead of revulsion. "When she wanted to kill the police, I provided another alternative."

"Blackmail," Kennedy breathed. "They keep your secret, and you don't kill them."

Hunter nodded once. "Yes. We drew in people from out of town."

Jeremy shuddered. "You used the house—the ads in the papers to draw in musicians, artists, writers...."

"She thought they were easier to tempt. More romantic. More... willing to try new things." Hunter began to look older as he spoke, his voice thickening with each word. "But they never stayed, even after we turned them, so we found an alternative—people who may want a way out of their current lives."

"Sad kids," Jeremy said. "People who are damaged and lonely."

"Yes." Hunter gestured at Jeremy. "Like Quince... and you."

"You don't know me," Jeremy whispered. "That's why it didn't work like it did with Quince. I've always been in love with Kennedy. You couldn't fucking change that if you tried."

The sad, damp glint in Hunter's eyes burned with something fiercer, and Jeremy remembered the night of the party—Hunter and Kennedy's standoff—and what had likely happened next. The rejection must have burned through Hunter and sparked anger that transformed into something darker. If Amy had really cut herself, the scent of her blood and pain must have lured Hunter to the kitchen.

"You're wrong." Hunter moved closer again. "It didn't work because you're special."

Jeremy staggered back to the wall. "Stay the fuck away from me!"

"I don't want to hurt people. When we changed, we didn't become killers. It just took away the layers that surrounded and restrained us. Now, it's easy to lose control."

"It also changed you into a monster that drinks blood," Kennedy spat.

"No." Hunter snarled the word. "It's not *food*. It's a way to transmit the changes, but it's also a connection. Like sex. And sometimes it goes too far... like with the girl. I never meant to kill her—and I would have never hurt you, Jeremy."

Hunter took a slow step forward, reaching out a questing hand.

"I think you're a liar."

Hunter halted. Behind him, Kennedy grabbed the ax.

"I think all of this was choreographed," Jeremy went on shakily. He tried not to watch as Kennedy moved closer. "I think you wanted a powder-keg moment once I walked away from you to go with Kennedy. You wanted something to send us all flying apart in chaos, and you knew exactly what to do to trigger me and my past. And you knew a kid's suicide would do it."

Hunter's lips pulled back to expose his curved canines. "If you believe that, you're a fool."

"If I trusted you, I would be a fool."

The ax came down, but instead of splitting Hunter's head open, the flat side slammed into the side of his face. He fell to the floor and went still, but Kennedy didn't stop there. He turned on his heel with the weapon held high and brought it down with an unforgiving crash. The sharp wedge of steel slammed into Laurel's skull in an explosion of blood and bone fragments. The ax's blade scraped against the floor.

Jeremy jerked away from the blood, the fragile skull shattering into pieces, and then toward Watts. He barely looked alive.

Kennedy stared down at the carnage and the ax fell from his fingers. "Fuck. Oh fuck."

Jeremy made his way to Watts on trembling legs and tried to find a pulse.

"You have to carry him," he said through a slick of tears. "We have to go before Hun—he wakes up."

Kennedy was still staring down at the gray bits of brain and sharp edges of bone.

"Kennedy, we have to go before he wakes up!"

The words pulled Kennedy from his trance.

He wiped his fingerprints from the ax with his T-shirt and very purposefully did not look at Laurel's body before kicking the weapon to the side.

They fled the cabin and left the prone bodies of the pale creatures behind, one shattered and one broken but still capable of hunting them down.

Neither of them spoke as they moved through the trees. They didn't dare to pause or acknowledge the blood and death they were leaving in the shack.

Jeremy ran until his legs throbbed and his chest burned, eyes darting and seeking an unseen threat in the dark. It didn't come, and the sounds of animals and insects filled the night air.

Maybe the woods awakening meant it was safe. Maybe they would get away.

The van's paint glinted in the shadow of the Caroway house. It was a pall hovering over them, balconies and arched doorways searing into the sky.

A thought crossed Jeremy's mind.

*Burn it.*

But there was no time.

He yanked open the van's door, sliding in, and found Quince still sleeping in the back.

Kennedy hauled Watts inside and arranged him beside Quince. His hands shook as he assessed Watts's wounds. "He needs a doctor. He's—"

Watts flinched, stirring. "Go, you fucking idiots," he rasped. "Hospital later."

Jeremy barked out a half-hysterical laugh through his drying tears. "My God, I've never been so happy to hear your bitchy voice."

Watts had already drifted back to unconsciousness.

They rushed to the front of the van and were speeding away from the house before Jeremy had clicked the lock on his door. As he stared through the windshield and gripped the sides of the seat, his mind tried to return to the blood and carnage, but Kennedy's hand sought his and brought him back to the present.

"I killed that woman."

Jeremy looked up sharply. "She wasn't just a woman. She was going to kill us."

"But she wasn't... she was still...." Kennedy held the wheel with one white-knuckled hand.

"If you'd let her go, she'd have hunted us down. Hunter at least seemed wary of killing us all. And if it wasn't for you—"

"No. We'd be dead if it wasn't for *you.*" With only the dash illuminating him, Kennedy looked washed out and wan, but his voice was strong. "We'd be fucking dead."

"I didn't do anything."

"You figured it out. You came for us." Kennedy squeezed harder before releasing Jeremy's fingers. "And I fucking love you too."

Jeremy's lips formed a brief wobbly smile. "What do we do now?"

"We stay together. It's the only way to stay safe. To deal with this." Kennedy drew a shaky breath. "I don't think I can do that alone."

"Me either," Jeremy whispered.

He curled into himself, staring out the window as the tree-lined roads and sparse buildings sped by. With the kaleidoscopic events of the night, of the past few weeks, spinning incessantly, it was impossible to bury everything that had happened.

But maybe that was for the best. They could leave behind the darkness along the Sabine, but Hunter was still there. And there were others like him. Repressing the memories of this night wouldn't change that. It wouldn't change the fact that there was still danger.

Jeremy balked from the path of his thoughts and zeroed in on a green-and-white sign along the Interstate. A beacon in the darkness.

*Houston—192 miles.*

They were going home. That was what mattered. The only thing that mattered.

Jeremy found Kennedy's hand again.

SANTINO HASSELL was raised by a conservative family, but he was anything but traditional. He grew up to be a smart-mouthed, school-cutting grunge kid, then a transient twentysomething, and eventually transformed into the romance-writing and sarcasm-loving guy that people know him as today.

Santino is a dedicated gamer, a former anime watcher and fanfic writer, an ASoIaF mega nerd, a Grindr enthusiast, but most of all he is a writer of queer fiction that is heavily influenced by the gritty urban landscape of New York City, his belief that human relationships are complex and flawed, and his own life experiences.

To learn more about Santino you can follow him here:
Website/Blog: www.santinohassell.com
Twitter: @santinohassell
Facebook: www.facebook.com/santinohassellbooks
Instagram: santinohassell

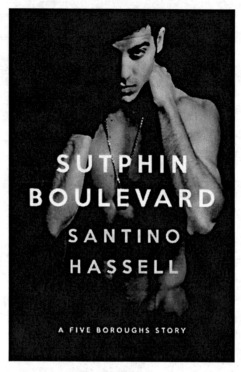

A Five Boroughs Story

Michael Rodriguez and Nunzio Medici have been friends for two decades. From escaping their dysfunctional families in the working class neighborhood of South Jamaica, Queens, to teaching in one of the city's most queer-friendly schools in Brooklyn, the two men have shared everything. Or so they thought until a sweltering night of dancing lead to an unexpected encounter that forever changes their friendship.

Now, casual touches and lingering looks are packed with sexual tension and Michael can't forget the feel of his best friend's hands on him. Once problems rear up at work and home, Michael finds himself seeking constant escape in the effortless intimacy and mind-blowing sex he had with Nunzio. But things don't stay easy for long.

When Michael's world begins to crumble in a sea of tragedy and complications, he knows he has to make a choice: find solace in a path of self-destruction or accept the love of the man who has been by his side for twenty years.

www.dreamspinnerpress.com

*Coming Soon*

# SUNSET PARK

By Santino Hassell

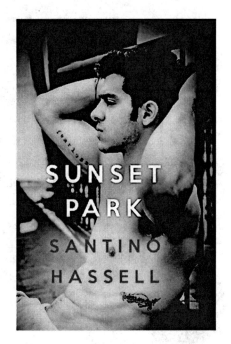

A Five Boroughs Story

Raymond Rodriguez's days of shoving responsibility to the wayside are over. His older brother wants to live with his boyfriend, so Raymond has to get his act together and find a place of his own. But when out-and-proud David Butler offers to be his roommate, Raymond agrees for reasons other than needing a place to crash.

David is Raymond's opposite in almost every way—he's Connecticut prim and proper while Raymond is a sarcastic longshoreman from Queens—but their friendship is solid. Their closeness surprises everyone as does their not-so-playful flirtation since Raymond has always kept his bicurious side a secret.

Once they're under the same roof, flirting turns physical, and soon their easy camaraderie is in danger of being lost to frustrating sexual tension and the stark cultural differences that set them apart. Now Raymond not only has to commit to his new independence—he has to commit to his feelings for David or risk losing him for good.

## Coming Soon to
## www.dreamspinnerpress.com

CPSIA information can be obtained
at www.ICGtesting.com
Printed in the USA
FSOW02n0909170917
38597FS